The Queen of Cups

Collette Yvonne

Enjoy the train wreck!

Cheers,

C. Yvonne

PANIC HOUSE

Library and Archives Canada Cataloguing in Publication

Yvonne, Collette
The Queen of Cups / Collette Yvonne.

ISBN-13: 978-0-9734623-0-2
ISBN-10: 0-9734623-0-2

I. Title.

PS8647.V65Q37 2006 C813'.6 C2006-902713-7

Cover illustration by Cindy Revell

Panic House Inc.
328 Beacroft Road
Little Britain, Ontario
Canada K0M 2C0

www.panichouse.ca
2nd printing

Printed and bound in Canada

For Peter McKeracher,

my Michael and my mate

One

No Duff

Stupid Friday meetings. I must choose now or be ridiculously late: do I get the braided leather platforms or the phenomenal metallic cork wedges? One pair is half price but the other ones are so *me.* I want both. I really *really* want both. Well, why not take both? Grabbing for my bag, I hand my card to the sales clerk saying, "I'm in a hurry."

Who the hell wants to work anyway, just before the August long weekend? Not me, but I'm chinning paperwork and there's an all-staff this aft. I try not to drum my fingertips on the counter. The clerk hands me a pen, I skid it across the charge slip and rush out of the store.

Rushing is difficult while wearing a vintage Chloe pencil skirt and my new wedges, but today's all-staff requires polish and begins fifteen minutes ago. As I go by, the workers on the street corner start whistling, shouting and waving. Ignorant knuckle-dragging jackasses. Averting my eyes, I pick up my pace. How irritating. Despite the progress of women and everything, men continue to exhibit vile and oppressive behaviours. One ape's even hollering, "Hey, Lady, come back!"

I won't look back. With stony indignation written across my face, I hammer straight on, hock deep, into freshly poured concrete.

The hollering man offers an arm to me as I tug one foot and then the other out of the muck. My beautiful new wedges remain embedded in the sidewalk. Only the shiny gold buckles are still visible above the surface. He has to yank the shoes out by the straps, hard, to extract them. I mumble my apologies and mush on to the meeting with cement feet.

***

I'm ridiculously late but it's okay. Everyone is still milling around the boardroom. The Head of Human Resources just jogged in, all decked out for the long weekend, wearing the InTecNor Global Positioning Vest and the matching InTecNor Bluefang Wired Hiking Shorts from our high-end summer lineup. He claps his hands twice and everyone turns toward him. He begins: "InTecNor needs to reduce duplication through the timely repurposing of resources. A challenging decision has been made to reposition the human inputs in this unit outside the structure."

Jaws across the room drop. We're being dumped. The man standing beside me is muttering, "No f'ing way, those bastards can't do this to me."

Shut up. The bastards can't fire *me*; I'm the company tech consultant, Sgt. Parril, P., Army Spec. (Ret'd.), military endurance expert. And all my survival expertise as one of Canada's finest went into the design of that head dork's ugly new hiking shorts. And the GPS vest—it actually repels mosquitoes electronically. Cutting edge stuff. I'm indispensable, I am. Because of me, that goof could go to battle in his swimming trunks if he wanted to. The HHR proceeds to stuff ten minutes worth of useful information about our repositioning options into the next two and a half hours. I've been repositioned all right. Bunch of cannibals.

I drift back to my office with a glossy, four-colour guide to choosing a good headhunter plus a skeletal severance package. We're to clear out our desks immediately. My desk is buried under a sliding mountain of fabric samples, catalogues, reports and file folders. Where to start? Dropping into my chair, I stare at the blinking light on my phone. Whoever you are, get lost. I don't have to talk to you; I don't work here any more.

I'm not sure what to think. On the one hand, a job loss represents a severe blow to my working woman ego and, even with E.I. benefits, a killer whack to my budget. On the other—well, well, well! A paid summer vacation! TGIF—Thank God I'm Fired!

While I'm still on company time, I better collect my stuff: my scruffy dayminder, a chipped coffee mug, an outdated framed photo of Donald and the kids. Inside the frame, the kids' innocent little faces smile at me: they will be devastated. Jack has been begging for a trampoline and Olympia wants a bigger splash pool. My poor babies. No new summer toys.

As I yank open my desk drawer, I look up to see a beefy security guard shuffle by my door. InTecNor is making sure no one snakes off with the computers, rolodexes and other useful consolation prizes. As if we're nothing but criminals.

Humph. Funny how seconds later, a cool, voice-activated hand-held computer just drops from the palm of my hand directly behind the torn lining of my purse. Then I fill a stack of boxes with my personal files, books, research notes, contacts and haul them one by one out to the parking lot. I stuffed them into the back seat of the old Jeep while the security guard looked on, arms folded.

It's baking hot outside. The Jeep is a broiler oven. Opening all the doors and windows first, I climb in and turn the key. While waiting for the air to kick in, I pull the handheld out of my purse and check it out. It's shiny and loaded with all the latest most attractive features. Very kewl. The guilt floods in: I'm a lowly thief now. I've never stolen so much as a gumball in my whole life. I ought to go right back in there this minute and return the goods. Or it's bad karma for me, forever.

But, hey, they stole my job. And what about the insulting severance package? I should march back in there and steal a laptop too. Whatever. I'll think about it, but right now I have to collect the kids from their day camp. I can play with this puppy on the way home. I plug the handheld into the lighter using Jack's Gameboy adaptor and press the ON button; right away the thing emits a strangled whine and smoke begins to curl from the pin ports. I yank the plug out fast, but too late, the handheld and the adaptor are fried leaving an acrid burnt-lead bad-for-the-lungs smell in the air.

Choking, I grab a file folder from one of my boxes and try to fan the smoke out of the Jeep. The folder falls apart in my hands and all its contents slip-slide onto the floor. Fuck fuck fuck fuck. I'm *not* going to cry. I slam shift through the gears and, as I pull out of the parking lot, I tip the handheld, still smoking, out the window beside the CEO row.

For some reason the air con won't work. I'm dying of heat. The highway is jammed with RVs and SUVs towing boats and trailers. The whole universe is going off to a cottage or a resort. Everyone except me, that is. Where's my long-weekend playground? Oh well. Maybe Donald will make me another one of his Triple Moby Bloody Caesars in Olympia's beach pail. We can set up the old Adirondack chairs in the kids' sandbox and bury our toes together. Or we could take the kids out for fish and chips at the Red Dog House and drink a bootful of limed beer.

***

Dammit. Donald's not home. I'm greeted by "Hi, it's me," on the answering machine. "I tried to call you, my meeting is going over, sorry, I'll call you later."

"Later" means midnight given the way things are going recently at Doubles Group Financial. Doubles is the critical word: Donald's hours at the firm have doubled lately;

he keeps saying things will ease up after the new Double-Double campaign winds down. Sure.

It's way too hot to cook and who can be bothered with a big Canada-Food-Guide-type effort? I'll microwave a few hot dogs for the kids. I'm not one bit hungry. Standing in front of the cupboard, I grab handfuls of Ritz crackers and gobble them down. How weird. Despite everything, I'm feeling calm, even upbeat. Most likely when the shock wears off I will rant and rave about appropriately.

After all, how dare they lay me off just like that? Who could blame me if I fix the kids up with a DVD and popcorn and skim across the road to Bibienne's house for a drink?

* * *

Sure enough, once I describe the indignities of my job loss to Bibienne, she declares her special Towering Mai Tai recipe is sure to soothe. I'm open to all offers of comfort. "I have Nirvana chocolate too," she says.

Bibienne is in top spirits as Bernie hooked up her new computer to the Internet yesterday. She's bookmarked dozens of interesting sites already: tarot, I Ching, horoscopes, numerology and Ouija. I wish I had high-speed access to the Internet. My crappy old computer usually drowns when I try to surf. I'm jealous but I try not to show it.

Bibienne's computer is lightning fast. I click on a bookmark for a cool tarot site and choose the Celtic Cross spread. Then, a question: *What does the future hold for me?*

The results show the Queen of Cups, the good woman card, seated in the terribly auspicious Position One, which represents the "Questioner in Her Present Situation."

"I'm a queen," I say.

Bibienne points to my glass and says, "Your royal drinking vessel is empty."

"Fine then," I say to Bibi. "Fill it up so I can analyze the rest of these cards."

Position Two shows the Three of Swords: a card suggestive of trickery and betrayal. My job loss perhaps? Possibly, except that the powerful and authoritative Emperor is standing in opposition to my Queen. Donald perhaps? But, if the Emperor is my husband, who is the Knight of Cups standing in the near future position? The Knight of Cups is a man of high romance, poetry and passion. Here, Donald doesn't spring to mind. How intriguing: the card drawn for the position representing Final Outcomes turns out to be The Lovers. I can't help but note that two cups makes a couple.

I'm itching to know more about this Knightly figure. Bibienne suggests I consult Ouija. At the Mystic Talking Internet Board, we pose the question: *Who is the Knight of Cups?*

Bibienne douses the lights and places her hand over mine on the mouse pointer. We close our eyes and concentrate. The mouse seems to vibrate ever so slightly. It feels hot to the touch. The mouse jerks into action.

The screen pointer skids in a straight line to the letter M, then D, and then, abruptly, Goodbye.

I wonder if *M.D.* could mean "Medical Doctor"? Bibienne says, "It might just be an amazing coincidence, but there's a hot new doctor in town and he's accepting patients!"

That's it. First thing next week, I'll book an exploratory checkup.

***

Donald greets my job loss announcement with a shrug and says, "You were sick of that job anyway. Find another one."

"Just like that?"

"Sure."

"But no one is hiring now, it's August."

"Take some time off then, do something with the kids."

Right. The kids' summer camp. How will I pay for day camp blessings without an income? The upside of losing my job is disappearing fast with the realization that last week's camp fees are still due and if I don't find something right away this week, I'm about to be saddled with full-time responsibility for my little darlings.

I better call Mom. Maybe she'll take Jack and Olympia for a week or two. No doubt Mom will leap at the chance to have the kids' company; she's been terribly lonely since Dad died last year. Now all she does is watch golf on TSN because she likes Phil Mickelson. She talks about Phil all the time. She's even been to his website and looked at all the photos. "He's so handsome," she says. "He looks just like your father did when he was a younger man."

Perhaps I'll stay on with her a few days myself. I'll let her pamper me. She'd like that. I wish I had more time to spend with her. Oh well. I can't help it if she insists on staying up in the godforsaken north, hours away, instead of moving closer to her own daughter who could help keep her active and involved. She could keep herself busy with Jack and Olympia. Thank goodness she has a few friends in her book club and delivering Meals On Wheels must make her feel more useful.

"Take the kids next week? Pauline, I already told you I'm going Elder Hostelling with the book club girls."

"But Mom, I can't look after the kids and job hunt at the same time. When do you get back?"

"I wish I could help out. Oh dear, I can't talk now, Brian just walked in."

(How dare she use that smoochy smooth "I wish I could" line on me. Does she think I was born yesterday?)

"Brian?"

"A fellow golfer. We're partnering today, with another couple. A foursome." (Muffled giggling at this.)

"I'll call you tonight then."

"I won't be in till late. Call me tomorrow. You know, he looks a bit like Phil Mickelson," she says, breathily. "Better let me get back to you ..."

Her voice trails off. I can hear sounds of more muffled giggling, then a disgusting sucking, slurping, slobbery noise.

"Mom? Mom? Are you there?"

"Yes, well—later."

As soon as I hang up, the phone rings again.

It's a collect call from Serenity, oldest daughter. "Guess what? We've got a ride all the way to Vancouver."

I grab a scrap of paper and a pen. "Where are you staying?"

"Don't worry about that. I'm gonna stop in to see Dad too," she says. Her father, my useless ex, is a tank specialist stationed in Edmonton. This is almost funny. No army base in the world can protect him from Serenity.

"Where are you now?"

"Thunder Bay."

Hanging up the phone, I feel panicky at the thought of my 15-year-old daughter hitchhiking cross Canada. Then, I feel pangs of sympathy for the truck drivers. There's nothing in Faber and Mazlish for this. Where are the useful references on raising extreme, no fear, generation Y-not teens?

* * *

Tuesday morning and Jack emerges from his bedroom, still wearing his pyjamas. He says, "I hate soccer camp, I'm *not* going."

"You're right," I say. "Hanging out with your friends

and playing soccer all day can get pretty boring, you might as well stay home and help me wash windows," an empty threat, as I have no intention of wasting my first job-freedom day doing housework.

Jack stomps off down the hall. Where's Olympia? There she is, wearing one of Jack's ratty soccer jerseys. It's raining. I dig out the rubber boots and raincoats. Jack soon reappears, ready for camp. I hand him his raincoat and say: "I want you to sit nicely with your sister on the bus today. That means *no fighting.*" Fortunately the bus driver is three hundred years old and practically deaf and blind. God forbid that the kids are expelled from the bus as behavioural problems, or I will be obliged to provide campground transportation myself.

Damn. I'm running late again. I have just fifteen minutes to deliver the kids before the bus pushes off.

A scuffle breaks out in the hall: Jack, enraged that Olympia is wearing his stuff, is attempting to strip her down. Yelling, "Just get in the car or we won't be going to Sugar Mountain tonight," I snatch up my keys, hustle the kids into their seats and peel from the driveway onto the road. There's an abnormal whirring sound coming from the motor, but I ignore it. Maybe it'll just go away.

I'm still in my comfy flannel Bugs Bunny pyjama bottoms, last year's birthday gift from the kids, topped off with Serenity's grimy rugby jacket, but never mind. If I make it in time, I won't have to drive all the way to the campground, way out in the middle of nowhere, and sign them in. En route, Jack stops pounding on Olympia and says, "I forgot my lunch." Performing a maniacal U-turn, I race home, retrieve his backpack, drive way out to the middle of nowhere and deposit them just inside the campground gates (to heck with late sign-in). The Jeep packs it in halfway home.

I'm stuck on the side of a deserted road with Bugs Bunny and my clogs. Stepping out of the car, I splash through a cold puddle to pop the hood and glower at the evil, miserable engine. I poke and prod at various greasy wires and belts. A passing motorist slows down. I hope he isn't a rapist, or worse, the camp director. I zip my jacket up to the neck. An unshaven man in a worse clunker than mine slows down, looks me over, then steps on the gas and disappears down the road.

All's quiet. The road is emptied of passersby. I lean against the rear bumper and fold my arms against the morning chill. At least the rain has stopped and the sun is peeking out from behind the clouds. Where is everybody?

Months go by on the muddy shoulder. At last, a leather-jacketed motorcyclist pulls over, unbuckles his helmet, leans back on his seat and grins. "Need a hand?"

Just my rotten luck, the kind motorcyclist turns out to be a sickeningly attractive man. I admire his crinkly brown eyes and then his tight blue jeans as he leans under the hood and fiddles with the lucky little engine parts while I pick surreptitiously at the grease on my thumb. The man calls out from under the hood: "Are you sure there's gas in it?"

Ah.

The man offers to go down the road for a can of gas. After kick-starting his bike (always so damn sexy to watch this manoeuvre), he turns to me and says, "Do you want to come with me for the ride?"

I'm astride the motorcycle in seconds. Immediately, the regrets flood in. What do I do with my arms? Where do I hold on? Would it be improper to hug the driver, a stranger? As the bike leaps forward, I almost fall off. Losing all my inhibitions, I hold on tight, my face pressed up against the soft hide of his jacket. The jacket and its owner smell wonderful: a mixture of sun-warmed leather, Ivory soap and a lemony aftershave lotion.

What a thrill! I'm perched on the back of a magnificent

motorcycle feeling the cool wind in my face. The bike is all shining chrome and soft leather seats, its dashing owner all mirrored sunglasses, clean denim and polished leather boots. My aging ride is swathed in grubby cheap fabric with stuffing poking through the holes. Obviously this freewheeling stranger isn't the parent of small children.

The only leather thing I own is my dog-eared wallet, which I just now realize is resting on my kitchen counter back home. At the gas station, my knight in shining armour waves off my promise of an IOU and ferries me back to my rusty wheels with a container of gas.

I dismount reluctantly. Once gassed, the stupid Jeep starts up with a healthy roar. Damn. There's nothing left to do but say, "Thank you." I suppose it's more appropriate than, "Why don't we do it in the road?"

"Any time," he says. Then he climbs on his bike, tips his helmet and rides away.

All the way home, I indulge in a dreamy fantasy featuring my rescuer as a rich sultan carrying me away on a magic carpet, then I lament the poverty of my imagination, no doubt a result of years of continuous malexposure to children's videos.

I walk in the door to find Bitesalot has experienced a hairball attack on the hall carpet. While I'm crouched down on my knees, scrubbing cat puke, I can't help but think how my life has become a real whirlwind of excitement.

A few minutes later I catch the sight of my flabby body in the bathroom mirror and I'm reminded of my abandoned workout schedule. My spirits are plummeting downwards. It's useless to fantasize, given my fanny size.

I'm losing my entire grip on the joy of my first job-freedom day. Guess I better get on with it, mosey down to the headhunter's office and see if they have anything for me.

***

Jack didn't give me a hassle about camp this morning because I slept in and let Donald take him and Olympia to the bus. That's the ticket: I woke up well rested and in excellent humour. Life is pretty good after all: the kids are at summer camp, at least for the rest of the week, and Serenity called last night; she arrived, safely, at my useless ex's hovel. Best of all (pinch me), I don't have to go to work today!

I should press on with my job search, but I'm not in any big rush to hit the bricks yet. The prospect of collecting Employment Insurance benefits for as long as possible is far more entrancing than landing another soul-sucking office job. There's one annoying catch: I must at least contrive the *appearance* of a job search. Another annoying catch: what if I was to attract an actual job offer? No worries, I'll circumvent that possibility by applying for decent, well-paying jobs only.

The latest ads in the paper were all disappointing. None of them read, *Wanted: Person to sit around all day reading. Top rates. Internet access.*

I was born too late—or too soon—everyone knows the boomers are still hogging all the top jobs and the GenYer's are snapping at my tatty GenXer heels, those sucky babies, forever adored and petted by the media.

But hang on. No reason to be glum. I'm still young and I have the rest of my life to look for work. Today I will take it easy. Pouring myself a scented bath, I sink in gratefully, taking care not to drop my cigarettes and lighter into the bubbles. I could become addicted to a life of blissful idleness on the dole.

I loll in the tub smoking until blissful idleness becomes boring idleness. What are my options? I could go hang out with Bibienne across the road—but her kids aren't off to camp. Scratch that. A workout would be good for my soft, flabby stomach, which is protruding unattractively from a mound of bath bubbles. What about sweeping out the basement or weeding the garden? But I'd better be careful; I might strain something. I'm out of condition. Everyone knows a person should begin with a carefully designed fitness program and ease into strenuous chores slowly, gently.

Hauling my body from the tub, I drag a comb through my wet hair only to find a wad of gum enmeshed at the nape of my neck. Where'd this come from? Probably Jack. This calls for a crisis visit to my hairstylist. I could take this opportunity to have a razor short punk haircut. And go blonde. It's time to reinvent myself. Yes.

I yank hard on the comb and the gum comes away, along with a significant chunk of my hairline. Ow. Man, that hurts. Maybe I'll reinvent myself later, say, after breakfast or tomorrow.

Downstairs, I see that Bitesalot and Scratches have clawed through the screen door again. Cat ire rises. For the umpteenth time I ask myself: why did I abandon the wise old motto of my youth: *Never have kids, pets or plants?*

Plants! Gasping, I run around watering houseplants, neglected for weeks. Two begonias and an orchid are beyond revival.

Glancing out the window, I spot the mail carrier going by.

Goody. I skip out to the mailbox hoping for fat cheques and letters only to find nothing but a phone bill and a credit card statement. Another maxed out card. My lip is twitching, signalling the onset of an attack of hives. Running for my hive syrup, I realize that my glorious good humour has slipped away, in the face of gum wads, dead orchids, shredded screen doors, overdue bills and my mounting resentments against the nearest generations. I try to cheer myself up with the thought that my older siblings are discovering arthritis and constipation and my heartless younger sibs will soon be in charge of administering their medications.

Antihistamine bottle in hand, I slump on the couch to watch the bumps heaving up on my arms and chest. One hive is threatening to block the vision in my left eye. To calm down and stave off a black depression, I attempt my favourite creative visualization: but this time, picturing the perky Valerie Pringle, Gone Grey and Longer-in-Tooth, is an insufficient pick-me-up. My life has gone flat and stale. I'm 37 years old, out of work and reduced to wearing a crumby bathrobe at 11:00 a.m. on a Wednesday. Wednesday used to be hair, salt glow or pedicure at lunchtime.

I'd consult my sagging shelf of self-help books but they're all the same. I already know how to combat anger and depression: affirmations, meditations, creative visualizations, massage therapy with the best bet being a solid crack at out-of-control spending. I should chuck the shelf out the window. Mom would say: *Buck up*. Thinking of bucking up, there *is* one thing left to try: I could have a Love Affair. I suspect that Mom bucked up a fair amount back in the day.

My lip stops twitching. I'm beginning to warm to the idea. A love affair could be just the play therapy I need.

I phone Bibienne to tell her about my freshly minted self-help scheme: "Seriously, I think I need to have an affair."

"You're just bored."

"Maybe. But don't you think any woman worth her salt has at least one romantic affair during marriage?"

"No."

"But you take in stray animals. Why shouldn't I?"

"All my strays get neutered, first thing. And, besides, sex is overrated. Come on over, I'll let you try out my new whirlpool tub."

"It's not the same thing."

"Then maybe you need to get away, take a trip, have

some fun," Bibi says. "But if you have *very* much fun, please don't give me any details."

Bibi already has too many married friends on flings at the moment, all of them moaning nonstop over their indiscretions while ransacking her liquor cabinet for solace. She can't afford another guilt-ridden, adulterous and sudsy friend.

"You're no fun," I say, feeling sulky. I say bye and hang up.

I can forgive Bibienne's attitude though, since she's a professional massage therapist. She's so burnt out that the very thought of a full-frontal skin-rubbing fling makes her flesh crawl. She's also way too complacent to have affairs; she prefers tennis and her pulsating water jets.

Oh well. I still feel that an affair could be a possible hedge against depression but there are no prospects in sight. He'd have to be rich. The job description includes long red fingernails and slutty hair. High heels and lipstick. I couldn't be bothered.

Considering the hot dates of my past, maybe Bibi's right. I could take a trip—there isn't enough cash in the budget for a real vacation but I could afford a campout with the kids, a feasible idea considering they've passed the impossible toddling-into-campfires stage. After all, I'm a certified Survival Expert: it's time they learn some basic skills. We could run naked in the woods and bathe in the lake. No housework, just a few paper plates. I haven't been camping in aeons. It could be entertaining: an escape to simplicity, far away from the burdens of clawing cats and dusty houseplants.

The prospects of a long stint on employment benefits are still appealing. Donald might object to the concept of Freedom 37; I'd better avoid gloating out loud.

***

The kids are horror-struck with my camping plan even though I've promised them swimming on pristine wilderness beaches and exhilarating hikes through the bush. Jack remains unconvinced and declares, "Hiking is lame."

"Camping is *fun*," I say.

Jack asks: "Will there be TV?"

"No."

"Xbox? Playstation?"

"No."

"I'm not going."

I persevere with a wild promise: mouthwatering meals cooked over an open fire. Then I mention the possibilities of sighting small animals of the forest: porcupines, raccoons, chipmunks, squirrels, etc. Jack runs off to find his slingshot while yelling something about hoping to meet up with bears. Olympia screams and clamps onto my leg: "I 'fraid of bears."

Recalling my own deep-seated fear of large carnivores, I remember a recent news item about a vicious bear attack upon a group of unlucky campers. "Bears are afraid of people," I say, while picturing Olympia being eaten up by bears. Cringing, I rush to lie down on my bed, in the throes of a sudden panic attack.

Now *I'm* horror-struck with my camping plan. Too late. I've got prepaid reservations at a wilderness park and a stockpile of brand new camping equipment, all financed with the severance money from my job. I have a red tent, a red lantern, a red cooler and three red sleeping bags. I've colour-bombed our campsite in a rabble-rousing hue sure to fire up all the bears within forty kilometres of the park.

After performing deep breathing exercises for ten minutes, I begin to feel slightly better—until Donald pokes his head into the room to ask if I have any thoughts on dinner. All I can think of is Goldilocks and porridge. Donald, with a cheerful wave of his hand, offers to go for takeout pizza; clearly he is pleased with the announcement of my camping initiative and the prospect of having the house all to himself for the week.

***

Packing up the Jeep for the trip is exhausting. The kids flip out as I fling their heaps of toys out of the back seat. Both of them demand to take along items like hockey sticks, video games, rock collections and giant boxes of stuffed animals. "We need the space for the pillows, sleeping bags and our clothes," I say.

"All useless stuff," Jack yells as Olympia slumps down in middle of the driveway, howling because I've removed her entire collection of Pokémon videos.

Hopes for an early start were wrecked hours ago. I'm spent. We push off. After twenty minutes driving, I remember I have forgotten my wallet on the kitchen table. I race home, retrieve my wallet and pause for a moment to listen to Donald singing in the bathroom upstairs. Singing? Showering? In the middle of the day?

Back in the car, Jack's screaming, "Limpy's putting her feet on me."

"Amn't."

"Get off. You stink."

"NO, YOU GET OFF. I HATE YOU TO DEATH."

I rearrange the entire Jeep so Olympia can hate Jack to death, in silence, from the comfort of the front passenger seat. Our Estimated Time of Arrival now coincides with sundown. I hope I can erect the tenting equipment and, most important, locate the campground's Comfort Stations before darkness envelopes us.

We arrive at the park and join the long lineup of vehicles ahead while the sun sinks behind the trees. All around us, massive SUVs grunt by, hauling trailers equipped with TVs, microwave ovens and private plumbing. Pointing out an RV hauling a trailerful of Sea-Doos, I remark to

Jack and Olympia: "These people are missing out on the Authentic Camping Experience. Tenting is best."

My sentiments escape Jack and Olympia who voice admiration for the trailers. "Look, those kids are playing Nintendo in that RV." Jack folds his arms across his chest and glares at me.

"Tenting Is Best," I say again, but the kids aren't buying it. After winding in circles through the park clutching an impossible map, I finally locate our campsite. Olympia demands to go to the toilet. I drive to the nearest vault toilet, which Olympia refuses to use. "It stinks like shit," she yells.

She's right, the smell could knock back a charging rhino, but a group of senior campers nearby are staring in disapproval, so I use my best authoritative-and-in-control parent voice, "I don't like it when you use bad language."

"But *you* always say *shit*, Mommy."

I hustle her back into the Jeep to search out the Comfort Stations, which promise flush toilets and hot water. We find one after another long winding trip around the campground: it's mobbed by young teenage girls, all wielding curling irons, lipsticks and hairspray. I hope Olympia won't notice the enormous spiders hanging about in all the spaces not occupied by teenage girls but, no luck, Olympia is already freaking out.

I plead with her: there are no other facilities available, spiders are harmless, spiders are Our Friends, the spiders at home are even larger, etc. Cringing at the prospect of sharing a sleeping bag with Olympia after she has peed in her own, I offer her five dollars to ignore the spiders.

"Ten dollars," says she.

"Done," I sigh. With the spider payola precedent set, Olympia yanks down her pants.

The campsite is no doubt picturesque but it's too dark to tell. The new flashlight batteries have mysteriously gone dead. I crash about in the darkness with the tent poles and pegs, while the kids complain: we're starving and we want to eat *right now*. Forget the bid for a healthy meal cooked over a crackling open fire. The kids are ecstatic, their impressions of camping profoundly improved by access to unlimited marshmallows and a family-size bag of barbecue potato chips. I'm not sure if my precariously pitched tent, let alone my sagging self, can hold up through the night. I'm tempted to abandon camp and go home but there's the problem of the rash bet I made with Donald: I must tough out camping for a period of one week. The loser has to organize Olympia's next birthday party while the winner gets to Not Attend.

Around midnight, tucked into a teetery tent, the kids asleep, I hear creepy noises outside the tent walls but I'm much too tired to care. I fall asleep to nocturnal sounds of the teens next door: furtive scurrying movements, sniffings, loud music and shouting: all soothingly reminiscent of home.

***

At dawn, with a flourish of tent unzippering, I release Jack and Olympia upon an unsuspecting campground. I re-pitch the tent and set up the stove to make pancakes and coffee. The site is enchanting: tall pines, a dear little chipmunk perched on an old stump, fresh air and wildflowers. Here the kids will be exposed to the wonders of nature, ah yes, this is the life.

The fresh morning air is pierced by screams: Olympia has fallen from a nearby tree. I rescue her from the bushes and apply first aid to her knee while hearing the first rumble of a thunderstorm on the horizon.

The torrent of rain swamps our campsite. I pass the day indoors, in the Visitors' Centre, learning about logging history, while attempting to mind the kids. Jack and Olympia swoop around the displays playing hide and seek.

The Visitor Centre staff is rather huffy with Jack over an experiment with toilet tissue in the recesses of the men's washroom. I feel huffy too but there's no use in demanding that the staff explain why the women's washroom isn't similarly equipped with the convenience of toilet tissue.

As the tent is soaked through, we're forced to take refuge in the Jeep for the night.

* * *

Another day, rain again. Between cloudbursts, the kids make friends with the neighbours' kids and they all hole up together in the neighbours' snug, watertight trailer playing board games and complaining. The trailer owners, Doug and Dot, are kind enough to take me in as well. The kids bitch nonstop that camping is *lame, lame, lame.*

Dot says, "We love this campground. We've come here every year for seventeen years."

Doug adds, "Just look out for the bears, haha."

"Pah. Don't listen to him," says Dot. "The bears won't bother you if you don't bother them. Just stay away from the poison ivy. There's tons of it here."

I explain that I already know what poison ivy looks like. I crouched in a patch of it last night during a sneaky side trip into the bush in an effort to avoid the vault toilet and the spiders. Now I have an itchy rash blooming across my bum.

Doug laughs and offers to rub down my backside with his special poison ivy preparation. Dot glares at Doug.

As the afternoon wears on, Doug slugs back a few more beers and starts in: "So this blonde walks into a bar ..."

Oh God, I want to leave but the kids are dug in and I can see that our tent has collapsed in the wind. I would be glad to decamp altogether despite my stupid bet but the Jeep is refusing to start. Doug, alarmingly attentive, sits beside me, draping his arm over the back of my chair, calling Dot "Old Girl" and insisting on our visiting them in Hamilton. Dot, in an enormous snit, retaliates with a dinner of greasy bacon and eggs.

After dinner, I insist that the party is over, to howls of protest from the kids, but I cannot take one more Viagra joke. Doug is determined to escort us back to our site. I say I can manage but to no avail. Dot purses her lips. She hands Doug his jacket and tosses me a switchblade glance of warning.

I'm grateful for the presence of the kids as Doug is getting right out of hand and is whispering urgent offers to scratch my itchy backside. I warn him to get his hand off my bum or I will stab him with my umbrella. Why, when promised the Knight of Cups, do I get The Fool instead? Thanks go out to the lousy stinking cosmos for bringing this horndog to my attention.

Sigh. I wonder where my magic carpet ride motorcycle guy is now?

We're forced to sleep in the Jeep again since the tent is submerged under a pool of water. My only consolation: the loud teens next door are long gone.

***

Finally, the monsoon is over. We slog down to the beach. I slather sunscreen on the kids and watch them frolic in the waves. Lying back in my beach chair, my sheet-white body draped with a towel, I read trampy pulp fiction. Periodically, I reapply sunscreen on the kids and turn a page. Nobody gets burned.

Later we roast hot dogs over the campfire and, again, nobody gets burned. The stars come out and I show the kids how to locate Cassiopeia, the Swan and the Northern

Cross. At bedtime, we call home to say goodnight to Donald but he is out. Humph.

***

Three days of R&R on the beach: I'm sick to my sandals of sunshine, frolicking in the waves and avoiding Doug and Dot. According to the trail guide, there's an easy Nature Walk to a Fire Tower Lookout with a spectacular view. The kids don't want to go. "C'mon, it'll be a blast," I say.

Two hours later, the kids are complaining bitterly of tiredness and thirst, so I reassure them that the Spectacular Fire Tower Lookout is just around the next bend. My back is in spasms from carrying Olympia around a hundred next bends and up the equivalent of three small mountains. At the summit, I collapse in a sweaty mound at the base of the Fire Tower and endure superior glances from a buff group of Professional Nature Trail Hikers. Jack and Olympia wheedle drinks of water from the hikers and then they scale the rickety tower, Olympia having discovered reserves of boundless energy for climbing. I would gladly jump off the tower into the rocky gorge below but I barely have the strength to stand.

After staggering back to the campsite to make a charming supper of peanut butter sandwiches with stale bread, I flop in my camp chair to inspect my blistered feet. I look up to see an enormous bear shuffling through the bush straight towards me. Backing up rapidly towards the Jeep with the kids in tow, we jump in, rolling up all the windows and locking all the doors. The bear makes a beeline for our picnic table and proceeds to ransack the contents of our cooler.

Trembling, I drive to the Park Office, to summon the park ranger. The ranger follows me back to the site where we find a dozen neighbour campers jostling for position with their cameras. The bear has, by now, destroyed the cooler and is tearing the breadbox to pieces. The ranger waves the onlookers back and employs a sophisticated ranger technique learned from long years at Forestry School: he throws a large rock at the bear. The bear runs away. The ranger leaves. The crowd agrees that the bear was handsome, but rather a small specimen, not much more than a cub really.

"Hey you guys," I say to the kids as they reach for the only item of food left, the marshmallows, "you might as well finish those up because we have to go home tomorrow." Both Jack and Olympia burst into tears, and declare that camping is awesome, not lame at all, never was.

***

I drive home slowly, holding up traffic so as to time our arrival home at exactly one week and not a minute less. Donald, with a glance at his watch, says, "I missed you." He looks tanned and rested.

I try not to display too much glee about winning the birthday party bet only because Olympia is in the room. I wonder how Donald will try to scam his way out of delivering birthday party joys to a dozen six-year-olds? I'm not sure my victory was worth a week in the bush but a kid's birthday party is, after all, the ultimate horror, so it remains to be seen.

***

All morning I lie in bed relishing freshly laundered sheets: obviously Donald went all out to welcome his camp worn wife home. A wave of tenderness overwhelms me. What a good, dear man he is. While I acted as bear bait, Donald acted like a sensitive new age guy keeping the hearth tidy and the home fires lit. Getting up, I spy a group of well-muscled dust bunnies attempting to break free from under the bed. No matter. Better that Donald misses a few domestic strokes than go Martha on me.

Shooing the bunnies back into hiding with my foot, I resolve to evict the troublemaking bunny gang with the vacuum before they rise up and demand their own bed and bath. I ask Donald if he could take the kids to the outdoor pool while I get out the vacuum and dust cloths. Otherwise, come September, we'll have to dress up the biggest bunnies in leather outfits and buy them Harleys to get rid of them.

Olympia shrieks at the idea of bikers under the bed. I tell her, "Don't worry," knowing full well that one day she'll be all in favour of whiskery hunks under her bed.

The eviction of the bunnies proceeds smoothly until a fragment of pale pink notepaper jams the vacuum nozzle. Dislodging the scrap, I toss it into the wastebasket.

Hold up a minute. I snatch it up again and scan the note:

Thanks for lunch! Let's do it again soon ~ L

On the top edge of the scrap I can see a scrolley embossed monogram: L.B. has nice memo paper. Who is L.B.? And what is *she* doing *under my bed?*

Oh my God.

My heart begins to pound. Hard. I wish I had never passed the vacuum—bikers under the bed might have come in handy.

* * *

At lunchtime, I'm still obsessing about the note. I could ask Donald but he is still at the pool with the kids. What's going on here? What the stinking-pale-pink-note-hell is going on here? Better go see Bibienne, right away, and see what she thinks. I charge over to Bibienne's and thrust the note at her. "Donald is screwing around on me. Just look at what I found."

Bibienne says, "Calm down and let's see what we have here."

She studies the note. "Circles over the 'i's," she says. "And look here—lying loops."

My blood is beginning to boil over. How dare he consort with a woman who makes lying loops?

"What are lying loops?"

"Dishonesty. There's a stinger in the 'a' here too. Very dangerous."

"Do you think I should confront him?"

"No way. He'll never admit anything, not unless you get some hard evidence. Who is L.B.? Laurie? Lana? Lolita?"

"I'm thinking it could be Leggy Bambraugh."

"Who?"

"Lindsay Bambraugh. Donald's new boss. I met her at last year's Christmas cocktail party."

I sure do remember her: Paris Hilton with a pink pager. Definitely a lying loops type. And Donald's eyes probably go loopy just looking at her.

"Quite the way to suck up to the boss."

"I thought I was the boss."

Bibienne nods her head slowly and says, "This means war."

two

cannot observe

War means tactical planning. Do I want open warfare? Underground-style freedom fighting? Nuclear Armageddon?

Extreme, no rules warfare is appealing—I could begin with a roaring bonfire of all Donald's belongings on the front lawn. But what if Donald is innocent of nothing but an unrequited lunch and a freak desire to launder sheets?

Even though my stalwart woman's heart knows the dirty, lowdown, lying, cheating truth, solid evidence is required prior to flaming his entire Conan Doyle collection. It would be best to heel in and remain on full alert for now. I can use a few satisfying underground guerrilla revenge tactics on Donald such as spilling a spoonful of bleach around the fly opening of his new designer boxers or letting Olympia play with his persimmon three-wood.

***

At the grocery checkout, I'm making my usual humble plea to the Interac Gods to flash their merciful "approved" message upon me once more when I'm struck by the thought that if Donald were to land a promotion at the firm, the sadistic Interac Gods could go stuff themselves. Good old Lindsay Bambraugh could be useful in this regard. Donald's select philandering could have its financial advantages. He would only be making my half bigger.

Maybe I should be supporting poor ambitious Donald

in his bid for advancement at Doubles. After all, we're in hock up to our eyeballs. Donald is always raving about The Need To Cut Back. He's a Certified Financial Planner (CFP) after all. His clients like to think they're buying shrewd advice from a sharpshooter with a fortune in offshores, timeshares and stock options. Good thing they don't know we cashed in our lone RRSP last year and our portfolio contains nothing but a promise to someday invest in a hot mutual fund if ever our seven maxed-out credit cards, swiping around town like windshield wipers in a deluge, can be paid off.

Sleeping with the boss is a dependable method for speeding your flag up the flagpole. Just think of all the wonderful material benefits. Maybe tomorrow I should go out and buy that gorgeous Ms. Gina suit I've had my eye on. I do need something decent for my job hunt. We can afford it as long as Donald's salary is inflating along with everything else.

Not to mention that this clearly frees me up. So, where the hell is my Knight of Cups? Nowhere in sight, that's where. I might as well forget about empty cosmic promises of dreamboats and concentrate on my nightmarish job search. I haven't made a single contact yet and I'm going broke waiting for my E.I. benefits to kick in. None of this means I have any intention of forgiving Donald or dropping my revenge tactics. They're too much fun.

Checking the mailbox as soon as I get home, I snatch up a brown, windowed envelope—oooh, my first E.I. benefit? Tearing it open, my high hopes are dashed—inside is an appallingly abbreviated assessment notice and instructions how to go online to fill out and file a report. Then I must wait two more weeks before I will receive a single penny of the piffulous compensation offered for an unsuccessful job search. Oh well, the promised pittance will at least cover the cost of regular squeegee look haircuts, guaranteed to scare off most prospective employers.

I sign in to the E.I. website and report my progress:

Did you start work during the period of this report? NO

Did you start a full time job during the period of this report? NO

Did you attend a school or training course during the period of this report? NO

Were you ready, willing and capable of working each day? YES (Well, sort of)

Did you or will you receive money? Definitely NO

No, No, No, Yes, No: I wonder how long I'll be chanting the pogey mantra?

I suppose maybe I better get down to brushing up my resume. My credentials: Basic Training plus a Skill At Arms Certificate. I'm a Certified Specialist in Reconnaissance and Survival from my regular army days. After eight years of getting lost in the bush I traded in my parade boots for civilian high heels. I know everything about making survival gear: I know where to buy top quality rustproof grommets for stringing hats and jackets. I know where to buy the best strings too.

These days job hunters are super competitive. I must find a way to stand out in the crowd. My employment counsellor wants me to request "information interviews" from prospective employers.

First I need prospects: progressive companies that offer respectable wages, benefits and advancement opportunities. This part of the research could take forever.

Then, at any time in the process, things may break down. The employer may "resist" the "information interview." Or the company is absolutely not hiring (it's more likely downsizing to the dimensions of a paper clip). In the unlikely case I score an interview I might botch it up by saying something inappropriate like, "Hello." Or, "Fuck off."

Then I'm supposed to follow up with thoughtful thank you notes to each person met during the information interview process including the receptionist who hates my sucky guts by now.

Gee, maybe the army'll take me back. They're desperate enough to take in any crazy broad who's prepared to wear Gortex and sleep in the mud. I'm sure I'm still a deadeye with a rifle and driving a tank's like riding a bike.

Back in the day, I toughed out basic training, ran obstacle courses, was gassed and learned how to crawl around in the dirt, all a perfect preparation for crack motherhood.

I played war games just long enough to meet Serenity's father. Who can resist a man in a uniform? Not I—especially when I'm rubbing up against a burly one in the depths of a snug foxhole. Never take off your thong in a foxhole unless you want to wear maternity combats. To this very day, Serenity's father still soldiers on, paid to stand prepared for the security of our nation. The nation sleeps at its peril.

This morning I called up all my best contacts: "Do you know anyone who is hiring?" Nobody's hiring.

Oh well, who cares, the thought of going back into uniform or slaving away designing hiking shorts makes me want to throw up anyway.

My E.I. agent suggests skills upgrading: benefits are widely available for students in full-time "Resume Writing" or "Choosing Your Career" programs. "Wait a minute," I say. "What about finishing my university degree? I could go back to school. That might help pump up my resume."

"Hold on," he says. He explains that full-time students learning actual skills at college or university don't qualify for assistance.

"But," says he, "if you aren't in a hurry to graduate—one or two courses are permitted. As long as you continue to look for work and report to me on your job search."

That's it. I'm going straight over to the university to reactivate as a part-time student. Suddenly, I can't wait to begin my serious scholarly lifestyle: challenging my intellect with cutting-edge treatises, the thrill of classroom discussion and debate, the stimulus of mind meeting minds, the on-campus bars.

***

It's been a long time since I've been on campus: there's not only two new bars, but convenient shopping too. Sir Oscar Dingwall University boasts a gleaming new student centre complete with banking machines, a variety of retail outlets and a fast food court. The classrooms and library are now tucked well out of the way of hungry student shoppers looking for a quick bite to eat.

***

Ratfarts. Maybe I think too much but now I think maybe I'm too old to be going back to school. The stress of second thoughts, a futile job search and secret revenge warfare on Donald is causing everything to get right on my wick. I yelled at the kids after catching Jack stuffing peas down the holes of the tubular chrome legs of the kitchen table. My investigation revealed that all four legs, including both legs on Olympia's side of the table, are almost filled to the top, mainly with vegetable matter such as zucchini, carrots and peas, which explains the awful putrid odour wafting around the house lately.

I had to remove the legs from the table with a screwdriver and try to rinse out the foul gunk. Later, I yelled at Bitesalot for traipsing about on the kitchen counters and licking the butter.

So far, intelligence confirming the mysterious "L.B." has been inconclusive: Lindsay Bambraugh called the house one morning looking for Donald. I told her he wasn't home so she said she'd "try him at the uptown office."

Very suspicious. I resisted the urge to say, "I'll bet you will, Honey Bunny."

To combat stress, I'm practising mild guerrilla tactics: when Donald gets home, I will prepare him a tasty ham sandwich—featuring a cholesterol-loaded slab of freshly cat-licked butter.

* * *

We're in the midst of another heat wave. Naturally, the air con has gone on the fritz again. My languidity is preventing further job searching or revenge tactics on Donald. In fact, in this kind of heat, I'm grateful he has a maybe-mistress—better he bother her for his sweaty sexual gratification.

I wonder what would I do if I caught him swinging his noodle down the street? No one would blame me if I tossed him right back out the gate. Single woman status is looking more enticing all the time. I will practise tonight and sleep solo on the couch where I can catch a cool breeze from the window.

* * *

I have to learn the art of self-restraint. Last night, while watching Jon Stewart, I ate way too many nachos, which resulted in an epic instalment of my favourite recurring dream featuring dreamboat Harvey Keitel. Ever since he dropped his pants in *The Piano* I've been hopelessly drawn to men who look like Maori warriors. In last night's episode, Harvey and I were starring together in the latest Tarantino film, but it all went horribly wrong when Holly Hunter showed up in a taxicab with Al Pacino. Holly Hunter always ruins everything. She was probably just a figment of jalapeno pepper sauce but still. I think I should try to do something interesting on a chopper with Dennis Hopper next time.

Will this freaking heat wave never end? Not only am I half dead from lack of sleep, but halfway through breakfast, I'm overtaken by knifelike cramps. I must lie down immediately. Donald can proceed with his plans to repaint the den without me.

Donald mutters darkly, evidently feeling that a monthly menstruation is a lame excuse for regularly staged episodes of laziness. He says he cannot possibly paint the den without an alert adult to run interference with "helpful" children. Fine then, I retort, the toilets are in need of a good scrubbing, certainly that task poses no risk of attracting little helpers. Donald quickly reconsiders. "So where do we keep the drop sheets, anyways?" he snaps.

I stifle my urge to remark that his regularly staged episodes of laziness tend to occur daily rather than once per month.

Downing a handful of pain meds, I rest on my bed in my bra and panties letting the fan blow cooling air across my tortured abdomen. Olympia wanders in: "Whutup, Mom?"

Ah ha—here's my golden opportunity to sensitively initiate that all-important mother-daughter discussion about our red tent time: "I have my period. Do you know what a period is?"

"I'm a boy," she says and runs away to prove it by peeing on the toilet while standing up.

All morning the kids scurry in and out of my bedroom with requests: Can I invite a friend over? Can I have a cookie/candy/freezie? Jack cut Scratchy's whiskers off—can I do Bite's? Can we help Daddy paint? You promised.

"Nooooo. I'm sick. Ask your father. No!—Wait! Stay. Away. From. The. Den."

Too late.

Wretched, wretched, bloody cramps. I roll over and wait to die. Death is uncooperative, so I hope to at least go into a coma, one that will keep going until the kids' summer vacation is over.

After waiting two hours for a half-decent coma, the meds kick in. I waddle into the washroom to check my supply of cotton ponies. All out. Donald appears at the top of the stairs to complain about the mess the kids made with paint in the den when he wasn't looking. Just when *is* he looking? Now I have to remember to avoid the den—the spaces worth visiting in this house have dwindled down to just the bedroom and the bathroom.

I feel like Oscar the Grouch. My house looks like his too. Peeking in the mirror, I sigh: Oscar the Grouch grimaces back. My period has made me green and fuzzy with blood clots.

I ask Donald to go to the store for tampons. Donald exudes an air of long-suffering.

"For heaven's sakes, it's *not* illegal for men to buy tampons you know—get *Tampax* Tampons, please, unscented, but *not* the ones with the plastic applicators, cuz I hate them, get the ones that come with cardboard applicators—they're biodegradable—the plastic ones grab you and pinch if you're not careful—that really hurts—oh, and make sure you get the *Super* size, Super Plus are even better but they're hard to find and make sure you buy a box, no better make it three boxes—they're such a rip those tiny boxes—they sure don't last long, who the *hell* do they think they're fooling? Check if there's a coupon deal—or if you happen to go to Loblaws, they have a store brand that I like for a better price ... You need to write this down?!? Oh forget it, I'll go."

I sneak away from the house when Olympia isn't looking. I have no patience today for long side trips to the toy store, McDonald's and every public restroom in town.

At Loblaws, I wonder: why not President's Choice Tampons? Maybe politically incorrect. Sounds too male. Even though women supposedly can be presidents too. I guess it would be too offensive to women, to remind us that we never get to be president. Not to mention the implications of creeping Americanisms. They could call them Madam Prime Minister's Plugs. I wish plugs were sold by the hundreds, instead of in piddly boxes of forty. If men had periods, plugs would be sold by the case like motor oil in the Canadian Tire store.

Wandering into the mall, I notice back-to-school signs draped over everything. A wonderful shiver of anticipation runs down my spine: school! The kids return to school soon! Then despair—proper school clothes will be necessary. Quickly, I snatch up a dozen pair of briefs for each kid.

Since I'll be heading back to school myself soon, I should grab some new panties for me as well, but it's too depressing. My briefs are less than brief nowadays. Perhaps it's time to visit the bookstore and check out the latest in the diet book section. A few years ago, I burned my entire diet book collection in a fit of feminist pique. I adopted a radical feminist perspective on doughnuts and gained two sizes.

I emerge from the bookstore clutching several worthy looking volumes with titles like *Set Free the Leviathan Woman Within* and *Meditation Guide to Mindfulness.* I'm afraid that my inner Leviathan Woman will slouch into full-blown view with minimum coaxing from me if my doughnut shop visits continue unchecked. The guilt inspired by *The Cavewoman Diet* on the seat beside me prevents a friendly rendezvous with Boston Creams. Time to make a serious vow: I will forgo all high-fat and high-carb foods forever, from this day forward, and eat properly, like my lean cave-dwelling ancestors did. I will cross-train every day. I would even give up smoking but I can't expect to tackle all my ruinous habits in one flush.

At home, I set the kettle on for healthful herbal tea but then I decide, based on previous experience, I'm in danger of homicidal orneriness if my caffeine requirements are ignored. A chocolate chip cookie would go nicely with the coffee. I'll get down with being a cavewoman tomorrow.

I must admit, I have also caved in to the purchase of the *Bedside Book of Astrology: Your Zodiac of Love Signs.* I can consult the stars for harmless diversion and then move over to the morale improvement business. My astrological forecast for the year ahead is promising indeed: *You may suffer betrayal at the hands of treacherous Gemini but not to worry, Scorpio-woman, a sizzling romance with Pisces is in the stars for you.*

Apparently, the occult world continues to toy with me. Romance? Where? When? I rack my brains but I don't know any Pisceans. How disappointing. But I do know a tricky two-timing twin: that would be Donald.

But how can this be? According to my star charts, I'm perfectly well matched with my current partner. Could the stars actually mean Donald? Inexplicably, the revelation causes a deep sinking feeling. I already exhausted the entire zodiac during my wild oats days. I ought to put breast to the nest and accept the best of a raggedy lot. Maybe all that business with Lindsay Bambraugh was just my imagination. After all, Donald stacks up well on the balance: he makes dynamite coffee every morning and bathes regularly. Many women don't even get that much.

***

Donald and Olympia are still struggling over final birthday party negotiations. Donald thought perhaps two little friends could pop by after dinner for a slice of birthday cake. "Half an hour is about right for these things, eh?" He looks at me for reassurance.

I look away quickly: it's critical to avoid eye contact in these situations; I wouldn't want pangs of sympathy to cloud my judgment and mess up the thrill of witnessing his final undoing.

Olympia is demanding a major Theme Party—say, pirates. With at least twenty-five piratic friends. And lots of Games. And Feasting. And a Sleepover. *Like all the other kids' parties.*

Donald is helpless in the face of birthday buccaneering. He is reduced to begging me for guidance. I relent (for Olympia's sake, natch, she deserves an extra big party this year). I offer a hint to Donald that he could organize a backyard treasure hunt and perhaps a sword-making craft.

Then, I add, cruelly, "Oh—and don't forget to do the loot bags."

Donald gives me a blank stare. He's doomed. My evil twin pipes up to suggest that he take Olympia to the mall to settle the selection of party hats and invitations. There is a God and she's premenstrual today.

After they leave, I have second thoughts—perhaps a sword craft is unwise; the runt pirates will no doubt slash around the house with the swords between attempts to keelhaul each other. I will have to stash all the breakables. I should've suggested pin the tail on the donkey. Donald could be the donkey.

Olympia is requesting drums for a birthday gift. I was thinking more in the way of a quiet little watch.

I'm diverted from thoughts of quiet little watches by the sounds of a gunfight and explosives coming from the vicinity of the driveway. Peering cautiously through the curtains, I see Serenity leaping from the driver's seat of a rusty pickup truck. The front door slams open and in bounds my prodigal daughter accompanied by a friend, two filthy backpacks and one enormous shaggy dog that appears to be a cross between a Newfoundland and a Cave Bear.

Both cats expand three sizes and begin hissing and spitting. The dog ignores the cats and heads straight to the cat food, devouring the contents of both bowls in seconds.

I greet Serenity and then I suggest that she return to the driveway and shut off the truck motor. Serenity scowls and mumbles something about faulty wiring and run-on. Then she introduces me to her new friend Dennis—formerly Denise—who she met at the Michigan Womyn's Festival (silly me, I thought Serenity was in Alberta all summer).

Dennis sets down a case of beer and grins. Serenity's new girlfriend is all out in favour of piercings and packing. Her style might best be described as chainsaw-positive. Serenity shares that she is also sex-positive, ain't that grrrreat? She adds that Dennis has no place to stay because her father changed the locks again, "so Dennis can stay with us, right?"

Dennis is the owner of the Cave Bear. "His name is George Bush," she says, as George Bush lifts his leg to pee on the kitchen chair. I shriek "No—bad dog," at which he flops down under the kitchen table to gnaw off its legs and beslobber the floor, while the cats crabwalk from the room in terror.

***

I wish Serenity and Dennis would go back on the road. Since their sudden arrival last week, all the decent electronics in the house including the cordless phone, the best DVD player and radio have disappeared up to Serenity's room. Serenity's door has been locked ever since. I can only assume they're having a sex-positive week as they emerge intermittently to plunder the contents of the refrigerator, the liquor cabinet and my purse. As for me, I spent the week luring George Bush back out doors while Olympia and Jack spent the week sneaking him back in and demanding nipple rings.

***

I receive a call from Mom, home from her so-called hostelling but I know better: Serenity ran into her at the Michigan Womyn's Festival. Apparently, she was wearing nothing but a floral loincloth and an ankh necklace. I didn't know the Elder Hostel program included unplugged lesbian lollapaloozas.

"Serenity tells me she bumped into you at the Michigan Womyn's Festival?"

"True story. You should go sometime."

Me, petulantly: "I would've except I only had to look for work and watch Olympia and Jack all summer, remember?"

My petulance is wasted as she launches into a description of what it's like to toast the sunrise with champagne at the trailhead just before backpacking through the Grand Canyon.

Then, in a chirpy voice, she says she's thinking of a fall trip with Brian to the Midwest where Phil Mickelson is supposed to be touring: "I'll be walking all the courses with Phil!"

***

Olympia's sixth birthday has arrived. The "emancipation" birthday, the long awaited coming of age that heralds full day, everyday, school attendance. Full day, everyday, school attendance is a huge developmental milestone. For me, that is. From now on, I can blame everything that Olympia says or does on her teachers.

Turning six also means Olympia's character is, according to the childrearing manuals, almost fully set. I'm terrified that this may be true. Last night at bedtime, Olympia announced firmly, "I don't believe in God." That's ten perfectly respectable commandments gone right out the window. I pity those teachers. They haven't a prayer.

All day today the crusty old seadog, Donald, lived up to his end of the bargain and entertained Olympia and her friends in the backyard with so-called pirate pizza, cake and games. One look at Donald's twisted grey face when I arrived home from a full spa retreat was enough to convince me: a kid's birthday party is easily worth a month in the bush.

three

chaff

Drat. It's only Friday of the first week of school and the kids are off already, enjoying a P.A. day. P.A. must stand for Parental Aggravation. While dressing, I hear sounds of a clash erupting over the breakfast table downstairs. Serenity is screaming at Jack: "Shut up, you spoiled little shit."

Summer's barely ended and I'm already facing down the barrel of another long day of crazed, snarling sibling rivalry. I can't help it. Listening to the kids' squabbling always makes me crazed and snarly.

I arrive downstairs as Jack howls, "You shut up, loser," and picks up a fork in an attempt to threaten Serenity. "Don't cry, it only makes me stronger," she laughs, at which he stabs her in the forearm with the fork.

Serenity lunges for Jack while I throw my body between the two combatants and yell, "What the hell's going on here?"

Olympia pipes up from the sidelines: "Serenity and Dennis ate all the Honeycomb in Serenity's room last night."

"What, the new jumbo box I just bought yesterday?" An eleven-bucker box of cereal. I'd like to jab Serenity with a fork myself.

I send Jack to his room while Serenity stomps off to find Band-Aids. Olympia is winding up to tears over the loss of sugary cereal. To keep the peace, I agree to go to the store to buy her another box.

Returning with the groceries and a conciliatory box of

doughnuts, I learn that while I was gone, Serenity locked Jack in the basement and Jack pounded the door with his hockey stick until the doorknob fell off.

I spend half an hour jimmying the door open. The whole time, Olympia nyea-nyea-nyea-na-na'd Jack into a rage through the door, knowing he couldn't get her until I threatened to get her myself.

While repairing the doorknob, I recalled last year's course in Handling Sibling Rivalry. I learned all about Acknowledging Their Anger and Describing the Problem Respectfully while Jack clobbered Olympia, Olympia bit Serenity and Serenity creamed both of them.

I take refuge in my bedroom and turn to my stack of self-help guides. I wonder where the *Meditation Guide to Mindfulness* has gone. I can't find it anywhere. It's a bit much when you lose your book on mindfulness.

The Leviathan guide for women looks idiotic but maybe it's time to sweep aside all negativity and open my mind. Skipping the boring introduction, I grab pen and paper and read the instructions in Chapter 1:

To become a Giantess you start with Baby Steps: Make a list of everything you must accomplish tomorrow.

On tomorrow's agenda is a visit to the in-laws. Ducky. Thanks go out to this dumb book for providing this annoying reminder and steering me towards another fit of depression.

I don't want to be a Giantess now. Tossing the book aside, I lie back on my pillow to think. The bright-side news is it's September and the schools are forced to open their doors again next week. Monday morning, I will launch into a tight new fall routine. But then, there's that downside to September: it's the first dismal herald of the oncoming dreadful fall season complete with Halloween and the vile Christmas climax. Perish the thought. I've already forbidden the kids to mention the words "Halloween costume" until 1 October. I must try not to think of the "C" word until December. Oh Lord. "C" is coming. I take a deep breath. It's essential to remain calm. Too late. I'm comprehensively depressed now.

What are my options? I could resign all my family responsibilities and run away to New Zealand, I could torch the house for the insurance money or I could become a Wal-Mart Greeter/Pickpocket Expert.

Or maybe I better just buckle down: after all, I'm returning to school next week. Maybe I'm destined to become a brilliant intellectual giantess.

***

Hearing pounding on the front door, I open it to find my next-door neighbour, Lewis Morris Boriston, going apeshit on the doorstep. He's waving aloft a large mangled hunk of blue plastic. "Your stupid mutt ruined my pool cover. That'll be three hundred dollars."

Sacre bleu. No point in demanding proof. In less than one month George Bush has devoured—besides a fortune in dog food—all the lawn furniture, the barbecue cover, the tires off two bicycles and a substantial section of wood siding, including four metres of eaves trough, off the back of the house. This is just the exterior damage. When he managed to sneak indoors he unstuffed the couch, shortened two tables and demolished a stapler, my favourite sweater and the dining room carpet.

I've tried everything. You never know what you'll get if you tie him up: crazed barking automaton, escape artist or frenzied backhoe. Usually frenzied backhoe: the backyard is well on its way to becoming a pond.

After ridding my doorstep of Boriston by pledging a pool cover replacement, I inform Serenity for the zillionth time that Dennis's dog is no longer welcome. I also insist they both trot outside this second to clear away the numerous poop piles and debris deposited over what's left of the yard.

From now on, when I go out, I will lock George Bush in the laundry room. He can make himself useful and eat the dirty laundry while I'm attending classes—I've enrolled in Canadian Literature on Tuesdays and Creative Writing on Thursdays, starting on the morrow.

* * *

The alarm didn't go off. Now I have to race around like a demented squirrel to get ready for my first day of school.

I make the mistake of going into the basement to look for a clean shirt. There are easily nine or ten loads of laundry piled in front of the machine plus the contents of the hampers upstairs. I feel a strong urge to cut classes on my very first day.

Jack appears beside me. "Where're my gym shoes?"

Where, indeed? Where's Donald? It's his bloody turn to get the kids organized for school. I could slay that man. He never does anything around here while I do absolutely everything. Well, things are going to change around here. He has a CFP designation and an MBA. It's time he learned to do something useful.

"Where's your father?"

"Uhaaihhaidoughnohoahuh."

"That's it, dammit. Go find him, wherever he is, and tell him I want him to come down here. Now."

Jack walks over to the bottom of the basement stairs and screams: "Daaaaaaadddddddddddeeeeeeeeeeee ..."

"I didn't say scream from the bottom of—never mind, I'll get him myself." I ship Jack off with clean underwear, heave an armload into the machine and shout upstairs to summon Donald. No answer.

Remembering my race against the clock, I sort everything into piles for later and sprint upstairs to dress in record time.

Frak. I forgot to add the soap to the washing machine: I tear back downstairs, while recalling pathetic old Prufrock who measured out his life in coffee spoons. At least he got a decent cup of coffee once in a while. My own life is measured out in cups of powdered detergent. Prufrock had it made compared to me. He probably had a cute French maid to rinse out his curdy shorts. I'm sure he never had to endure the sheer torture of accidentally snorking some of those powerful blue detergent beads up his nose like I did just now.

"Ow oww owww owww ..." Where the hell is that useless bloody man? As the Great Goddess is my witness, if I'm to ever remarry, it will be to a man who has been properly raised and socialized to women. I scream upstairs again. Donald's head appears at the top of the stairs and he says, "I'm sorry, I was running the dishwasher just now. Did you need me? I'm making the kids' lunches and thought you might like a sandwich for school—do you want egg salad or chicken?"

***

I've arrived well in time to select the best seat in the lecture hall. It's a smart move to sit near the front of the hall but slightly off to one side in the lecturnal blind spot so I'll avoid attracting unnecessary attention from a reputedly sadistic CanLit professor. Professor D. Greshen has a reputation for carrying grudges; therefore, I will take all possible precautions to keep myself out of the line of academic fire. I'm fully armed to defend myself with the exceptional notes I intend to take with my new fine tipped roller ball pens and notebook, neatly dated and operationally ready on the desk before me.

Scanning the roomful of babbling students, I can see

that none of them are prepared to take proper notes and all appear to be decades younger than me. Hair fashions have changed: everyone is wearing intricate braided styles, coloured spikes, dreds or no hair at all. I may be the only person in the room with organic hair.

Ducking my head behind my notebook, I inspect foot fashions. I note that Birkenstock'd feet outnumber Nike wearers. I can congratulate myself on a savvy fashion sense as I wiggle my stylin' toes within their awesome vintage Birkenstocks.

"Cool shoes," remarks the young dredlocked man beside me. I award him with a winning smile of gratitude, and then I grasp that he is speaking to a young woman beyond me. The flush of embarrassment spreads down to the tips of my toes and beyond. The room is unbearably hot and stuffy. I realize I'm having a hot flash and I burn comprehensively with annoyance that the onset of an early menopause should coincide with my first day of school.

Gathering my tote bag, notebook and pens, I fumble towards the door, bumping into a man in my hurry to exit. Retrieving his spectacles from the floor, I excuse myself and hurry to the women's restroom.

My hot flash takes forever to subside. Splashing my tomato-red face with cold water only causes my "waterproof" mascara to streak. I slink back into the lecture hall while ducking the saturnine gaze of the venerable and rebespectacled Professor Greshen, who is now well into his introductory lecture. Midway through the row, I find my seat taken. Now I must slouch at the back of the room and hang my head in shame with all the other latecomers.

***

At lunch, I review the course syllabus for my CanLit class. I'm required to attend one lecture plus one tutorial per week, plus I have to read sixteen million books, prepare three essays, and undergo one midterm and one final examination. In addition, a portion of my grade will be based upon participation *and* weekly assignments in tutorials. Not to mention the supplementary readings available at the library. Man, this will be even tougher than real work.

It's soon time to go to my tutorial class. According to my schedule, I'm assigned to a class led by an M. Doorite. I hope Doorite is a woman. I've had enough of men in my life trying to lord it over me.

Entering the tutorial room, I spy a man sitting at the desk in front of the room, shuffling through papers. M. Doorite is male, after all, but he is also distractingly attractive. Like a young version of Harvey Keitel. I wonder if he's younger than me? I hope not.

I had never considered the possibility of being older than my tutorial leader. What an appalling thought. It's weird to be older than the teacher, even if he's merely a grad student dressed up to look like a real teacher. I feel ancient and matronly. However, there's still the opportunity to intimidate. I can project an air of wisdom and mature intellect. From now on, I will wear my studious looking reading glasses and avoid makeup.

Doorite's hairline is slightly receding but this only gives him a more appealing mature look. On second thought, Doorite is probably around my age after all and a small, discreetly applied quantity of mascara and lip colour is very becoming on the gracefully aging woman.

Funny, the man looks familiar too. Where have I met him? I scrutinize Doorite as he closes the classroom door and begins blathering on about course outlines and essay writing. Neat denims, blue shirt and tie, leather jacket. On the chair beside his desk, I spy a motorcycle helmet.

Good grief. It's the magic carpet ride motorcycle guy. I hope he doesn't remember me stranded on the roadside in my pyjamas. Probably not since today I'm superbly pulled together with flat-ironed hair and wicked new low-rise jeans. I'm not a bit like the frumpy mud-spattered grunge I was a few weeks ago.

As I leave the classroom, Doorite smiles disarmingly at me and says, "Hey, no Bugs Bunny today?"

***

Creative Writing class: an easy credit, no doubt. All I have to do is just show up in class wearing black and scribble out a few twisted stories, ha, ha, roses are dead, Violet is a porn star.

Professor Stanley Stool informs the class that he prefers to be addressed as "Coach." The poor man must have a Kinsella complex. I'm afraid I'll have to conjure up sportive metaphors such as hockey arenas representing the vast twin pads of life: playing your position and trying to survive against the great goons of existence.

It's not so bad—an Irving complex would be much worse—I would then be obliged to deliver the World According to Stanley Stool and ensure that I include at least one bear as a pivotal character in every story I write.

Stool wants two pages of prose or one of poetry ready to go for next class. Like I said, roses are dead.

***

Where are my brains? I have agreed, reluctantly, to become a Tawny Owl for the local Brownie unit, as Olympia is newly enrolled. An exemplary Tawny Owl must provide guidance to girls on their journey to young womanhood by role modelling, teaching new skills and sharing life's wisdom. I have promised to Help Others and Do My Best. Instead, all things considered, I ought to raise my right hand and swear that I will Try Not To Screw This Up.

Memories of my own days of Girl Guiding are dim: I

dropped out of Guiding to pursue boys—a dismal waste of time; however, now I can heal my Inner Brownie and buy one of those sharp Alfred Sung blouses we leaders get to wear. Visions of campfires, sing-a-longs, cooperating and sharing inspire misty eyes as the first actual meeting begins.

Brown Owl, a twenty-five-year veteran, has a whistle, no neck and a fiercely determined look. A grubby-looking papier-mâché toadstool is whisked out for the opening circle; we all join hands and skip around singing, "We're the Brownies ..." I feel really silly but skip around gamely. The toadstool disappears and we all gather to make crafts.

I'm in charge of the mouse craft: the girls must glue bead eyes and string tails onto the body of a mouse, half a walnut shell. This afternoon I devoted four hours to cracking 357 walnuts in an attempt to procure twenty-seven intact walnut shells. Olympia chooses craft time to cling to my forearm as my demonstration of the craft proceeds.

How annoying: the strings and bead eyes won't stay stuck to the walnut shells. I advise my Brownies to try to be patient but they're bored of my cute little mouse craft within seconds and are demanding better adhesives. The Smallest Brownie is in tears as she has somehow managed to paste her walnut shell to the surface of the table and has tons of glue in her eyebrows and hair. I pry her shell off the table, managing to crack it into pieces. I must then console an anguished Smallest Brownie while attempting to pry Olympia off my forearm without cracking her in pieces.

I'm receiving numerous jackboot glances from Brown Owl's craft table—which hums along efficiently. I'd like to rip Brown Owl's eyebrows back down to proper position.

Will this meeting ever end? After the "Going on a Bear Hunt" song I hope. *Can't go over it. Can't go under it. Can't go around it. Gotta go through it.* As soon as the last tube of glue is packed into the craft cupboard, I bolt home to lend a hand to a restorative glass of wine. Gotta go through it.

***

Goody. Doorite cancelled tutorial class today to give us an opportunity to attend a computer lab, as he thinks computer knowledge is the key to success in university courses.

In the lab, I begin my online session by reading a long list of earnest email postings sent by desperate students trying to fathom how to retrieve messages, save messages, delete messages and decipher the software, etc. Some queries appear to be misdirected from students trying to post to online class discussions for other courses, in one case a posting appears to be from a discussion at another university.

No one has progressed to the point of discussing the assignments and readings.

I'm heartened by the conspicuous lack of contributions from Doorite. He probably hasn't figured out how to post messages yet himself.

I'll give it a shot:

Subject: Baffled

To: CANLIT@ding.u.com.edu

From: pauline@ding.u.com.edu

> *Anyone want to discuss the first assignment with me? I don't get it.*

~Pauline

***

Returning to the computer lab, I discover twenty-eight new postings in my mailbox. Most of them add to the favourite thread of class discussion: the stupidity and futility of conducting class discussions via computers. I open a message, *privately sent*, from someone named Michael:

Subject: Re: Baffled

From: michael@ding.u.com.edu

To: pauline@ding.u.com.edu

Hi Pauline. If you would like to meet me after class next time we can discuss the first assignment.

~Michael

I am flattered by this personal attention—but who is this Michael??? He writes like he *knows* me. And, the cheek of this young man, asking me for a study date. I like him tremendously already but—sigh—it would be best to avoid temptation and nip this flirtation in the bud:

Subject: Have we met?

From: Pauline@ding.u.com.edu

To: Michael@ding.u.com.edu

Who are you? Re. meeting after class: sorry, I'm married. I don't do study dates.

~Pauline

How sweet to think that young "Michael" has a crush on me. Because of him, my battered heart has been airlifted from the fender-bender zone of marriage and plopped on a happy little cloud. I run home and spend the remainder of the day trying to figure out which one he is and looking for my contact lenses.

***

Before class, I run over to the computer lab. My heart does a mini back flip to see *another* private email from Michael! I open it quickly:

Subject: Re. Have we met?

To: pauline@ding.u.com.edu

From: michael@ding.u.com.edu

I wasn't asking for a date. I am your tutorial leader. You may email me your assignment if you need any help.

Michael Doorite, T.A. (Teaching Assistant).

P.S. I am also married.

My heart descends from the clouds and lands back in the parking lot with a thump. Cringing with shame and humiliation, I email my apologies and the assignment immediately. No way can I go into that man's tutorial class today given this embarrassment. How can I look him in the eye? I will beg off sick. I'm all queasy now. I better go home and lie down for a bit. A little Crème de Menthe on crushed ice is always stomach soothing. I still love email: I can use it to deliver my regrets.

* * *

Two pages of actual creative prose are due tomorrow. Or one page of poetry. No story ideas spring to mind but how hard could a single page of poetry be?

After a gruelling morning spent staring at a blank sheet of paper, I decide to tackle a compelling topic for the contemporary poet:

Top Ten Reasons to Quit Writing Poetry.

Number Ten: You realize your obscure and incomprehensible poetry really is obscure and incomprehensible. [For an ultra-cool postmodern twist, I will write this sentence out backwards which will render it almost impenetrable.]

Number Nine: Thheerreee aaaarrreeee bzzzzzzzzzzzz alll ovrrrr uuuuuuuuuuu

Number Eight: You're sick and tired of taking out the heaps of bro ken images.

Number Seven: Your agent tells you that Vince McMahon finds your work "inspiring of perspiring" and wants you to give a reading on the next Wrestlemania

Number Six: yr dogder hz infirmed yu that yr hart probily cunt stand th incitement enymore

Number Five: you find out that e e cummings had no upper case on his typewriter

I can't think of any more reasons. What to do? I could change my title to *Top Six Reasons.* Or, I could always say my poem is a work in progress rather than admit it's unfinished; yes, that sounds so much more writerly.

***

I feel superior to fully half the students who came to class with half-baked excuses rather than completed assignments ready to hand in. Coach Stool, in a profound and erudite response to queries regarding the art of writing and creative blocks, grunted: "Let the shit flow."

Evidently, he's a raw writing enthusiast. I feel relieved: he's bound to like my shitty unfinished poem.

***

I assemble with thirty-five eager Brownies and Leaders in the parking lot of Clearview Conservation Area. Brown Owl, a woman quietly referred to as "Gestapo Owl" by the other Owls in the district, is crisply uniformed and offensively cheery. She checks her wristwatch, toots her whistle and raises her hand in a snappy Girl Guide salute. The entire Brownie troop, plus a few startled passersby, ceases milling around the parking lot and snaps to attention. G. Owl folds her arms and maddogs Smallest Brownie who is giggling. Smallest Brownie blanches.

She begins, in a foghorn voice, "Good morning, girls. Remember: there's to be No Fooling Around. Don't dawdle. Stay in your activity groups, don't chat with your neighbour, be quiet and don't pick the flowers. Laura! Park that gum in the garbage. Where's your guide hat??? Well. Put. It. On. Your. Head. *Everyone* must wear her guide hat …" G. Owl stops yelling long enough to scan craniums.

I swallow my gum and duck my head. Damn. Forgot my stupid guide hat.

My group is going for a hike. My shoulders are already aching under the weight of a backpack stuffed with trail guide, field guide, compass, binoculars, camera, first aid kit, sunscreen, snacks, bug spray, water flask, notepad and pencils.

G. Owl continues with much sniffing probably owing to her miffery about absent hats. "I want everyone to reconvene here in one hour sharp," she says. "*And don't forget to have fun.*"

I charge along the path with my assigned group of Brownies to seek the wonders of nature and shatter all the peace in the forest.

We arrive at the first checkpoint having spied no signs of bird or mammal. All the wonders of nature have fled upon hearing our noisy approach. I remind everybody to keep together, and offer merit points to Brownies who can walk the most quietly. Then I discover that three Brownies are missing from the group. I speed back down the trail only to find them poking sticks into a humongous pile of dog droppings near the trailhead.

The second checkpoint opens into a lovely grassy meadow. "Be especially quiet so you won't scare away any wildlife," I say.

Dividing the group into smaller patrols of three, I send them off to seek mushrooms, wildflowers and interesting birds, saying, "Blow your whistles if you see anything you want to share with the other patrols."

Within minutes, a round of vigorous whistle blowing arises from the patrol at the edge of the meadow. I hurry over importantly, clutching my field guide and binoculars. All my patrols are peering over the edge of an embankment, still blowing their whistles, and pointing and shouting at a naked teenage couple below, scrambling to snatch up jeans, shirts, shoes and socks. All the Brownies are jostling for a choice viewing angle and are hollering: "What're they doing?" "Why was he lying on top of her?" "I know what they were doing. I saw my Mom and Dad do that once." "I saw that boy's dinky." "Do we get a badge for finding them first?" Two patrols begin arguing about who saw them first.

I hustle my charges away from the scene. Smallest Brownie is frightened and about to cry. The older Brownies are giggling and smirking. One pipes up to comment that the couple was mating like dragonflies do except dragonflies only stick their tails together. Her comment spawns a rash of enthusiasm for describing unusual sightings of animal couplings such as the time someone's neighbourhood dogs got "stuck" requiring her Dad to hose them apart and did you know gerbils bite each other when they do it? One little girl shared the interesting fact that boy horses have very long penises.

Steering the conversation away from descriptions of unusual kinds of penises found in the animal kingdom, I suggest to the girls that the young couple ought not to have been naked in the woods. The Brownies wax enthusiastic about contributing to the new thread of discussion: "They might get sunburned." "Or poison ivy." "Or people might see them. Like we did." "Or they could hurt each other bouncing around like that."

I assure the Brownies that no one was getting hurt and that the couple was simply enacting the mating behaviour of our species, end of discussion. If you have any more questions you may ask Mother or Father or, better yet, Brown Owl.

Olympia immediately peppers me with more questions, e.g., "Mommy, mating is yucky, do I have to mate, do I, do I?" I secretly agree that mating is all too frequently in the category of yucky. I don't have much to go on at any rate. Smallest Brownie disintegrates into tears, and sniffs, "I don' wanna mate." I restrain myself from expanding on the concept of No Means No and resist commenting that, in most circumstances, a headache is all they'll ever need.

As a matter of note, I can feel the onset of pounding in the region of my temples, like a young bull moose rutting at my skull.

There are five more checkpoints left to complete the Nature Walk. By the fourth checkpoint, Smallest Brownie stops weeping and demands to go to a toilet. She refuses to pee in the bushes. By the fifth checkpoint she has wet her pants and is weeping again. By now, two Brownies have scraped their knees and a third has bonked into a tree earning herself a large bump on the middle of her forehead.

I wonder whatever happened to the sixth checkpoint? Perhaps we took a wrong fork somewhere back along the trail? I'm fed up to my Brownie pins with Environmental Appreciation: unchecked clear-cutting of forests is beginning to seem like a reasonable idea. Several Brownies recall a fork in the path: I was too busy handing out first aid to notice. We double back to the fork and find, praises be, the sixth checkpoint.

As we emerge from the bush, I can see G. Owl. She looks put out. Her face curdles with the revelation of the events of the hike as chatty Brownies recount to the group their experiences with horse penises and nudity in the woods. At this, all the leaders and parents turn to me, with pointy pitchfork faces.

Smallest Brownie begins to giggle and point. Coming off the trail are the two young lovers from the woods. All eyes turn to check out the red-faced pair. From the stony expression on the girl's face as they hasten by us to their car, I can tell her boyfriend is already forked over and hanging in the gallows.

four

Bona Fides

Coach Stool failed to grasp the profundities of my "Top Ten" poem even after I explained them to him. Evidently, he would prefer a serious poem containing serious words. Judging from Stool's vocabulary, any word related to a substance oozing or, better yet, spewing from a bodily orifice would do. I'm doomed. Another major assignment is coming due and I can't think of any fresh metaphors for things rotten and disgusting.

***

Picking up my latest efforts between two fingertips, Stool leads the discussion: "Lose the stink-heads and stink-tails."

Me: "What do you mean?"

"I *mean* the superfluous extras. The beginning and ending. Redundant. The middle could be cut way back too."

The "A" students smirk and lean forward to offer further critical response: "Why so many characters? I think your story might work better without characters. Characters are so derivative."

"I could tell right away that you're a 'thesaurus' kind of writer. Roget is so, well, you know …" (At this everyone nods their heads in agreement.)

"Did you have any sort of plot in mind?"

What a bunch of trolls. My Creative Writing workshop is fast becoming a complete write-off but it's too late to drop out without incurring serious academic penalties. I must face the awful truth: I'm stuck with Stool.

I have also given up on online discussions, at least for Creative Writing. The discussion board, or "Writing Wall," is fraught with technical problems. Many students are unable to access the wall. The Wall often goes missing. Messages disappear or get scrambled.

Whenever a student ventures cautious criticism of the course, Stool posts messages asking others what they think of so-and-so's "shit-for-brains" remarks. Stool's technique is effective: it cuts down on unwanted questions and comments; although last week, two students became frustrated to the point of wall abuse and screamed back at Stool using all capital letters and rude emoticons.

The best thing I can do is lay low and watch The Wall go up in flames.

***

Justifications for buying a new personal computer: the lineups at the school computer lab are becoming a nuisance. I would much prefer to lose files and crash programs in the privacy of my own home. Plus, the kids are lacking the academic advantages conferred by access to a decent home computer (and are tormenting my life away for access to computer games with names like Sim Decapitator, Crush Face II and Marrow Quest: The Legend of Buddy Bonesucker).

At the computer store, I fork over my entire E.I. cheque as a down payment on a new computer and printer. And another justification: I can fend off the E.I. claims inspector with a dazzling worldwide job search effort. I'm sure he couldn't run me to ground on the web.

After dinner, I lead the family into the den to admire the new system. I inform them that the computer is locked and loaded, and brimming with educational software to boot. The kids groan but proceed to show Donald and me how to download a headache in three minutes or less.

***

The new computer is also brimming with preloaded games including several addictive card games like Solitaire and Mahjongg. Bibienne warned me about the dangers of dependency on FreeCell but I heeded her not.

While playing Vegas-style Solitaire, I recall that in the recent rush of buying and installing the new computer system, I neglected to update my E.I. claim on time again.

Two months ago I designated Wednesdays as Job Search Day. But it's too late now—I'm on a roll with $550 against the house and I have to try to beat Donald's record. If the Great Goddess meant for me to work, she would've provided me with a real job by now.

The computer beeps at me. It's Bibienne with a text message: "Don't forget exhibition game tonight."

I almost forgot. Hockey! Where are my skates? Man, I'm so down with that: the crunch of bodies against the boards, passing the puck down the ice to victory, the beer celebration in the locker room. So what if my joints can't take it any more? Even though Bibi and I are the most senior players on the bench, Bibi is still the best right-winger in town and I can still clean out the corners for them. No body contact means wait till the ref turns her back, then BAAAAM! At least on the ice, my moby Venus hips will be valued.

***

As I glide around the ice, warming up, I feel fantastic. It's so good to be back. I've got my groove on now. Look at those babies on the opposition: so young, so innocent, that little left-winger over there thinks she knows how to play hockey. We'll show these young'uns what it's all about. Bonzai!

***

Groan. I'm forced to skip classes again today. I can barely move. My neck is broken. And both my shoulders. And I think that whacked little left-winger dislocated my middle finger. Plus, early-early this morning, Olympia appeared beside my bed complaining she felt hot and her stomach hurt. I tried to ignore her for five more minutes of shut-eye and then she threw up on my pillow. I've missed all but one of my CanLit tutorials so far. I wonder if Doorite has noticed my poor attendance?

***

I've just finished applying the black stripes to Olympia's "escaped convict" costume. She refuses to be anything in a costume I could buy at the store. The felon design and production has taken days while a good old traditional ghost costume would've meant five minute's worth of ripping eyeholes in a threadbare white sheet. I never get to do a ghost.

I'm dressing up as a clown. Donald pops his head around the bathroom door to observe the application of greasepaint and a large red clown nose to my face. He surveys my costume, borrowed from Bibienne: a purple striped bodysuit, red patent miniskirt and tarty little white boots. He glances at the glass of wine on the counter beside me and smirks: "Boozo the slut-clown. That's hot."

I tell him that seeing as he is such a comedian then he can wear the clown costume and take Olympia to the Community Centre costume party himself.

I suffer his swift apologies including a fumbling attempt at a peacemaking kiss resulting in the loss of my red clown nose into the toilet. Plucking my nose from the bowl, I reattach it with the uncomfortable feeling that this is symbolic of some core aspect of our relationship but I cannot face what it might be.

Jack The Raptor is already long gone with his friends to rampage and gnaw on candy in distant neighbourhoods. I hope he's very distant (as promised).

Serenity and Dennis frittered the entire day away, upstairs in their room, preparing for the Sapphic highlight of the season. I peek in to find they look same as always, with the minor addition of a few extra whips and chains. Dennis inquires if I wish to come along on their witchy revels, reiterating her firm belief that I'm simply pre-lesbian (as are all straight women and perhaps even some men in her eyes).

I wonder if perhaps Dennis is onto something, but I'm afraid at my age and stage I am no longer *pre*-anything, except menstrual, more like I'm *post*-everything except *mortem*.

Donald drops us off at the Halloween party and speeds away. Before entering, I beg Olympia to demonstrate self-control at the refreshment table.

"I threw up on a princess last year, didn't I?" recalls Olympia happily.

"Yes, yes, you did," I nod with what I hope is an adequate measure of frowny-facedness to cover up my prideful smirk.

Inside the doors, Olympia disappears into the fray of screaming ghosts and goblins. My eyes are having difficulty adjusting to the "spooky" atmospheric lighting provided by electric strings of little plastic jack-o'-lanterns. Blind, I step forward and somebody's brat kid dressed in a vampire costume and on roller blades runs over my foot. I wonder who brought this little bloodsucking monster on wheels? I'd like to tell them to teach their kid some manners.

The refreshments table is covered with orange cake crumbs and sticky juice box spills. I wish the organizer parents would act their age and licence these nasty events. How can I get into my clown character without substantial improvisational enhancements? I deplore the lack of enhancements. I'm sure that parents in more advanced nations wouldn't stand for it. My nose smells funny and itches. Removing my nose and floppy hat, I slump against the wall in misery.

"Hi there," says a man dressed in a Mountie costume complete with fake handlebar moustache and sideburns. The mounted man salutes me with a tip of his felt hat and proffers an opaque plastic cup filled with—beer!

"Sam Steele, at your service, Ma'am."

I can't quite place the tall handsome lawman in the dim light but I feel an instant bond. He's most likely a local garage mechanic who has serviced the Jeep recently. I've always had a soft spot for garage mechanics. Such handy guys to have around. And what a fine fellow to rescue me, a damsel in distress.

I drain my plastic cup and feel cheered. The cheerful feeling increases as my dashing Mountie slips away to his secret filling station every so often and returns with more. What luck.

The Mountie attempts to point out his son in the crowd. "He's over there, the one with the vampire costume."

"What an adorable child."

My contact lenses have gone all blurry from beer and greasepaint but I can tell he's just like his adorable father. The evening has turned out to be very congenial. Nothing beats a man in a uniform: they hold their liquor well and know how to amuse the ladies.

After my third cupful of beer, I ask my Mountie if I can see his gun.

"Sure. Would you like to hold it?"

"Sure. Why not?"

"But if you start clowning around with it I'll have to cuff you."

"Just you try. Bang bang shoot shoot …"

The Mountie takes me by the wrist and is about to apprehend me—"I always get my man!"—when Olympia tugs on my sleeve: "Mummmmmmeeeee, I feel sick."

I sigh and tell my fearless Mountie I have to go, while hoping aloud I might bump into him again sometime.

The Mountie frowns and looks perplexed. "Pauline, I hope so. We've missed you in tutorials."

Oh brother. It's Doorite. I'm such a dough-head.

five

Garrison Force

How embarrassing. I should never have clowned around with Michael Doorite last night. I just knew I'd manage to make a fool of myself in front of this man. Again. He's too delicious. It's always been my fate to parade my unshaved pits in front of the cutest lifeguard. Speaking of fate, why do I keep bumping into this man all over town, as if I were a character from a James Redfield novel?

So much for my carefully cultivated studious image. What if he thinks I'm a bimbo now?

I lock myself into the den to begin work on my CanLit essay. So what if Michael Doorite thinks I'm a bimbo. He'll know the truth soon enough once I submit my first essay.

***

Today's tutorial class was discouraging: Doorite reminded us about the upcoming essay submission deadline: we only have two more weeks and should have concluded a first draft by now. I have twenty-two pages of notes but no thesis. Humph. Michael's not as cute as when he wore scarlet and siphoned beer into me.

***

Today's my birthday: Freedom 37 gives way to Freedom 38, if you can call two bratty kids, one rebellious teenager, a roving husband, a heavily mortgaged house, piffulous family income and hamster wheel lifestyle "emancipated."

A critical peek at my backside in the bathroom mirror this morning revealed suspicious lumpy bits where smooth skin once existed. Cellulite.

Five years ago was the "First Grey Hair" birthday, last year, the "Chicken Neck" scare and now this. I've yet to come to grips with the aging process. Seems like only yesterday I was toothsome and plumy; how quickly one becomes long in the tooth and pruney.

I have to try not to be bummed out about symptoms: grey hairs, wrinkles, random urges to play golf, strange new preferences for pants with elastic waistbands and goose bumps over the recent announcement of a giant new drugstore in town. In an effort to head off the rapid onset of birthday depression, I will skip Creative Writing Class and go big box drug store shopping.

My pulse quickens at the sight of endless aisles stocked with wart removers, analgesics, deodorant, shampoos, wrinkle creams, vitamins, cold remedies, perfume, lipstick, hair dyes.

Perusing the perfume aisle first, I test a different fragrance for each pulse point, then I stumble towards Cosmetics, demented by a mushroom cloud of Poison, Obsession, Calvin and Passion. I'm waylaid by a Cosmetics Advisor who is brandishing a coupon for a "free" Beauty Makeover—with a minimum purchase of $50. I won't tell her that my bikini line has descended beyond my kneecaps and my standard hair accessory these days is a rubber band that once adorned celery ribs. I'll treat myself to my own head-to-toe Beauty Makeover at home as a do-it-yourself birthday gift: to the sixth ditch of hell in a lead cloak with Naomi Wolf.

I'm ill-prepared for the hair dye section. After a spell spent gaping at the wall of choices before me, a woman with flamethrower red hair and pink highlights offers some guidance. Apparently, I need to decide what kind of statement I am planning to make. It's a good idea to begin by investigating my skin tones. Then I should go in for some hair colour personality testing.

There's no hair colour called waffle so I settle upon a red henna. Henna is safe and washes out according to the flamethrower woman.

I load my basket with all the latest transmogrifying products: Botanical Gels to get a grip on static, Moisturizing Hot Oil conditioner for controlling the frizzies and Volumizer Mist for restoring natural-looking bounce. And let's not forget this morning's cellulite scare: I toss in Cellulite Thigh Cream, Cellulite-fighting bath beads and Cherry-Flavoured Lip Gloss with special ingredients for lip cellulite. Hurrying home to tackle the beauty products, I feel sure they will provide, if not a permanent youthful glow, the means to temporarily lighten the foot of old crow.

First I prepare a cellulite-fighting bath: leaping in I try to meditate away the lumps, as suggested on the box, but I'm twitching all over with impatience. I want to get on with the primping.

Congratulating myself on my excellent birthday plan, I scrub my body down with a loofah to remove the layer of dead skin cells and lather up with the Anti-Cellulite soap. Drying off, I apply a dose of Cellulite Thigh Cream right up to my buttocks. Then, following the directions on the box, I mix the henna powder with hot water and apply the mixture to my hair.

After allowing the minimum fifteen minutes, I wash the green muck from my hair, the mixing bowl, spoons, floor, sink, walls, shower curtains, hands, face and neck. Everything the green muck has contacted is stained a bright pink. Except my hair—it looks exactly the same and numerous grey hairs are still plainly visible. Checking the mirror, I can see my thighs and buttocks appear exactly the same as before. What in the …?

That's it. No more fooling around. Grabbing the thigh cream, I smear on a triple-thick layer and, seizing the henna box, I mix up a second batch and slather it into my hair. I spread Perfecting Cream on my face and smear liquid wax on my legs, armpits and bikini line. Striking an appropriate languid pose on the couch with the latest Vogue magazine, I await my miraculous transformation.

The *Vogue* models are impossibly thin with skeletal limbs, gaunt faces and tiny concave stomachs. Of course, it would be easy to remain that thin when it only takes one lousy cheese puff to fill up your entire alimentary canal. Thoughts of junk food drives me from the couch to liberate a can of Pringles from the snack cupboard. After all, it's my birthday. I deserve chips. I'm worthy of many chips.

Tearing the lid off the can and holding a chip aloft like a priest with a communion wafer, I vow: "From now on, I leave the water and toothpick diets to Kate Moss."

I'm going to eat all the Pringles and rest my head.

An intense stinging sensation on my face interrupts my nap. I've been zonked out for two hours. Rushing to the bathroom to remove the henna from my hair, I discover my ears and the back of my neck have gone shocking red, a hue that persists after scrubbing fruitlessly for ten minutes. Rivulets of red henna have left permanent streaks down my cheeks. My hair has turned greenish-orange with vivid pink strands where the grey strands previously existed. So much for "Evening Sunset." More like "Sailor Take Cover."

All the parts of my face untinted with henna have gone pink and puffy from the peeling effects of Perfecting Cream. Worse yet, my cellulite has gone to war with the anti-cellulite cream: the cellulite is winning, my thighs and buttocks are swelling up with itchy red spots all over. I slop pink calamine lotion on my spots in an attempt to reduce the itching.

I don't look one bit better than before. In fact, I look

about as attractive as boiled rhubarb. Damn. I forgot to purchase headache tablets at the drugstore.

Lying down on the couch again, I hear the door slam—Serenity and Dennis prancing in from school early—cutting classes again—obviously they figured I wouldn't be cutting classes too. It's bad enough to discover that someone has replaced your thighs with bags of cottage cheese but it's even worse to find yourself the parent of a rebellious teenager before being done with the rebellion stage yourself.

In a touching display of concern over my adverse reaction to beauty products (and certainly with no concern over my adverse reaction to their truancy), they collapse onto the floor in laughter. Between snorts, Serenity says, "I've got killer munchies."

They wobble off to the kitchen. I suspect they're on drugs. All the signs suggest that they're rarely *off* drugs. As all seven layers of my skin are still burning intensely, even after the removal of all traces of creams and powders, I can only envy them at this moment.

Actually, I'm sorely tempted to ask them if they could spare me a few pills or a joint. Why feign ignorance? On the other hand, responsible parents don't get stoned in front of the children. They wait until the kids are in bed.

Before I can make up my mind, Dennis wanders in. "Hey Pauline, isn't it your birthday today? C'mon, get baked with us." With that, Dennis drops a stubby joint into my lap.

I'm about to ask *where'd you get that?* Then I remember the old adage: Never look a gift joint in the mouth. And it's my birthday after all. Seizing the joint I say, "What's this? Marijuana? Hash?"

"Homegrown. But it's sweet stuff. You'll get a sick mind stone with a tight finish on the body stone."

"Drugs aren't permitted in this house," I say.

Dennis and Serenity collapse once more on the floor, squealing and gasping.

"Okay, we were bouncing anyway," says Serenity and holds out her hand for the joint. I tuck the joint away in the pocket of my dressing gown and cross my arms. The girls shrug and disappear out the door. Right on: here's my chance to slip out to the back deck and smoke up before Jack and Olympia arrive home from school.

Ahhh—best birthday present in years. Right away I begin to feel better about my pink hair, puffy face, growing older, homegrown poverty, third world poverty, nuclear proliferation, global warming and even the national resurgence of the Tory party.

Studying the fingers on my right hand, I'm reminded: They really are lovely. I've always had attractive, long slender handmodel fingers. I should be thankful for my blessings. I wave my beauteous fingers in the air: Oooh, trails!

I'm not sure what kind of weed this is, but Dennis's homegrown is better than any imported stuff I ever managed to get hold of in my teenage years.

At supper, I'm just coming down off of the body stone when Donald asks what in world is wrong with my legs? The wax strips are as yet attached to my shins and bikini line: now it will be impossible to remove them without the aid of a blowtorch and high quality painkillers.

***

Inventory of birthday gifts: I smoked most of my gift from Serenity and Dennis but I've saved the roach for an emergency. From Jack and Olympia, I got fuzzy slippers; from Mom (sent by post from somewhere near Phoenix), a signed photo of Phil himself and a note, "Brian and I met Phil and Amy in a bar and we had dinner with them.

Amy's sweet but Phil could do better." From Donald, a magnum-sized bottle of bubbly to go with the fluted glasses I asked for but didn't get. From Bibienne came geranium-scented aromatherapy bath oil with coordinating soap and shampoo.

I'm furious with Donald and my so-called best friend Bibienne. Neither of them bothered to organize a party or anything else nice for me this year. Nobody in my worthless circle of friends even telephoned. I've locked myself in the bathroom to sulk. I'm refusing to speak to Donald. I yelled at him to go stuff himself when he hammered on the bathroom door just now. Who needs any of them?

Instead of lending my mind to unprofitable thought processes such as reflections upon my disloyal, uncaring, selfish friends, family and husband, I will meditate on something calming, Zen-like and mind-expanding, say the stupid koan about the stupid tree falling in the stupid forest or suchlike.

***

I have soaked an hour and twenty-five minutes in a geraniumized tub and scrubbed down with the geranium soap. I'm terribly relaxed from drinking all my bubbly and smoking the emergency roach. I don't care any more. I smell like a big geranium and I'm well potted. With no place to go. Yes I do care. Weeping tears of self-pity into the tepid geranium-scented water, I wish someone cared enough at least to abandon me on a sunny patio in Peru.

I emerge from the bathroom to learn that while I was soaking, Bibienne called to find out why I'm not at tonight's game, especially since they're having a Locker Room party in honour of my birthday?

It's not too late. I peel from the house to the arena and fall in. It's my party, and I can drink all night if I want to.

***

It's late. I tiptoe unsteadily into the house. Everyone has gone to bed. I'm not sleepy so I check in to my MSN. No one is online. The time has come for me to venture into chat rooms. I sign in as, "Birthday Girl," and scan the online list of chatters.

Soon, I receive a call from *CamperMan, divorced male, clean chat* from Wisconsin. I decide to throw my ports wide open and accept a keyboard connection. We chat cleanly for a while about camping, gardening and parenting. CamperMan is rather promising as a net friend: he describes himself as tall, fit, and university-educated.

Come visit me in Wisconsin, he says.

I remind him that I'm a Brownie leader, a *married* Brownie leader.

I'd like to go camping with you, he says.

My husband might not like it.

CamperMan explains patiently that visits aren't necessarily accomplished in reality, this is the Internet after all, one may *imagine* visits.

Ah. I get it now. The conversation takes a sudden and abrupt turn. I explain that I'm a newbie; I've had no experience in "visiting."

Experience isn't necessary, I can show you how …

My fingers tremble across the keyboard. I should terminate this connection immediately but curiosity propels me onward.

What do I do?

Are you alone?

Yes.

What are you wearing?

I'm wearing jeans and a sweaty hockey jersey but my imagination can do better, right? What, though? I tap my fingers on the keyboard and try to think of something fetching, but not overly revealing.

A fuzzy sweater and purple nail polish.

Perfect. Slowly I unbutton the top two buttons of your sweater and slide it back just enough to reveal your beautiful bare shoulders. Now I kiss you. I catch you in my arms and brush my mouth slowly across your shoulders and up your neck to reach your slightly parted lips.

I imagine CamperMan's perfect Harvey Keitel-like lips caressing mine. Within four seconds I'm back online wearing a pink lace negligee and perfume, my short brown hair has transformed to long blonde hair sweeping loose down my back.

Your perfume is intoxicating whispers CamperMan. *I'm unzipping the tent. Come on in …*

Does it have to be a tent?

Whatever you want, you got it.

My messy den morphs into a mountain chalet with a huge roaring fire. With his offer of a massage, a bearskin rug appears, perfect for a long slow body rub. *We're snowed in for weeks,* I insist, slipping him a bottle of massage oil. CamperMan applies the oil expertly, slipping the straps of my negligee down my shoulders to my waist while whispering compliments about my gorgeous soft skin and hair, and running his slippery fingers across the small of my back, edging dangerously close to my buttocks. My heart is pounding and I realize that this "visit" is possibly growing out of control. I'm at risk of losing my net cherry.

I don't know what to say next so I type back that CamperMan has a nice haircut. CamperMan, carried away now, whispers, *turn over so I can nibble your …*

Oooooh, go on, nibble my … Nibble my … What, WHAT???

My blood runs cold as the computer screen freezes. My Internet connection has inexplicably vanished. I inspect the telephone cord: it looks fine. I redial and try to log in again but where did our chat room go? I can't find it. Maybe if I … But it's too late. My rumply jeans and t-shirt reappear, my silky blonde hair droops back to brown. I wonder what CamperMan is doing now? Maybe I don't want to know.

Pulse racing, I hurry upstairs to confide my depraved encounter to Donald, who is sound asleep in bed. Shaking him awake, I whisper: "Guess what? I just had cybersex."

Donald's eyebrows hit the ceiling. "Come again?"

I provide a detailed account while gauging Donald's reaction. Perhaps I've gone much too far; however, Donald appears interested, very interested, and he inquires if perhaps a reality-based encounter might be the recommended follow-up. I'm game. Donald throws the blankets aside and I jump in.

Reality-visit concluded, Donald smirkingly remarks that further well-managed cyber visits could be just the thing for a ho-hum married life.

***

I'm in a complete frazzle. Internet fever is causing me to get behind in both my courses. The kids are both home from school today, sore throats and feverish, but still upright and combat ready. I spent the entire morning at the doctor's office collecting prescriptions and at the drug store filling them. Now the afternoon will have to be devoted to holding the line at home.

After constructing a giant fort with the entire household supply of cushions, pillows and comforters in the middle of the living room, Jack starts teasing Olympia by singing over and over, "Barney's dead, Barney's dead" until she screams and punches him. His nosebleed creates convincing evidence of a massacre in the fort. At least I can get out tonight for my hockey game.

At dinnertime, the babysitter phones to say she has too much homework and can't sit for me tonight as promised. It's Friday night; too late to find anyone else. Serenity and

Dennis are gone off somewhere and Donald left hours ago for another weekend conference.

I'm resisting the urge to cry. At last, the kids are tucked into bed, their compliance an accomplishment clinched with heavy-handed doses of cough syrup. While watching *Trailer Park Boys* from the comfort of the cleanest section of the kids' fort, I succumb to garrison mentality, and fortify my defences with a substantial shot of brandy.

***

Explosions and screaming from a nasty cartoon soundtrack at top volume commenced at dawn and the kids are still coughing. Looking outside, I see last night's snowfall melting, turning to grey-brown slush. Relief. No need to shovel the driveway. My head could use a shovelling though.

Stats show that the average Canadian child passively consumes an estimated 30,000 acts of violence on TV during their formative years. I wonder where Jack and Olympia stand—well on their way to mass-murderhood? Oh well. TV is an important element of mainstream culture so it's also valuable for well-rounded child development. Actually, I hope like hell they consume mainstream culture all morning, no, all day, then they will remain passively occupied so I can cram for my CanLit exam, write a Profound and Original short story for my creative writing workshop and decipher an impossible chapter in my brutal Postmodern Theory textbook. I run a rapid detour through the bathroom for a quick PTA (pussy, tits and armpits) with the Sponge Bob sponge. Yesterday's jeans will have to do. I run downstairs and pour cereal into bowls.

The kids begin grumbling. "Yuck, we hate cereal, we want pancakes. Daddy always makes us pancakes on Saturday." Maybe I could serve pancakes soaked in cough syrup?

We're out of cat crunchies. Cornering Bitesalot and Scratches, I toss them outside. They can brush up on their mousing skills today. No guilt allowed. I slouch into the den with a mug of coffee.

Soon Olympia appears in the doorway demanding pop. In the kitchen, I pour her a glass of milk. Olympia doesn't want milk, so she pouts, crosses her arms against her bunny cup and sinks in a heap of discontent to the kitchen floor. Leaving the bunny cup on the counter, I step over the pouting heap to return to the den, resettle and resume efforts to write.

Out in the hallway, Jack yells, "Lumpy spilled her milk."

Olympia screeches back, "I'm *not* Lumpy."

I negotiate a truce between the kids and mop the floor while holding a tenuous Thread of a possibly Serious and Creative Thought Process. Pouring Olympia a second glass of milk, I cave in, adding a huge dose of chocolate syrup. I grab more coffee and head back to the den.

Jack yells, "Lumpy spilled her milk again."

"Thank you, I'll be right there."

I try to ignore them while typing furiously for two minutes. Reluctantly I tear away to investigate the spilled milk. Where'd the kids get to now?

Bitesalot got to the milk first with his muddy paws (who let him back in?). The muddy milk tracks across the floor, the table and the counters. I mop up the mess while my grasp on a second, possibly improved, Serious and Creative Thought Process slips away.

I find the kids watching a Terrible Awful Whacked Show on TV, so I change the channel. The kids shriek so loud I turn the channel back to the Terrible Awful Whacked Show and settle for lowering the volume a bit. Back in the den, I toss Scratches off my chair, which is all sloppy from her muddy wet paws.

The phone is ringing. After a gazillion rings, it stops.

Jack bursts into the den. "I'm invited to play at Harold's house after lunch. Can I go?"

Harold's mother is barely speaking to me since the last time Harold caught one of Jack's colds. On the flip side though, the punishment of silence from Harold's mother isn't such a bad thing, and the opportunity to offload Jack for the whole afternoon is much too attractive. If the house is quiet, Olympia might even take a nap.

The kids give me mad props for serving them canned pasta two days in a row. I wipe the crumbs and Scratches off the counter onto the floor. As a peace offering, I give Scratches the kids' leftovers. She spurns the leftovers and stalks away in a huff.

I hustle Olympia into her coat. Jack's coat is still wet and mud-covered from yesterday. I forgot to put it in the machine. I hand the coat to Jack anyway. Harold's mother would never. Releasing Jack onto Harold's doorstep, I drive away hurriedly, like a terrorist after planting a bomb. Speeding to the grocery store, I scour my memory to recall the items on my shopping list, still magnetized to the refrigerator door. Home again. I put away the groceries. Damn it all. I forgot the flipping cat food.

Olympia, bored with TV, roller-skates through the den with my hockey stick, showing off her slashing and high-sticking skills. "Go play an away game in the hall," I say, at which she bonks into the door, collapses on the floor and bursts into tears. Producing paper and markers, I say, "Here. Draw a pretty picture for me."

My throat feels sore. No doubt I'm getting the kids' cold.

"Mommy, look at my picture." Olympia holds up a drawing of two kids with green ears watching an enormous purple TV. A big smiling yellow sun shines grandly over all. I'm relieved there's no blood, gore, flamethrowers, automatic weapons, etc. The drawing will make a perfect—and easy—cover page for my CanLit essay.

Olympia miraculously agrees to go for a nap. Back in the den, I'm bored to the pins with my Profound and Creative short story effort. My characters are stubbornly refusing to Have Lives. Exiting the word processor, I log in to my favourite new chat room.

***

By evening, I'm felled by the kids' rotten cold. Bibienne calls and suggests a scotch cure, her top remedy for colds, depression, broken bones, stubbed toes, chipped nail polish, etc. "I'll bring you a slurp of Lagavulin—it's the best brand for sore throats."

The Lagavulin is soothing, my head clears, and my sense of smell returns. "See what a mess this place is? It stinks. The cats have peed in basement again, but so what, the basement is a dump anyway. My whole life stinks."

Bibi shakes her head. "Say, 'I hate my life'."

"I hate my life."

"Excellent. Get it out—say it again—louder."

"I hate my life, I hate my life, I hate my life."

"See, doesn't that feel better now? It's a healing mantra."

I drain my glass. Bibienne looks so beautiful. I could hug her.

"Marry me, Bib."

I lub my life.

***

I avoid eye contact with Michael as I hand in my completed CanLit essay. The man is disconcerting. I'm not certain but I think I saw his eyes light up when I walked into class today. Every so often during discussion he flashes me a look. A *smitten* look. It's probably just my imagination but I'm positively flattered and this could be useful at marks time.

Trouble is, Michael has dimples in his cheeks. And attractive crinkles around his eyes. I blush like a fool under his gaze.

six

Stand Down

I hate always being late. The parking lots are jammed so now I have to park away out in Lot ZZ and run for class through a snowstorm. As I arrive inside and hurtle around the corner, I spot Doorite ahead, also running late it seems. He waits for me at the lecture hall door, holding it open. What a gentleman. As I pass, I notice the snowflakes melting on his hair make it curl up at the ends. I suddenly want to run my finger through one of the dark rings on his neck.

I listen to the lecture, which is suspiciously similar to the airless speech we heard last week. I ask around afterwards but everyone dozed off again. No one can really be sure if Professor Greshen repeats the same lecture every week.

Later, in tutorial class, I receive my research paper back. I can feel my mouth go all baggy: the last page is marked with a C+ and a scrawled comment: *A good start on a thorny topic, but not much more than a start. If you wish to try to improve your grade, you may take three days to rewrite and resubmit your work. Great cover page!—M. Doorite, T.A.*

No wonder I scored such a crappy mark: lazy Professor Greshen leaves the marking of my work to an incompetent grad student.

I'm furious. Where's my A? My essay was brilliant. Doorite must be mistaken. At class end, I wait behind to protest my mark.

Doorite glances over my paper for a minute and says, "Sorry. I don't think I can increase your grade as things stand. You know, I may even have been a bit too generous."

I can feel my face becoming hot. "What do I need to do to improve this paper then?"

"I have time right now to go over the weaknesses if you like, in my office. Or we could go to the Dingy Cup."

The coffee shop is packed but we manage to grab a tiny table at the back. Doorite begins: "Your essay has potential but you really need to take the time to think things through."

He begins jotting down titles of papers that he thinks I need to read. "Who are you reading?" he asks.

I can't possibly tell him that stacked on my bedstand is the latest Diana Gabaldon novel and the current *Reader's Digest*, courtesy of a gift subscription from Mom. What have I read lately that isn't on the assigned reading list? Wait, relief, there is something worthy here: "*The Stone Diaries*! Carol Shields!" I say.

"Yes, good stuff. How about writers like Milan Kundera, Jose Saramago, Gao Xingjian ..."

I confess I haven't got round to them yet.

He adds more names to a growing list of titles. I pledge to go to the library right away and take out all the books. Squeezed into the corner beside Michael, shoulder to shoulder, poring over the list that contains names like Rilke, Proust, Flaubert and Joyce Carol Oates, I recall the thrill of the motorcycle ride and the feeling of the warm summer breeze in our faces. Now, we're having coffee and Camus.

***

My bum is sore from sitting in front of the computer for endless dead-boring hours. Blast that man for making me rewrite my essay. It was excellent as it was. Doorite is a fool. I can't imagine what I found attractive in him the other night. No doubt all this typing will turn my beautiful piano fingers into ugly stubs.

***

Three in the morning. Essay finished. Fall into bed. Eyes won't close. Mash pillow about. Get up and take headache tablets. Lie back down. Heart is pounding. Feel hot and sweaty. The classic hallmarks of a full-on panic attack. I've not purchased a single stocking stuffer and Christmas is but three weeks away.

In the dark, mounded beside me, is a soundly slumbering lump of a husband. No fair. He is snoring the untortured snore of a man who has no clue how to "do" Christmas.

The cruel light of morning comes and the Christmas panic has subsided to grinding anxiety and a measure of grim-faced resolve. This year I will make sure Donald does his fair share. I wait until Donald wakes up and I say, "We're not ready for Christmas." Donald gives me a blank look and offers to go downstairs and make me a cup of coffee. It's a start.

I sit up in bed, feeling groggy and light-headed. No wonder. Seizure-inducing busybodies keep asking me the "Are you ready for Christmas?" question. If I were Queen of Defence Staff for a day, I would immediately order an air strike on them and all their kind.

I can't escape the onslaught of tinsel and icicle lights. All of our neighbours have long since spun into a full-bore decorating assault: every home on our street is bedizened with tacky plastic Santas and thousands of twinkling, blinking bloody lights.

We don't have any lights up yet. But who needs lights anyway? After all, I spent an entire afternoon last week constructing a tasteful birch log deer family for the front lawn, complete with cute tree branches for antlers and Christmassy red bandanas around their necks.

I jump out of bed and look out the window to admire them and—they're gone.

"Donald," I streak downstairs and cry, "someone stole our deer family. It's those rotten thieving delinquents from down the road. I'm calling the police. I'll have them charged with property damage."

As I snatch up the phone to dial, Donald blurts out that the deer family has been stabled in the kids' playhouse. Apparently they had an "accident." Something to do with Jack and Harold playing Santa Goes Psycho.

I rush out to the playhouse. The deer father's legs are broken, the deer children are missing their red bows and baby antlers and the deer Mom has lost her head. Psycho Santa will have nothing on me when I get my hands on his lawless elves, Jack and Harold.

Indeed, 'tis that most wonderful time of the year when strangling all family members is a constant obsessive thought. Mom is on top of my stranglee list. She's back from her travels, is taking pole dancing lessons and has lost fifteen pounds since September.

Last night on the phone she went on and on about how allover liposuction can work wonders, and then said, "You might at least want to have your thighs done, dear."

Sharing her spot as list topper is my E.I. worker who cut my benefits last week in a merry fit of pre-holiday claims investigation. When faced with a demand for a list of employer contacts, I had to admit that my job search has ground to a halt. The claims guy then muttered that my job search never got off the ground, period. He then informed me that E.I. claims might be reinstated if a formal application is made and proof of a job search is produced. Furthermore, claimants better be aware that legal action can be taken against fraudulent claims.

At least this freed me up to register in a couple more classes. In January I start two half-credit courses: Feminist Interpretations of Drumming and Thigh Chi: Walking Meditation.

I pour a bowl of cereal for breakfast. A wave of nausea passes through me. Is this the latest miserable flu bug going around? Hope so. The shivery kiss of influenza would provide bedrest and a blameless excuse to shake off Christmas duty.

Speaking of pre-Christmas taskings, I better start drafting up a Christmas shopping list. Groan. Both the jalopies need winter tires. My puny cash reserves mean a pitiful budget for shopping. I could easily go into the red on stocking stuffers alone.

Snatching up paper and pen, I try to think of bulky inexpensive items that can fill up stockings: family size tins of Beefaroni could do the trick and provide that exciting heavy stocking rush. It's perfect—Jack and Olympia worship Chef Boyardee.

Last week, Mom, trying to be helpful, suggested I give budget-conscious homemade gifts.

She's nuts. Homemade gifts are way more expensive than store-bought what with the expense of buying the materials and tools and factoring in costly wastage in the form of all the botched items. Maybe I could come up with ideas for acceptable gifts that could be cleverly crafted from inexpensive materials found in abundance around the home: dust bunnies, newspaper, cardboard boxes, holey socks, driveway gravel, rust scraped off the cars, leftover Halloween candy kisses, beheaded action figures and unpaid bills. Here's a thought:

**E.I. Claims Investigator: the "gag" gift—a "simulated" hairball in a hand painted Popsicle stick container (can use REAL hair from bathtub drain)*

**Bitesalot: a preserved teabag, festively spray painted gold and glue gunned to long string for "active" play*

**Scratches: ground glass concealed in a tasty fish sauce*

**Mom: a homemade bird feeder made out of head portion of well-dried roadkill (take the head of one cat—pry the jaws open, fill with birdseed, and attach a gaily coloured string)*

Jack would enjoy making the bird feeder. Or I could just give Mom a budget-conscious Big Jar O' Nothing.)

Time to stop obsessing about Christmas and get ready for school. As the Jeep is going in for its new tires today, I'll get Donald to drop me off at the campus and catch the bus home later.

In class, I hand in my English essay and Michael launches into a long discussion of metafiction and what it is; for example, he says it can be characters in a story who do things because that's what characters ought to be doing in a story. Duh? Not sure what he means but thinking so much makes me tired. The story here is I would like to lay my head on my desk for a nap. On the way out to the parking lot, it turns out that I'm the loser character in an existential novel who is endlessly looking for a vehicle, which appears to be missing.

Where's the SUV? It's bloody freezing out. I trudge around the entire parking lot until icicles begin to grow out of my nose. I'm about to call the campus police and report a stolen vehicle when Michael pulls up alongside me in his car.

"Everything okay?" he asks.

Suddenly, I remember about the Jeep but I can't admit any of this to Michael. "Fine. Fine. I'm looking for, uh, um, the bus stop."

"It's back that way," he says, pointing away across the lot and giving me a quizzical look. Oh God, I hope he didn't see me zigzagging around the lot, stupidly searching for the Jeep just now. I can feel a hot blush winding like a scarf around the base of my neck.

"Would you like a ride?"

The scarf tightens and I wipe the nostril icicles onto my mitten as I choke out an answer, "Yes, thanks."

Halfway home, Michael points out his street. Oh my. I had no idea we lived so close together. Close enough, in fact, that I could easily ride my bike over to his house. I wonder if Michael owns a bicycle? We might well bump into each other while pedalling in that quiet part of the park near the river ... At this thought, the blushing scarf mounts higher up my cheeks. Michael grins at me. I hope he thinks it's just apples from the cold.

Thanking Michael for the lift, I run into the house. A hot cup of tea and a sandwich might help defrost me. I'm just sitting down to my lunch when Donald walks in the door, carrying a suit bag.

He unzips the bag and pulls out a new silk suit. A Canali. An early Christmas gift. From Lindsay Bambraugh.

"Lindsay Bambraugh bought you a designer suit?" I ask, incredulous. "Why?"

Donald can explain: managing his image is part of Lindsay's job. She's simply making sure her team looks poised, professional and polished. After all, Lindsay is *a visionary* and knows how to do business.

And, according to Donald, Lindsay is also "a generous and big-hearted woman." Hmmm. All I was planning to give Donald for Christmas was a shirt and tie.

He goes upstairs to try on the suit. I follow him into the bedroom. Oh my. Obviously Lindsay is trying to turn my man into a metrosexual. Thank God! The suit looks absofucking smashing on him. Makes me want to tear it off him and have at it. Which I do. Nice. Nice.

Later, after Donald goes back to work, I think what a perfect indulgence it is to have a middle-of-the-day bonus romp when the kids are in school. Ironically, all thanks to Lindsay. Maybe I ought to send her a Christmas card or something.

Ugh. Reminds me—it's time to get on with sending my Christmas cards. I will begin with making a list of all those who have sent me a card so far this year. They will get their cards first. I better remember to hang on to my list—it will come in handy if I win the lotto next year. Only those of my real friends who remembered me with a card will be rewarded with new sports cars; I will righteously snub everyone else.

I'm sidetracked with drafting a version of my Personal Christmas Manifesto which I will ratify some year if I ever get the personal nerve:

I will not bake, I will not shop
I will not work till I drop drop drop
I do not like this Christmas thing
I do not like it, ting a ting ting
I will not plan, I will not wrap
I will not take more Christmas crap
Refrain: nah nah nah nah nah nah nah nah nah

***

Hooray—today is the final CanLit class of the fall term.

Michael handed back my rewritten essay. I jumped for joy to find my mark upgraded to a B+. Michael's scrawled note at the bottom of my paper is especially gratifying: *Pauline: I found this essay much improved. It was interesting and insightful. Keep up the fine effort.—M.*

Michael's not such a despicable guy after all. I think he's brilliant.

I linger after class with several other students to wish Michael a happy holiday. Everyone agrees the proper way to handle the well wishing is to propose a toast to him down at the campus pub.

At the pub, while waiting for a table, the students crowd round Michael. I'm shunted off to stand by the bar but I don't mind at all as three frat brothers are buying draughts for anybody who dares to arm wrestle them, win or lose. I lose three times in quick succession and am about to go arm to arm with Bubba Slam when Michael taps me on the shoulder. "Would you like to dance?"

***

It's 9 a.m. I catch myself humming as I empty the dishwasher and refill it with breakfast dishes. Last night was so much fun. Is it possible Michael *likes* me? He asked me to dance but then he danced with all the females in attendance from tutorial class. It's hard to detect any favouritism on Michael's part but it's easy to see that the female students favour Michael greatly with a drop-dead redhead leading the pack. I soon gave up trying to get near him as Bart Slam kept asking me to dance and, compared to jostling with Drop-Dead, dancing with the Slam Bros. looked far less risky.

No wonder I am happy. The fall term is over. No more classes till January. I close the dishwasher door and lean on the counter. Suddenly, I feel empty. What's this? Next term is weeks away. Why am I so glum at the thought then? It can't be that I will miss old Greshen and Stanley Stool. But a long break without, dare I admit, chances to see Michael seems less than appealing.

Good grief. I have developed a crush on Michael. The thrill of my brief dance with Michael last night rushes through me: I thought it was the beer that made me want to wrap my legs around his waist. Yet, a sobering layer of ice on my windshield this morning failed to restore rational, nonlustful thinking.

Perhaps a break would be for the best. I wouldn't want to allow a baby crush to balloon out of proportion. A little time will let the air out of any puffy attraction.

At any rate, it shouldn't be too hard to keep my mind off Michael what with the hell of Christmas storming down upon me.

***

The queasy sensation in my stomach apparently wasn't the flu bug going around as I have recovered enough to make and consume a bucketful of shortbread dough. In addition, I whipped up a batch of Chocolate Chip Snow-drops as a measure against the oncoming landfall of a Category 5 Christmas PMS although nothing less than Chocolate Chip Avalanches will prevent my hormone-induced desires to disembowel the next person who tells me that they "finished all their Christmas shopping in September."

Bibi calls just in time to stop me from gobbling down another plateful of cookies. Do I want a ride to hockey practice? Oi.

I love hockey. None of the women on the team have started their shopping either. At the start of the season, our team captain warned us that if she finds out any player is doing more domestic stuff than her partner, she will be kicked off the team.

After practice, Bibi and I head over to the Puck Stop Lounge for the annual Christmas get-together with the team. After consuming too much punch, I blabbed to the whole bunch about my recent cybersex experience and pumped up the story to boot. Now I've earned myself a fine new reputation as a computer slut. I should've gone all the way.

***

My slender purchase of some holiday good cheer disappears upon arrival home. There's a note on the kitchen table:

Mom

Dennis and I had to borrow your ride, truck wouldn't start. No one was around so we traded. Back in a couple weeks. Peace.

Serenity.

P.S. Merry Xmas!

My ride. If only I could get my hands on Serenity, I'd boil her in oil. She didn't tell me they were pushing off today. At least Serenity remembered to leave behind the keys to Dennis's truck—which is not really a truck any more, but truck-ish. It's a bit of a stretch to apply the term "truck" to ten thousand rusty bolts hurtling down the road in loose formation.

***

I'm in the grip of another Daley-Parril Christmas At Home. Donald is in the grip of a long winter's nap on the couch awaiting a critical NHL game on TV. Only five hours remain till face-off time. Jack and Olympia are watching TV specials nonstop and issuing updated Santa demands during the endless commercial breaks. If I were Queen for a Day, I would cancel all holidays that involve prolonged school breaks. I would outlaw jolly old Santa and toy advertisements on TV too. I wish someone would organize a Holiday Hating Competition: I could win a prize.

To coax Jack and Olympia away from the tube, I suggest a merry outing to a tree-cutting farm. Donald shudders awake from his nap.

Jack and Olympia, in a rare moment of agreement, shout, "No Way," in unison. "Too cold out." "Boring."

Donald nods his head and thoughtfully suggests I might make a solo outing to purchase a tree from the local Boy Scouts at the gas station: it's important to support worthy community fundraising efforts, etc. I insist that the ritual of felling evergreens is an important step to promoting Christmas spirits, a lovely walk in pine-scented woods will perk us up, Boy Scout trees are no doubt more costly than cut-your-own, and why let the Boy Scouts have all the fun of cutting down our own special tree?

Jack perks up at the thought of hacking down trees. "Can I chop the tree down please, can I, please?" He bolts from the room in search of hatchets, axes and saws. Olympia tears after him, howling, "No fair, I want to chop the tree down."

I urge Donald from the couch to supervise the search as an axe murder in the basement appears imminent. The expression on Donald's face as he storms by indicates that sending him into the fray can only advance the probability of bloodshed. Nevertheless, I run upstairs to seek sweaters and to escape the sounds of a heightened uproar emerging from the basement. I wonder anew at the strength of my personal power to transform a tranquil family scene into a riot in mere seconds.

Back downstairs, I find Olympia parked in front of the TV again and Jack and Donald arguing about the necessity of snow pants, hats, mitts and jackets.

We set out for the tree farm with grim determination to provide the kids with touching memories of jolly family Christmas traditions beyond watching *A Simpson's Christmas* on TV. I urge Jack and Olympia to sing carols to pass the time. Jack and Olympia know a new one called "Rudolph the Shit-Faced Reindeer." Repeat. Repeat. Repeat.

The tree farm is mobbed by shrieking kids and resolutely cheerful parents, all armed with axes. Donald longingly eyes a stand of precut trees. Too late, as Jack and Olympia are already hurtling into the woods. Donald and I lunge after them.

Daylight is rapidly disappearing. I remember—too late—last year's forgotten resolution that from now on Christmas tree-cutting excursions will include Ye Old Traditional Flashlight. When I inquire which tree have they chosen, each kid points to a different specimen. Jack's choice is tall enough for the Sistine Chapel, while Olympia's preference is a young maple.

Patiently, I explain to Olympia the importance of evergreens as the solstice symbol of life, hope, and the promise of spring to come. Olympia is unmoved, and promises tears and recriminations to come if the maple sapling is left behind. Jack and Donald howl "timber" behind us. A monster spruce slams into the snow beside me. Olympia clamps her arms around the sapling declaring her refusal to leave the farm without a personal solstice symbol. My feet are frozen and the bush is dark and creepy after sundown. Capitulating to the demand for the maple, I grab the axe and hack it down myself.

Olympia instantly bursts into howls of rage as she wanted to cut the tree down herself. I try to console her, saying "I'm sorry, darling … baby … sweetchops; you're too young to handle axes anyway; c'mon, tree cutting is supposed to be a Fun Thing; awww honey, please don't cry any more," and "Dammit, if you don't stop crying this second the blessed tree stays in the bush."

I avoid eye contact with Donald as dragging the enormous spruce down the trail is a near-impossible task. The forgotten flashlight would be useful to locate the trail pointers. Donald halts our progress several times to lop another metre off the tree. The spruce is in danger of becoming a table decoration. Jack and Olympia are tired, tearful, and griping about their cold toes, the long walk in the dark, hunger, the lack of junk food or Better Things To Buy at the farm than "boring stupid trees."

Hearing stealthy footsteps approaching behind, we see a hooded man with an axe and rope gaining rapidly upon us. Turns out to be an employee who informs us the farm is closed. Stone-faced, he points with the axe to indicate the exit.

Donald's wallet empties at the front gate; the charge for cut-your-own trees turns out to be steeper than precut

Boy Scout trees, the tree farm man charges us extra for the maple and for the saw we lost in the bushes.

***

Dennis's truck won't start so we have to ask the tree people for a boost. They seem much less smiley and friendly now. A few tries and the truck roars to life. Donald tips the tree man, while announcing, tight-lipped, that it's my turn to drive as his head is pounding.

It's getting late. The kids start yelling and shoving each other in the back seat. Low blood sugar. I speed down the highway towards fast food and then notice the flashing red lights behind us.

After making deep sucking noises to the patrol officer, I insist that Donald take over at least to the portals of the nearest burger place. A tight turn into the drive-thru lane results in the pruning of the side-view mirror from the driver side of the truck and damage to the drive-thru speaker post. Olympia chooses that exact moment to comment on the progress of male pattern baldness on Donald.

The rest of the drive home is uneventful except for the sudden final loss of the spruce on the highway. So much for Donald's assertion that we didn't need to tie the tree: "It will stay put," he said. The truck behind us just ran over it, instantly bonsai-ing the remains.

Donald detours to a Boy Scout concession for a hasty replacement. The selection is well picked over. Strictly budget. We choose one of the remnants: the poor thing is losing its needles so fast I tell Donald we better hurry it home for a drink. I'll take mine shaken, not stirred.

Dennis's truck sputters and quits just as we pull away from the curb. I call the garage to tow it away with strict instructions to the mechanic to *troubleshoot only—do not go ahead with any repairs.* Then we have to drag the trees home on foot, several blocks, with the kids complaining all the way.

As we wrestle the trees through the front door, I can see that the replacement pine may wind up resembling Olympia's maple now that millions of pine needles decorate the front entrance carpet. This merry excursion has all the hallmarks of another benzo Christmas. I slip up to the bedroom and locate my stash of Ativan. Horrors: I'm almost out. Maybe Mom will cut me a few from her stockpile; how she talks her doctor into keeping her in clover is beyond me.

Back downstairs I find the pine leaning from its stand at an impossible angle in the corner of the living room. Donald is wild-eyed in deadly combat with a hopelessly tangled nest of Christmas tree lights. Knowing better than to offer helpful suggestions, I attempt to back from the scene as Donald hurls the lights to the floor, kicks them across the carpet and declares with a strangled roar his absolute refusal to participate in any further Christmas decorating for the rest of the evening; he'll deal with the tree trimming some other time, preferably next June or July.

I pack Jack and Olympia off to bed, visions of Toys R Us dancing in their heads, and flop on the living room couch with my martini nightcap. The tilting pine has disproportionately long branches that jut out into the room. Donald is forced to hold several aside to maintain a full view of the television set and the final gripping plays of the hockey game. Scratches passes the remainder of the evening clawing Olympia's maple to shreds.

***

Tree decorating: it's the same story every year. Jack and Olympia always fight about whose turn it is to hang the angel and Donald always fuddle-duddles the lights. "Donald," I say, "this year can you please arrange the plug so we don't have to crawl around under the tree to turn it *on* and *off*?"

I don't add that, for once, I would like a tree that doesn't require chiropractic treatment before and after use.

I tell Donald that Boriston's multimedia Christmas tree whirls around on its base, has hundreds of pre-programmed blinking lights and an original soundtrack. All without blacking out the neighbourhood and no extension cords in sight.

Donald glares at me. "Then why don't you just move in with Boriston for the holidays if you admire his big flashy tree so much?"

"Fix the lights, or I'll rip them down with my teeth."

"All right, keep your shorts on."

"And while you're at it, do something with the angel. She's not supposed to be sitting on top of a red light."

***

The truck repair bill: $624.95 for a tune-up, new battery and brakes, plus labour. I'm desperate for wheels, even the hell on wheels that is Dennis's truck so I wordlessly pay up and wish my mechanic a Happy Holiday. Once out of earshot, I employ the checkpoint swearing skills I learned long ago on a peacekeeping tour. Survival swearing warms up the air, a good thing, as the truck heater is dinked all of a sudden.

***

Christmas Eve: My cyclic calculations were spot on: my period snuck up on me at dawn while I was still sleeping. The cramping woke me up. Now I have to strip the sheets.

I would rather face the cramps facedown in bed but I have too many last-minute Christmas errands to do.

In the bathroom I discover that Serenity and Dennis plundered my entire supply of tampons for their trip south, so I'm forced to stuff in wide wads of toilet tissue. The toilet tissue stuffing brings on acute pangs of paranoia—could toilet tissue cause toxic shock syndrome? Recently Bibi gave me some sea sponges but I can't quite bring myself to use them: should I sterilize them first? How? I'm afraid I could catch some invasive sea disease from them, say, a colony of sea snails or slugs.

On my way downstairs to the kitchen, I see the house is a complete, top-to-bottom mess: unmade beds, coffee cups strewn in the living room, papers, toys, books everywhere, jam on the counters, sticky spots and those sneaky sock soakers on the kitchen floor. My period is the same: a top-to-bottom mess with sticky spots all over. A sock soaker.

I'm nearing the peak and pinnacle of my seasonal ill humour. I will have to exhaust the day in ticking off a long list of last-minute errands several of which mean breaking last year's vow to never again shop on Christmas Eve. It can't be helped—yesterday Jack broke Donald's mother's Christmas gift and now it must be replaced along with my pilfered supply of tampons.

Partway through the afternoon, while inching through the crowds at the mall, I recall how, at breakfast, Donald declared an urgent need to wrap up some business calls at the office. I would add *file for divorce* to my to-do list if I had the time but I'm too busy replacing *his* mother's Christmas gift. He can just forget the Mommy Kissing the Santa Claus Thing tonight, that's for damn sure.

Christmas day: we battle our way down the highway towards the big smoke and the in-law's house. Upon crossing the threshold, Donald morphs into a Traditional Christmas Man: he spends the day doing crossword puzzles between napping, playing with the kids' new electronic games, snacking, watching football, etc. I'm trapped with His Mother in the kitchen. H.M. is exhausted and suffering frequent frowning attacks: these are the wages of cooking and baking for a solid week. I told Donald he ought to at least help her with the turkey, i.e., stuff it. H.M. waves him back to the couch.

Olympia and Jack spend the day smashing their new breakable toys with old unbreakable ones.

I can hardly stand any more joy and holiday cheer. I succumb to a migraine headache as the family sits down to the table. Thanks to my crampy period, I have an unimpeachable excuse to escape the family dinner to the comfy couch in the basement rec room to watch my favourite Christmas video, *Apocalypse Now*. I can only envy Martin Sheen during the beach bombing scene. I wish I were bombing down south towards a tropical beach, sans family. I'm sure I'd love the smell of native palms on Christmas morning.

Boxing day: we set out through the annual Christmas snowstorm to Mom's. I have to suppress my rising "unploughed road" rage. En route, I tell Donald 'tis my turn to be a Traditional Christmas Man, as he got to be one at His Mother's. Donald takes offence at my remark resulting in a heated argument. Jack interrupts the stony silence portion of the quarrel to inquire if this might be a sign that we will be getting a divorce and, if so, that's right on, since all the coolest kids come from broken homes plus they all get twice as much good stuff at Christmas and birthdays.

I question Jack further only to discover that both he and Olympia feel deprived of step-parent experiences. Serenity has all the advantages in this regard; couldn't we be reasonable and at least consider a trial separation?

A glance at Donald confirms that he would be open to suggestions. Typical. I just organized Christmas and now I get to mastermind a split-up? No dice. However, if he wants to make all the divorce party arrangements then I will gladly attend.

We arrive at Mom's three hours late. Mom is snappish and complaining about having to hold dinner until 9 p.m. Well, shoot me. Geez. It sure doesn't take much to put snarls in her tinsel.

***

After devouring Mom's dinner, we open our presents. I'm excited about the large box tagged with my name. I tear off the wrapping with great expectations only to discover an electric grill that looks like a giant clam. Just what I wanted: a waffle iron for meat. And, come to think of it, it looks exactly the same as the one I gave Mom for Christmas last year.

How touching. My own mother has regifted me.

***

Wonderful to wake up in your own bed. Donald is still slumbering away. Last night, after driving into the small hours to get home and then hauling a trunkload of bags and boxes into the house, Donald and I glanced at each other and headed to bed wordlessly. Donald is still barely speaking to me since I accused him of being too lazy to bother with taking advantage of our irreparable differences.

At least tonight is New Year's Eve, best holiday of the year. For one, the whole sparkling slate thing kicks in but mostly I love it because it's all about drinking. I better get cracking and begin the celebration with some Baileys in my coffee. You can't drink all day if you don't get started first thing in the morning.

seven

Beaten Zone

My firm, personal belief: whatever one chooses to do on New Year's Day sets the tone for the following year. So far today, I haven't got around to joining Amnesty International, Chi Kung or the Tai Chi Society, or volunteering for Green Peace, local Arts Committee, School Council or even to fill the vacant post as Cookie Convenor for the Girl Guides; thus, all these worthy organizations are likely to be left waiting in vain for me for at least another year.

I spent the morning in bed and the afternoon playing Carcassonne and Bean Trader with Olympia and Jack. After supper, I made the mistake of writing down my New Year's resolutions regarding smoking, drinking, fitness and study habits. Donald found them, read them and laughed himself stupid.

Bibienne said that at the beginning of the new year, it's self-revealing to write out a summary of the past year in fifteen words or less. I grab a pen and write, "Lost job. Lindsay Bambraugh. Went back to school. Got drunk. Cats are fatter. Me too."

I wonder if it's okay to add a postscript. I would put, "Met Michael."

***

I wake up overjoyed: no, it's not just a dream, "C" is a whole year away! The kids return to school in a few short days! Winter sunshine is streaming through the bedroom windows and I spy, with disbelief, the kids playing outside, unprompted, both romping in an abundance of new fallen snow. Donald whistles into the bedroom, dewy fresh from a shower and shave, and I recall, as he towels off, that it's been a long time since ... of course I forgive him for being too lazy to split up with me. Batting my eyelashes, I whistle back at him. His wet towel drops to the floor.

Ahh—ecstasy! Take me, take me fast! "C" is a whole year away—who needs foreplay? 'Tis the most wonderful time of the year.

***

Dennis and Serenity arrived home, tired and broke. Better yet, my car's home, with all its tires, not broke.

***

Mom dropped in today on her way to play golf in Pebble Beach. Phil might be there and she "misses him." I have reluctantly agreed to look after Montrose, her fat, spoiled designer Poo-x (Poodle x Schnauzer) while she is snowbirding it down south. According to Mom, Montrose dislikes kennels. And kennel owners.

Donald's taken to calling Montrose, "Mongrowl" because Montrose is a mongrel who growls. A lot. Montrose especially likes to growl at Donald. He must think Donald is the kennel owner.

Mom's heading out just in time: Environment Canada is predicting heavy snow for the next three days.

I sure hope so, since I haven't yet cracked the assigned text for CanLit class tomorrow. I could use a class cancellation for reasons of snow. What a treat: I will place my trust in the Weather Gurus, flake out on the couch and watch 24 tonight.

***

Environment Canada, the Philosopher Kings of Meteorology, was dead wrong. Not a flake fell last night. Therefore I'm forced to attend class today enveloped in ignorance.

Despite my lack of preparation, I must admit I'm looking forward to seeing Michael again. I want to test my theory that I have overcome my silly crush.

In class, Michael zones in on me with a question regarding feminism as it is expressed in *The Journals of Susanna Moodie*. I reply that when Moodie wrote the text, her feminist voice was emerging from within a social context of harsh demands vis-à-vis daily life as a pioneer in the Canadian bush, the ongoing oppression of women and the general suppression of the female voice in the literary canon of the times.

Congratulating myself on such a brilliant and unrehearsed response, I sit back in my chair smugly. Who needs to read these snorey texts anyways?

I do, apparently. Michael quickly points out that when Margaret Atwood wrote the text, she might well have felt that the issue of women's oppression hadn't much changed since pioneer days, and next time I should try to come to class better prepared.

How dare Michael rudely dress me down like this in front of the whole tutorial group? To heck with his sexy blue eyes, I'm determined to delete him from my thoughts as of now.

I arrived home from class to find Donald waiting for me in the driveway, shivering in his car. Turns out Montrose guarded the doors and growled so threateningly, Donald felt safer outside. Meanwhile, the kids sat inside, all warm and cozy in front of the TV, completely oblivious and well-protected from intruders.

Hee hee hee.

***

First thing this morning the school buses were cancelled due to a record-breaking snowstorm so I'm stuck at home with the kids.

A mountain of snow fell overnight and more is on the way. Donald left all the snow shovels outside after the last storm, so I was obliged to use Olympia's pretend shovel to locate and dig out the real shovels.

Montrose continues morose, missing Mom and exhibiting sure signs of depression. He won't eat or drink; he just lies there and bares his teeth at Donald. I slip him an Ativan and drop one myself as lately I'm exhibiting my own signs of depression: the desire to lie there and bare my teeth at Donald. Eating is never a problem but drinking might be if I were to test drive my growing speculation that life would look much better as viewed through the bottom of a daily tumblerful of vodka.

I'm desperate to get away. Fortunately, Mom left me her house keys and a brilliant suggestion: her house might be an ideal place to escape for a few days all alone.

Mom's house: the lap of libidinous luxury. Two fireplaces, a plasma TV plus DVD player, a well-stocked liquor cabinet, a king-size bed, a hot tub and the possibility of meeting Mom's new next-door neighbour Jesse, *a real hottie*, as Mom described him, adding that he is a young, rich and single dentist. Jesse might well be useful to help me keep my mind off Michael who continues to intrude, unwanted, into my thoughts.

To Donald, I refer to Mom's house as an austere, solitary and quiet study nook where the preparation of two essays and assiduous preparation for midterms might be facilitated. And who knew Feminist Drumming could be so bloody demanding? I'll have to take my new tom-toms and practise. Upon mention that I'm willing to take Montrose and George Bush with me, and that Serenity and Dennis are willing to help with Jack and Olympia, Donald sighs and agrees.

***

The weather report is grim. The winter travel advisory declares northern highways to be icy to snow-covered. I'm terrified at the thought of challenging road-hogging tractor-trailers on treacherous highways all the way to Mom's but I set out anyway as I'm even more terrified at the thought of missing out on my opportunity to escape the family bosom for a few days.

Halfway into my journey, I change my mind. It would be better to be embosomed than embalmed. But it's too late to turn back. Visibility is extremely poor because of the Star Wars effect of snow on my windshield plus there's more snow billowing up from the rear wheels of the tanker just ahead of me; therefore, I can barely make out all the warning stickers pasted on the rear of the truck: skeletal hands, shrapnel and erupting flames plus stickers indicating the onboard location of an Emergency Spill Kit. The tanker is no doubt secretly transporting radioactive waste fluids, the kind I could tune in on with my radio. I would ease back more but a second transport is bearing down hard on me from behind; if the tanker up ahead brakes I'll be instantly squished into road kill with a half-life.

I'm caught in the northern version of a *ménage à trois*, the ten-ton trucker sandwich, the True North Tango. Ah, relief, the second transport pulls out to pass. It would be a lasting relief, except we happen to be on a curve and if the road wasn't snow covered a double line would no doubt be visible.

I wish I had left instructions with Donald: female pallbearers please and, for God's sake, don't play Elton John tunes at my funeral. Also, I would prefer cremation but if the transport driver has his way, there won't be anything left of me anyway.

I wish my fingers weren't paralysed or I'd snap that loathsome Eagles tune off the radio. It's no surprise that a tiresome seventies band will be prominently featured in my death scene. I'm sure that at least nine out of ten highway fatalities are scored by a stupid Eagles song because at least nine of the top ten golden oldies is either "Hotel California" or the dead-boring "Life in the Fast Lane."

Funny. The Life flashing before my eyes is brief, and strangely unfamiliar. Perhaps I was sent the wrong one by mistake; I must check on that first when I get wherever I'm going. The Life is boring too, so I must rely upon figments of my imagination to provide some juicy bits. I hope my imagination can come up with some concrete erotic figments involving Harvey Keitel but my cursed imagination prefers to deal up a vision of the kids and Donald, graveside, garbed in bright yellow decontamination coveralls. Oh well. It's probably better like this since Jack hates dressing up. He'll enjoy my funeral more this way.

Also, I think I better open my eyes and pay attention to the road; maybe it's not yet my time to slide off this icy mortal coil after all. The transport is pulling away on the curve, and I can just make out the notice on its rear panel: *If this vehicle is speeding, please call ...* The truck gears up, passes the tanker and roars out of sight before I can determine the number.

I arrive at Mom's as the snowstorm abates. Her steep narrow driveway looks icy. In a hazardous situation like this, it would be a smart move to leave the Jeep at the top of the hill. But, considering the effort required to haul a staggering quantity of gear—groceries, suitcases, books, Montrose and George Bush's kibble, plus two crazed dogs from the top of the icy hill to the house—I realize I'm looking at three trips, minimum, in the dark. I decide to risk entry. Halfway down, my brakes give the nod to the ice, the drive transforms into a luge run, and I lose control of the Jeep as it picks up thrust and spirals, neatly severing four moonlights and three mugho pines at the sides of the drive and coming to rest firmly within a six-foot snowdrift at the bottom, mere inches from the front deck but pointing in the proper direction, uphill.

Incredible: I've no broken bones and, better yet, Mom's dentist neighbour probably didn't witness my graceless entrance as his driveway appears empty. Montrose and George Bush are okay too, rolling their eyes in terror and whining to be released from the luge. I have trouble opening the door, as it's jammed by the drift, but I manage to wriggle out the passenger side after the dogs. I'm grateful that the only fatalities are the moonlights, and mugho pines, yet Mom will still clobber me when she sees the damage. Locating a shovel, I dig a path and extract my gear from the trunk, all in all a feat comparable to five or six portages from the top of the hill.

Upon entry into the house, Montrose figures out that Mom's not there, and sinks into profound funk, laying across the doorsill like a sack of wet Prozac powder while I try to haul in bags over him. I offer him a dish of kibble. Montrose sighs and shuffles back to the front hall to wait by the door for Mom's return, two weeks from now. I unpack and go to bed hoping, in vain as it turns out, to enjoy a dream of a good drilling from a handsome dentist. Instead, I endure a dream of my old craggy dentist, Dr. Argyle, leering at me with toothbrush and dental floss …

***

I awaken much later than usual because of the lack of standard morning stimuli: Jack and Olympia quarrelling, Donald yelling at Jack and Olympia to pipe down and Serenity and Dennis attempting to drown everyone out with what sounds like est-test-punk-rap-fist-fusion-meltdown. Mom's house is pin-drop quiet, perfect for studying, and I certainly intend to get cracking on that right away, right after I snoop through Mom's closet and all her drawers.

Mom's walk-in closet is an eye-widener what with its total lack of stained sweat suits or, for that matter, any garment that is tasteless, outdated or in less than perfect condition. Garment bags, hatboxes, shoe racks and immaculate cubbies ensure that the toe of one strapless shoe will never so much as brush the hem of a raw silk suit. Mom is a neat-clean-freak, even worse than I ever previously suspected. I'm seriously questioning my parentage, for with such solid evidence before me, how can I possibly be her child?

In the nether reaches of the closet I discover a box containing dusty photos, including a selection of snaps taken of me as a pudgy child, then a sullen teen, then a pudgy and sullen adult. Clearly, I have always been massively unphotogenic. The only sensible thing to do is tear them all up. Not a single photo of me as an infant exists in the lot. I will have to scour the whole house to see if I can find the adoption papers.

In a bureau drawer, I'm taken aback to find a wealth of lingerie from Victoria's Secret, all lace and underwires, frills and satin bows, in a rainbow of colours—shocking enough until I chance to uncover a set of oriental Ben Wa balls. I can't explain the presence of unabashed erotica. Okay—Mom likes unusual objects, she probably bought the balls for the cunning hand-carved box they nestle in. She can't possibly know what these are actually for.

It's a bit more of a riddle to explain the presence of a red-and-black lacy bra with peekaboo cutouts and matching crotchless panties. Trying them on, I find they're a perfect fit. Surely I'm not the same size as my mother? I paw through mounds of silky nothings frantically. If I don't find an ugly, shapeless, moth-eaten granny gown soon, I'm going to need some potent mood benders.

Under the bed I find the mother lode—a flat decorator box containing a serious assortment of sex toys: vibrators with studs, vibrators with rotating heads, slim-line and super size vibrators, ankle and wrist cuffs, massage oils, edible gels and *edible underwear*. The underwear reminds me that I haven't had breakfast. The thought of Mom prancing around in edible underwear is taking my appetite away though.

I scrabble through the box looking for an explanation: where did all this come from? Does she know what to do with these gadgets? I'm puzzled by a few of the gizmos myself: what are they for? What do they do? I'm afraid to ask. I thought I was beyond requiring this sort of explanation from my mother.

Scouring the entire house mightn't be such a bright idea after all. I've had just about enough revelatory experiences for one morning. I'm in a complete frazzle now. A hot tub bath would be just the thing to restore a proper relaxed mood for studying. The hot tub is fired up and waiting out in the screened porch where the temperature is at least minus ten. Stuffing my hair under a toque, I slip on Mom's pink Victoria's Secret movie starlet heels and dash across the freezing porch to submerge myself in steaming hot water.

Bliss. I float in the tub until the tips of my fingers are puckered like raisins. Fat raisins. Hot tubs are reputed to be good for weight loss; I should stay in for a week.

I hate to leave the delicious warmth of the bath to press the books. There are a variety of nozzles to play with, reminding me of Bibienne's whirlpool tub. Well, why not? The pulsating jet offers real possibilities. Spreading my legs, I advance towards the spray. I wonder what Mom would make of this—or if she herself, has been making out with the hot tub already. Trouble is, the jets aren't strategically positioned. The smooth sides of the tub keep me at bay.

Despite many attempts to take the tub firmly in hand,

I can't quite shimmy into the sweet spot. Tremendous flexibility, like that of a tree frog, is required for a touchdown. I should never have quit that yoga class.

With a tendon-stretching shove that will cowboy my gait for days, I manage to pinch in close enough. I feel awkward but the jet is really quite sensational and I'm determined to see this through. Closing my eyes I imagine what it would be like to spread out in a hot tub with Michael. Yes. Oh. My.

I step from the tub slowly, so as to stay in the present moment of perfect relaxation. Every pore on my body is wide open, pumping out loads of toxins and stress. My skin will be amazing for weeks. I glide across the porch only to find the sliding glass door frozen shut by an accumulation of ice crystals from the steam. Thumping on the door to loosen the ice, I gape in helpless horror as the latch suddenly snaps down, locking the door. Montrose pads into view. He stares at me quizzically and then flops his body down on top of my pile of warm towels and terry robe. I bang uselessly on the door as my pores snap shut and begin to freeze.

Quickly, I hop back into the tub to warm up while considering ways to get back into the house. There's not much choice: I could stay in the tub until someone finds me—could be days, perhaps the entire week—or I could run around to the front door wearing nothing but a toque and pink starlet slippers.

But what if someone sees me running naked through the yard? The screened porch is furnished with nothing but two plastic lounge chairs and a plastic palm tree. The only possibility is the round hot tub lid lying on the porch floor—I could roll it alongside me, keeping my nakedness between the lid and the wall of the house, giving me protection from the wind and full public exposure. This time, I climb from the tub in a less than regal manner, and set off through the snow drifts wielding the lid, on the side of the house opposite to the dentist.

I plough my way to the front door, only to find it, too, locked tight as a frozen fist. Heaping curses on the evils of Canadian winters and screened-in porches featuring hot tubs, I scurry with the lid back to the warmth of the tub to consider my next move. There's an extra key hidden in the shed on the other side of the house—in plain view of the dentist's house but the situation can't be helped.

I retrieve the key from the shed and struggle on through deep snow. The lid is catching in the shrubberies. As I try to force it along, I accidentally drop the key. Heaving the lid aside, I begin to dig, furiously, with frozen fingers.

"Excuse me. Do you need some help?"

Looking up, I see Jude Law standing at the corner of the house. Wait, no, must be the neighbour. He's wearing a warm sheepskin coat and a dismayed expression. While I blurt out an explanation, the man quickly peels off his coat and gallantly hands it to me, and then kneels in the snow beside me to dig. Eventually the key is uncovered and the stranger accompanies me to the house, unlocking the door as my fingers have turned bluer than his eyes by now. Inviting him in, I promise to return his coat momentarily, after I've slipped into something more comfortable.

In the bathroom, I despair over the shivering spectre in the mirror. I have a red beak where my nose used to be. My hair is tangled and frozen in crazy Celtic-style knot formations. My cheeks appear frostbitten, on both ends. I comb my knots out and dress in several layers, but I think a return to the hot tub may be necessary to restore warmth to my frozen body.

The stranger turns out to be, as suspected, Jesse, Mom's dentist hottie. Clearing my throat, I hand over the coat.

Jesse makes motions toward the door. I can't think of

any intelligent words, let alone a sequence of intelligent words resembling speech. I splutter out an offer of a cup of coffee which, citing work and the possibility of a rain-check, Jesse declines, to my vast relief.

Waving bye and thanks I close the door and swoon onto the living room couch for the afternoon with a stack of Mom's tabloid magazines and her e-blanket cranked on high.

***

Mom's king-size bed is magical, all pillow topped and feathered and fluffed. How does she ever get up in the morning? I'm fully restored from my naked romp in the snowdrifts. Speaking of naked romps, wouldn't it be fine if Michael were here to ...? No, wait. I have to stop thinking about that man. Perhaps it would be better to arrange my daydreams around Jesse next door. He's much too young and baby-faced for me but surely he could stand in as a suitable object of lust while weaning from Michael. Fortunately, most silly crushes don't last; I hope I can detox from this one by next Tuesday's tutorial class.

Lighting up a smoke, I nestle back into the pillows to contemplate my day's schedule. It's time to tackle the books. No more hot tubbing. I will begin with a strong cup of coffee and a brisk shower.

The showerhead comes with seven inspired nozzles. The flexible hose makes things way easier than hot tub jets. What if Micha ... Oops, I mean if Jesse were to fling back my shower doors all of a sudden and offer to scrub my back? There's a thought. Mmmmm.

Or better yet, Jude? Or Harvey Keitel? Four nozzles left to go. I can't help it. I'll use them on Michael.

Always save the best for last. Turns out he's a four-nozzles kind of guy.

After downing a cup of coffee, my head clears a bit.

Good grief. Now the baby crush is a monster crush. And on a man who is capable of annoying me more than Donald himself. It doesn't make sense. But I can't help it. His disarming brown—or are they green?—well, so what—his dreamy blue eyes swim in front of the page when I try to write.

Help. I'm *in love.* Madly, deliriously, inexplicably, head over cracked frozen heels in love.

***

I return home to find the house a disgusting mess, a reliable indicator that Donald remained in a guiltless Bambraugh-free state during my study retreat. And, according to Serenity, Donald remained in a grouchy state the whole time as well.

Maybe he's gone off her. What crummy timing. I need to remain free from my own guilty conscience so I can continue to revel in highly impure thoughts of Michael. My lowly pelvic chakra is spinning right out of control. I'm sorely in need of an Energy Worker but the last time my chakras were exposed to healing influences, I ran out and spent $200 on recordings of the kind of music you would hear if you were stuck in an elevator in the middle of a forest.

Tomorrow: tutorial class with Michael!

***

Driving home from Dingwall, I conduct a review of today's tutorial class. Oddly enough, nothing happened. Instead of ecstatic leaping towards me as if we were in a field of daisies, Michael acted perfectly normal.

What in the world did I expect? Now I can see, with the sickening thump of a reality check, that to him, I'm merely a student he sees once per week. I'm no doubt in la-la land to dream that he has any feelings whatsoever towards me. So now what?

Aversion therapy might work. I will try to picture Michael being incompetent in bed. Yes. He has a little teensy tiny one. I wonder, really, how big is it? Wait, wait, wait. I'll be going off the road here. I better get Michael out of bed. I'll picture him in a drunken stupor beating up his wife. That's better. Yes, he's a beast. I hate Michael. I will repeat this every morning, ten times. An affirmation.

Lighting up a cigarette, I wonder if Michael finds smokers unattractive. I thought I detected a slightly raised eyebrow when I lit up at break today. Perhaps he is disappointed with me? That's it—I quit as of right this minute.

Well, maybe not right *this* minute. Rather than be wasteful, I should finish up the pack. There's only four smokes left anyhow. I will chain smoke them to disgust myself, and enhance my resolve.

Walking in the door and, crumpling my empty cigarette package in my raised fist, I boast triumphantly to Donald: "I'm going cold turkey."

Donald lifts his eyebrow on high. "What? With or without the cigars this time?"

* * *

Quitting smoking is a nightmare already. I'm all tense and nerved up. It doesn't help that the kids are jumping up and down with excitement over a bulky parcel, just arrived through the post from Florida and addressed to them.

They go wild to find a heap of fireworks within: Li'l Red Devils, screamers, rockets, roman candles and giant Mexican sparklers. What else did I expect in the mail from Mom? A picture postcard?

Doesn't Mom know it's illegal to send explosives through the post? Doesn't the postmaster know? Obviously not, as the customs declaration is marked, in Mom's neat handwriting, *fireworks—value $10.* A big fat lie. I happen to know that the street value for just one of those hefty M-80s is ten bucks. Jack is jumping up and down in glee. He says he can get $15 apiece for the screamers at school. Olympia immediately shrieks, "If Jack gets to take his screamers to school, I wanna take mine too."

I assure Olympia that she takes her screamers to school every day already (thank goodness) and then, sternly, I warn both of them that under no circumstance are fireworks to be taken to school nor are they to be used without proper adult supervision. Under penalty of death. In the meantime, I will store them away safely in the back of the hall closet and no one is to touch them.

"NO. NO. NO."

Jack and Olympia go nuts. They want just one little M-80 right now to blow away Olympia's stuffed dinosaur, the purple one with the pull string on his neck who croons on trustingly about kindness, love and caring. Olympia thinks it would be a nice touch to let him sing his happy little song as they sit him on the rocket and light the fuse.

I think so too.

***

As the side effects of Higher Education include a desire to infest others with a knowledge and appreciation of the arts and sciences, I can no longer suppress my urges to expose the kids to the classics of music, art, literature and film. Thus, to commence the cultural incubation of my philistine offspring, I have announced Family Film Classics Night and, despite vigorous protests from the kids, I borrowed *The Miracle Worker* from the local library and lured them towards the television room with soft drinks and bowls of popcorn.

I soon regret the drinks and popcorn—I forgot that

the theme of struggle in the film is expressed primarily through violent food-hurling fights and dinner table confrontations.

I soon regret the whole film fest idea too, as Olympia is hiding her face in my lap during the interminable screaming parts while Jack comments that Anne Bancroft, as teacher Anne Sullivan, is "almost as good" as Arnold Schwarzenegger in *Terminator 2: Judgement Day.*

At long last, we cheer at the final scene where Bancroft hauls the rotten brat, Duke, under the water pump. The screaming stops, the credits roll. Fearing that Olympia is too traumatized, and Jack too thrilled, by the violence, I attempt to offer a thoughtful filmic perspective by explaining that the remarkable Sullivan freed the young, untamed Helen Keller from a life sentence of terrible ignorance and human isolation by employing sign language and her unrelenting persistence.

Jack shrugs and runs away to play video games, free at last to enjoy terrible ignorance and human isolation in the comfort of his own bedroom.

***

Parenting and quitting smoking don't go together.

For the past two days, Olympia, intrigued by the concept of sign language communication, has been unrelentingly persistent in refusing to speak in words, preferring to point and grunt at me in her own private and quite incomprehensible made-up sign language. I warn her that if she persists with imitating the untamed Helen Keller, I might stage my own dramatic improvisation of the Bancroft/Schwarzenegger character.

***

Quitting smoking is much harder than anticipated especially now that I must sneak around behind everyone's back to light up. Smallest Brownie caught me sneaking a smoke before tonight's meeting with the result that all the Brownies solemnly declared they will "help" me in my effort to quit.

Thanks to a bright idea from Brown Owl, the Brownies spent craft time creating anti-smoking posters for me to take home—most featured drawings of withered, blackened lungs and sad-faced carcinomas but Smallest Brownie decided to go with a hideous representation of me lying in my coffin looking decidedly fat.

Now I'm smoking more than ever.

***

Mooning around over Michael is becoming a full-time occupation. The detail that he is married only raises his stock. After all, a married man is generally motivated to maintain a high level of discretion, Donald being such a fine example.

I caught Michael *looking* at me during class today. Could this crush actually be requited? If so, I haven't the foggiest notion what to do about it. I have vowed to *really* quit smoking again, starting this minute. Okay, first thing tomorrow.

I'm experiencing all the ridiculous symptoms of being in love: hatred of all my clothes, hatred of my skin, hair, nails and nose. Hatred of weekends and days (Monday, Wednesday, Thursday and Friday) when I don't see him. Hatred of being unable to concentrate.

Especially hatred of all my clothes: everything in my closet looks frumpy and worn out. Choosing an outfit to wear to class takes forever. My usual jeans and sweaters won't do. I would prefer to appear in class as today's smart, pulled together woman of sensuality. This morning

I rejected four ensembles before opting for a swishy skirt with a clingy low-cut jewel tones top. Then I wondered if the jewel tones top was too revealing so I changed into a clingy skirt with a swishy low-cut blouse.

I would shop for new clothes but, thanks to Dingwall, it looks like I'm closing in on my freshman fifteen. I refuse to restock my closet in larger sizes. Oink, oink. So now I'm on the latest serious fad diet; I will reward myself for weight loss with an attractive, seductive new wardrobe.

The silly fad diet book recommends exercise. Ugh. I'm too fat to move. However, after an afternoon in the presence of angel eyes Michael, I vow to begin my daily exercise program as soon as I get home.

After class, I run to a sports boutique to purchase the proper exercise fashions: I love the latest styles in yoga wear. Within minutes I've found an adorable pair of zipper shorts. And the camisole top with the matching fold-over-waist swing pants was made for me. And I ought to get the running pants with the matching jacket just in case I take up running in springtime. In the change room, I enjoy imagining a pumped up scene of myself—taut and firm of course—running into Michael in the leafiest section of the park while wearing my sexy new tear-aways. No sense in having all these new clothes without purchasing an updated workout video also. The workout video jacket advises that all women should be engaged in weight training programs so, at the last minute, I cave in to a barbell set plus matching ankle and wrist weights. I better start training right away—I can barely lift the shopping bag out to the Jeep.

I rush home to get into my sweet new yoga pants, ignoring the incredulous expression on Donald as I pass him on the stairs to the basement. The slug. I slide the mini trampoline out from behind the furnace into the centre of the family room and dust it off. After warming up with some stretches, I follow up with a few reps of pec-carving weight training with my new barbells. Next, I leap onto the trampoline for my fat-burning cardio. Immediately the trampoline gives way and, instead of bouncing up, I thump straight down, hard. Every vertebra in my back feels as if it were rammed up into my neck. I can see tiny white lights fizzing around in front of my eyes.

Donald and the kids come down to see why I'm moaning.

I can already tell that everything from my ankles on up to the top of my head will be sore for weeks. Donald winces. "Sorry, Pauline, I guess we forgot to tell you that George Bush ate the under supports."

I yell, "That's it—where's the damn mutt?"

Everyone chases me upstairs. Donald tries to talk me down from beaning the dog with my barbell, saying, "It's way too late for a correction, you have to catch him in the act," until I shout, "Then maybe now's the perfect time for you to take a good look at your golf bag," at which Donald lunges for the dog himself.

I spend the evening on the couch wearing my nifty new outfit as I'm too traumatized to climb all the way upstairs to change. Donald is kind enough to offer a heating pad for my wrenched spine. I think perhaps once I've recovered, it might be a good plan to keep the barbells beside the couch in case the urge to weight train should come over me during commercial breaks.

***

I'm afraid even love cannot conquer the urge to smoke. I must have a smoke, right now. I'm totally stressed out: I just received a vexing call from the school principal. Jack is suspended from riding the school bus until further notice as yesterday, when getting off the bus, he tossed a lit screamer under the front wheels and ran. It scared the bejeesus out of the substitute bus driver.

Why oh why did he have to play stupid pranks on a substitute driver? The regular bus driver is so shell-shocked he would never have noticed.

***

My Daily Regimen to Enhance Slimming and Restore Healthful Beauty From Within: I start with a high-quality "green drink" for improved cellular health. Then I fill a large tumbler of water to facilitate choking down the daily palmful of pills recommended by my straight-faced holistic health practitioner: six Omega-3 caps for glowing good health, one pinch of ginseng for energy, two mega E for heightened libido, six mega C in memory of Linus Pauling. Then I follow with an astragalus and liquorice supplement for my adrenals, evening primrose oil for hot flashes, B complex for stress, calcium and chelated minerals for insurance, and sometimes vitamins A and D—because I might as well have those too. I down as many as possible in one holistic gulp, in reckless disregard of recommendations to stagger intake for proper absorption.

I have found it's a good trick to mix a little bicarbonate of soda into the water to help settle my discombobulated stomach.

***

Donald just came back from picking up Mom at the airport. He went off to meet her quite cheerfully as he can't wait till she takes Mongrowl away.

As usual Mom swanned in, laden with highly unsuitable gifts for the kids: for Olympia, a marionette with a million billion strings that tangle as soon as you look at them, for Jack, a pellet rifle, and for Serenity, a Smith and Wesson handgun with a sweetheart handle. Olympia immediately protests that she didn't get a gun.

Mom says, "I'll get you a real pretty one as soon as you're just a little bit older, dear."

After the kids ran off with their weapons and such, Mom opened her handbag and showed me the "lady-like" Saturday Night Special she'd copped for herself. A month in Florida and she's packing a junk gun and handing pieces out like candy.

Damn. All I got was a bag of cutesy citrus "bath bombs" shaped like lemons, limes and oranges.

I don't want stinking bath bombs. Where's *my* cute little gun? Or at least some duty-free booze so I can get blitzed in the bath?

Mom also picked up one sick tan on Pebble Beach. And another new boyfriend. He looks like Fidel Castro. I don't know how she sneaked a Castro-look-alike across the border along with all her other illegal goodies. I can't remember what this one's name is. I can't keep them straight any more. They're all rich and apparently can't keep their scuzzy hands off her. It's disgusting.

Then, she dropped another bomb into my lap: she's planning to sell the house and travel the world with Fidel Whosit.

"What?" I wish to hell she'd go back to stalking Phil Mickelson.

"First we're going back to Cuba and then it's on to Portugal."

She's really starting to piss me off.

"By the way Pauline, I've also decided to let you keep Montrose until I get back."

***

Serenity and Jack were in massive snits all morning because I confiscated the handgun and the pellet rifle and after they calmed down, Olympia freaked out because I accidentally cut all the marionette strings off when trying to untangle them for the seventeenth time in twenty-four hours.

I'm holding firm against Jack who downloaded stats from the Consumer Product Safety Commission Report that show more injuries in the 5–14 age range are caused by pencils and pens (64) per capita than by pellet rifles and BB guns (43).

It's a good thing I don't know which end of a pellet gun to hold up. Stats can shift and quickly too.

* * *

Post-Superbowl Sunday: the in-laws phone up to say they're thinking of dropping over, thereby inspiring a furious round of crisis cleaning. Donald and Dennis are socked onto the couch, doing some male bonding and watching mid-season basketball and curling bonspiel wrap-ups. Serenity, in a sports widow sulk, has slogged off to her room to do homework. If it weren't for Dennis's sports mania, Serenity would be flunking miserably.

Poor Donald, he's obviously suffering his annual post-football season, no-big-game-on-TV-blues lethargy so it's safe to leave the vacuum running and sneak onto the deck periodically for smoke breaks.

While I'm passing a dust cloth across the top of the television, Donald props himself on his elbow and smirks at me: "I didn't think you could kick the habit."

Indignation leads to a rash bet: I'm forced to quit for good, starting tomorrow, or I'm bound to vote right wing in the next federal election, projected to be called this spring.

I'm flat out determined to survive quitting smoking even if it kills me.

***

Day 1 Cold Turkey: I so regret my quit smoking wager with Donald. I would do anything for a smoke. I would happily contribute to the ruin of our nation and vote for a right wing party except the thought of Donald snorting in triumph is a powerful deterrent. Plus, of course, I'm hoping to impress Michael. Donald was unmoved by my suffering until he learned I'm employing the dreaded 24/7 Pampering Method of quitting.

Bubble baths, chocolate bars, afternoon naps, shopping, soap operas and Oprah will be the order of the day until I have conquered smoking for good. No housework or cooking allowed. In other words, one hundred per cent laziness and self-indulgence will be required to kick the habit.

I made a brief attempt to contribute to an online CanLit discussion but I was soon forced to stop: I felt stressed by the clicking of the keys on the keyboard.

Today's goal: a hassle-free afternoon nap. I will skip tonight's Brownie meeting. Dissipation is a far better bad habit than smoking; I could get rather addicted to it. I wonder how long withdrawal takes? Days? Weeks? Months? Must I remain totally shiftless and self-indulgent forever?

***

Day 2 Cold Turkey: I couldn't sleep last night—nicotine withdrawal is causing intense nightmares—like Salvador Dali and Picasso are having a fight in my head—there are severed eyeballs flying all over the place.

Tobacco use is seriously bad for the health. I nearly had a smoking-related coronary when Michael, waving a pack of Players, said, "Hey, Pauline, aren't you coming outside for a smoke today?"

***

Day 3 Cold Turkey: I waited after class yesterday to demand Michael explain why he never smoked during breaks before. "I can take it or leave it," he shrugged.

"But I'm really glad that you quit," he smiled. And then he *squeezed my shoulder.*

***

Day 4 Cold Turkey: My shoulder is still emitting sparks where Michael squeezed it. I can just imagine the fireworks that might result from the rest of me if further squeezing were to occur.

***

Day 5 Cold Turkey: The nicotine withdrawal is getting worse—I'm hearing voices now. Yesterday, all day, they went: *you've been so good, after all you put up with, you deserve a smoke, you're worthy of a smoke.*

Today's voice sounds like James Dean: *go on, screw the world, if you feel like smoking, go ahead and smoke, smoking is cool, be a rebel.*

At this, Ms. Practical chimes in: *sure, choke chain yourself to a pack of smokes. Can't you find something more radical to take a rebel stance on? Since when does smoking make you cool? Plenty of dorks smoke. Get serious—you don't have to keep supporting rich blood-sucking corporations just because you have dumb old James Dean in your head.*

I wonder how I can shut these maddening voices up?

I hope they will get lost by tomorrow, as voices are the last thing I need when I have the golden promise of the house all to myself: Serenity and Dennis are going to a Queer Arts Festival and Donald's taking Jack and Olympia for a birthday visit to H.M.

I inform Donald that, since this is Cold Turkey Week, I'm feeling out of sorts and H.M. will have to celebrate her birthday without me this year. I didn't share with him my conviction that in-law exposures ought to be strictly limited for the immediate critical withdrawal period, say for the first Cold Turkey Decade. I'm determined that quitting smoking will have its advantages.

Also, to Donald, I cite the mounds of schoolwork that await me: no exaggeration here, as my schoolwork has indeed mounded to unprecedented heights.

However, I neglected mentioning to Donald my plans—confirmed this very moment via email—for an afternoon cram session tomorrow with Michael who has offered to drop by to help me prepare for next week's midterms!

eight

Ruse

I twisted and turned restlessly all night due to the prospect of the private study date with Michael. The result is a nasty kink in my neck. I can barely move my head. I tiptoe, wincing, to the bathroom and rifle the medicine cabinet for muscle relaxers and painkillers while wondering: How did I get myself into this? What if I make a full fool of myself? What if Michael were to fall on his knees before me and declare his undying passion? What would I do? What if I happened to be wearing my sexy navy sweater with the zippered front? Or, better yet, the blue chambray dress with the pearl buttons that go all the way down? Best sleepless night I've ever had.

Despite the debilitating kink in my neck, I'm as helpful as can be to assist Donald and the kids out the door and on their merry way. I feel somewhat guilty about my prevarication with Donald over the private study date. Perhaps I'm futzing with the rules by inviting Michael here, into the private recesses of Donald's own scruffy little castle. But, this is innocent, right? I've no plan to actually seduce Michael. My intentions are entirely honourable: to enlist academic assistance from my teacher. Guilt is for actual wrongdoers. I have done nothing wrong. Why do I feel so guilty, like some little kid hiding misdemeanours from a strict parent? I'm a grown woman after all. Why should I report to Donald every time I invite a friend over to the house? I'm beginning to feel resentful towards Donald for tracking my every move. Who does he think he is, anyways? No wonder I have a pain in my neck. It's all Donald's fault.

Michael will help me prepare for the exam and then he'll go home. End of story. This will be nothing but a friendly cram session.

Thoughts of friendly cramming with the help of angel-eyes Michael are causing a racing pulse, shaky hands and feelings of faintness. Or maybe it's acute nicotine withdrawal. Why oh why did I ever make that boneheaded quitting-smoking bet with Donald? I can't possibly cope given first study date jitters.

Besides, who cares what Michael thinks of smoking women? Who cares if Michael squeezed my shoulder? I must sneak outside for a puff. Just one. Or maybe two puffs, just to take the edge off.

Driving in haste to the convenience store to buy a pack of smokes, I vow to smoke only one and jettison the rest. Racing home again at top speed, I tear open the package with my teeth. I better smoke outside on the back porch rather than risk smoking indoors as the smoky smell evidence lasts for days. Donald might suspect.

The best part of quitting smoking is the deeply satisfying nicotine rush after several days' deprivation. All the jitters and unpleasant guilty feelings dissipate with the second cigarette. I'll have just a few, two or maybe three more, cigarettes today and return to the quit tomorrow. After Donald returns. One teensy tiny lapse on the smoke-free path doesn't constitute a total failure.

Halfway through my second cigarette, I hear a car pulling into the driveway. Michael's not due yet; could it be Donald returning for some forgotten item? Panicking, I stub out my cigarette, and hide the butt in my coat pocket. Now, I'll rush indoors to sit before my desk and assume an innocent pose with my textbook. Wait a sec though—Donald wouldn't be ringing the doorbell. I jump up from my desk and run to the door to find—Michael!

Michael apologizes for arriving so early expressing hope that it's okay ... Hey, was I on my way out? I'm still wearing my coat. I nod yes and no with what I hope looks like nonchalance but with the result that my bobbing head assumes the aspect of a head-wagging rear-window car toy.

I invite him in with racing pulse, shaky hands and feelings of faintness. After taking Michael's coat, I remove my own coat feeling that removing any article of clothing in front of Michael is too suggestive and, possibly, a slightly indecent act. We've a shortage of hangers, so I must hang the coats wrapped together on one hanger in the hall closet: I'm enraptured at the sight of his coat hugging mine.

Michael goes into the living room and looks at the bookshelves while I make coffee and chatter madly about the upcoming midterm. I return with a firm objective: to sit in the safe single chair with the safe coffee table and safe mugs of hot coffee between us, but Michael is still more interested in checking out the book collection.

"Maybe we could start with reviewing notes and then move into sample exam questions," I stammer.

Michael turns and glances at me with *that look* again. The room is becoming unbearably hot and cold at the same time. With any luck, Michael won't notice my red, flushed face covered with white goose-bumpy blotches. To avoid eye contact, I bend my head down over my books and flip through my binder, pretending to be searching for pertinent study notes. He says nothing and turns back to the bookshelves. The silence in the room makes the rustle of the turning pages insanely loud.

He pauses for an age or two in front of the poetry corner (which contain, thank God, several volumes by Leonard Cohen). Then he asks, "Who is your favourite?"

Michael likes *poetry*! Of *course* he does. I just love this man. In a flash, half the afternoon has drifted by in conversation about poetry, novels, movies, restaurants, food, wine. It's amazing. We like all the same things. And all afternoon, Michael keeps on looking at me with *that look*. All I need to do is twist my head sideways to gaze into his wonderful eyes. I must be careful not to outright stare.

Instead, I practise half-glancing under my lashes just like Princess Diana used to do with such devastating effect on millions. Shouldn't be too difficult—I only need to look demure and charming for one person. It's hard to be Princess Diana what with a sore neck but I don't care. For an hour now, I've been sitting right beside Michael, cross-legged on the floor, our backs leaning against the couch, one thrilled knee twitching against his. I'm painfully aware that if I were to accidentally shift my hand over two inches, my fingertips could be brushing against Michael's luscious thigh.

My fingers are aching to tango over there. Just thinking about touching Michael causes my neck to kink up more, my face to flush and giant beads of sweat to spring up on my forehead. I'm sure Di never went through anything like this.

With a quizzical look, Michael says, "Are you okay? You seem tense."

Me? Tense? No, not at all, tense, no, not me. I assure him I'm fine, perfectly fine, it's only a stiff neck, I probably slept on it wrong, that's all, and all would have continued fine until—he reaches over and places a friendly hand on the back of my neck and squeezes. Every last tiny goose bump on my body is activated and grows until there's no room left and many bumps are forced to migrate onto my teeth, nails, hair and floor.

"Whoa, your neck muscles are tight, try to relax, Pauline."

I'll try to not faint. A surge of electricity bolts down my spine and burns holes through the soles of my feet.

I've lost all my ability to speak, thank heaven, or I

would be moaning uncontrollably: "Give it to me, baby."

I must get a grip. It's only a friendly neck massage. I remind myself that Bibienne recently showed me how to do similar massage techniques. No actual line of propriety is, as yet, crossed.

Michael's fingers are working the nape of my neck into slush, while the rest of my body is frozen solid. My eyes are zooming in and out of focus. All lines of propriety are becoming dangerously fuzzy. Time to review the specifics: I'm alone in the house with a captivating man who is turning my vertebrae into a vibrating zone of burning desire. I lose sight of the line as it sizzles off to the distant moral horizon. I wonder if offering to remove my blouse to facilitate the massage might be interpreted as sending out signals.

The neck massage is phenomenal: all my soreness has magically vanished, but Michael says I'm "still tense" and, slipping behind me, proceeds to vibrate my shoulders.

The shoulder vibrating produces extraordinary tension in all zones. Perhaps I should try a Lamaze breathing technique. If I could recall any. If I could actually breathe. Michael's warm breath tickles my cheek as he leans closer and gently brushes my hair aside to whisper in my ear, "Would you like me to do your back too?"

Perhaps Michael is sending out signals. At a critical time like this I had always thought that I would probably balk. I ought to balk. I ought to at least *consider* balking. To facilitate the back massage, I think it would be helpful if I stretched out on the floor. I dive for the carpet, landing face down, panting slightly and getting dog hairs on my tongue and up my nose in the process.

Michael places his hands on my back, and begins a lovely stroking motion but I'm getting distracted by the mouthful of dog hair. I attempt to spit the hairs out, surreptitiously.

Abruptly, Michael removes his hands. I snap my head

around and stare as Michael stands up slowly and sighs. "I think I better go."

I jump up from the floor. "Why?"

Michael rubs his forehead. "Damn. All I can think about is grabbing you and kissing you. I should never have come."

I cannot believe my ears. Michael wants me! I blurt out that I, too, share the same feelings. He can go right ahead and kiss me, if he wants to, please ...

A wonderful, long, standing-up kiss ensues. My knees are turning into mush. I better do something before they buckle out from under me.

It's too late. My knees are long gone. The wonderful, long, standing-up kiss has somehow turned into a wonderful, long, lying down, rolling-around-beneath-the-coffee-table kiss. I can't believe this is happening. What if Donald were to walk in on us? I can explain—it's only a friendly massage.

Michael's kisses are incredibly sweet but this floor is uncomfortable, I should really suggest a move to the couch and, besides, the carpet has an unpleasant smoky odour—I'll have to rent a steam cleaner soon ... I hate this nasty carpet ... Perhaps I should buy a new carpet ... That new Heritage Green colour would be ... Good grief, how can I think of home decorating at a time like this? My stream of consciousness is showing galling signs of middle-aged pollution.

Purely immoral thoughts are forced into the forefront again by Michael's hands slipping under my blouse and sliding it upwards. Even better, Michael is employing an exciting nuzzling tongue technique in my ear region. I can't recall Bibienne ever doing a nuzzling tongue when massaging my back.

Michael whispers that he can't help himself, as he has wanted to nibble on me since the first time he saw me.

Yum yum. Please go ahead and make a good meal of me then.

The thrilling love bites are causing a loud ringing in my ears. All my senses are exquisitely heightened. I can even hear a wailing siren sound like one of the kids' screamers going off. My eyes are beginning to smart and tear. Michael abruptly stops all biting, nuzzling and tickling, and I'm about to protest when I realize the loud ringing is the smoke alarm going off in the hall.

My eyes return to focus. The air is filled with smoke. I glance down below—I've heard of things like this but never before believed it possible. The house is on fire not my ... Snatching myself up from the carpet, I scramble to the hall to see thick plumes of blue smoke and fiery balls rocketing out of the closet, down the hall and into the kitchen where they explode into hundreds of brilliantly coloured stars and streaks.

Grabbing the cell phone, I duck my head and run outside with Michael, while calling the fire department. A throng of neighbourhood residents and passers-by scramble to watch the pyrotechnic display and the progress of the blaze. Every few seconds another explosive round of crackers or out-of-control pinwheels comes careening out the side door, making the crowd shout "ooh" and "ahh" appreciatively. The unpredictable rockets slow the progress of the volunteer firefighters but they run more hoses and foam. They manage to extinguish the fire, which the Fire Chief pronounces to have begun *somehow* in my hall closet where, by the way, a large number of banned fireworks were obviously improperly stored; fortunately they were able to contain the fire. I tell the Fire Chief I'm mystified as to how the fire could have been started.

I'm lucky to have a home left according to the Chief. Not to mention that I should also be thankful for the safe deliverance of all my cherished household pets now furiously barking and hissing and squabbling in the back seat of the Jeep. I'm not feeling lucky or thankful at all. The closet side of my house is destroyed, as is, I fear, my newborn relationship with Michael given the pained expression on his face as he inspected the charred remains of his leather coat before heading home. Perhaps some nicotine will soothe away these unwelcome feelings of tension.

As I pull out my smokes, I remember the butt hastily shoved in my coat pocket earlier this afternoon—but I won't volunteer this clue to anyone, especially to the insurance adjuster who has just been called and is on his way over here along with Donald. I sit on the curb and light up quickly, closing my eyes and sucking deeply, another pea-brained mistake as I open my eyes to discover Donald pulling up beside me in his car and rolling down the window.

We meet with the adjuster who says the smoke and water damage extends throughout much of the house; however, he promises to send in a crew and compensate for all affected areas. I'm doubtful, especially when memory recalls Michael's hand brushing my neck.

Now I'm forced to accompany Donald back to my in-laws as my wet, sooty, reeking house is temporarily uninhabitable. Most disappointing of all, the fire has extinguished my chances of further amorous encounters at least for today and possibly forever.

***

Serenity came home from the arts festival without Dennis. Apparently Dennis went on the pull with another participant. Now Serenity is locked within her uninhabitable bedroom and is refusing to come out.

Thank goodness, as I can justify moving back home myself—I volunteer to move back into the house, explaining to Donald that support and supervision of Serenity is essential. Meanwhile, the rest of the family members will remain quartered at the in-laws at least until the insurance company agrees to pay for motel accommodations. I would rather be drawn and quartered than stay under H.M.'s nose a second longer. I'm sure she could sniff out sneakiness through a smokescreen a mile thick.

***

The fire was, perhaps, a lucky turn of events. The insurance payout means new Heritage Green carpeting plus a top to bottom cleaning of the house by a team of fire-damage specialists. This promises to be the best (and only) spring-cleaning this house has ever had.

Second thoughts are as persistent as the disagreeable smoky odour in the house. What might've happened if not for the fortuitous fire? While emptying drawers and closets of smoky clothing for the cleaners, everything comes clear: last Saturday's study date with Michael was a close call. I must never let my guard down again.

After all, the state of my underwear is truly shocking. A review of my dresser drawers reveal that my entire supply of bras is in tatters and most are at least a cup size too small. I must avoid all possibility of further close encounters with Michael until I have had an opportunity to replace my greying and shabby stock of bras and panties.

***

In class, Michael's eyes undress me from across the room, reminding me of yesterday's plan to shop for a new bra as soon as possible. I flash him what I hope is a disarming sorry-darling-but-I-really-must-dash smile and flee from his gaze to run to the mall as soon as class ends.

I'm dreading the prospect of bra shopping. I can't bear the thought that I'm a "D" now. When it comes to bras, "C" is for Creamy Enough, Thank You Very Much. "D" is for Disgusting.

The time has come to seek support. It wouldn't do for Michael to be faced with an aged old crone of a Maidenform bra.

In the lingerie department, I admire an endless array of styles and colours in the "A" size section: dainty spaghetti straps, pretty eyelets and sexy lace trim. In the itty bitty bikini boutique the bra is just a whimsical fashion accessory.

The lingerie staffer takes a brief visual assessment of my chest, shoos me out of "A" and sternly directs me to the dreaded "D" zone, well past the cute matching bra and panty sets, way at the back of shop where the "D" size bras all come with bulletproof spandex, steel rivets and an optional beige forklift.

There are no playful polka dots here. This is the serious support outback where the big girls come to ride the range. The bras and matching bloomers look like they belong in a saddle shop. I could accessorize with spurs, I suppose.

With a sinking feeling—no doubt just my boobs sagging past my hips—I select an underwired balconette bra. The staffer suggested that, for best presentation, I need to prop up my Broadway girls on a solid marquee. In the privacy of the dressing room, I pry open the carton and attempt to apply the undergarment to my chest. I'm tempted to ask the staffer if this thing comes with an installation manual, and then I discover my mistake: turns out I've turned the bra inside out and upside down. Trouble is, the bra is equipped with a frontal fastener, cunningly hidden under a gigantic rosette. (Ah—thought that was the "on" button.)

Also, the confounded garment has six strap fasteners,

fourteen hinges and a special attachment that looks like a battery compartment. I wonder what the compartment is for and contemplate that a power pack might be kind of fun. Built in zoom control or an overdrive might come in handy. The word *handy* in relation to my chest naturally makes me think of Michael.

"D" is also for Despair: What if Michael prefers cute little perkers?

***

I love living in an uninhabitable house. It's better than going on retreat: no cooking, no cleaning, no laundry, no kids or pets underfoot. I've remained in a blissful state of solitude all week: Dennis and George Bush are gone, Donald and kids are housed at a motel, Serenity is still refusing to come out of her room and even Montrose and the cats are safely kennelled out of harm's way while the team of cleaning specialists work their special magic.

***

Curses. The racking fracking cleaners have worked so rapidly and efficiently that the house is once again fit to receive Donald and the kids. They all troop in marvelling at the gleaming walls and floors. "It's fantastic, isn't it?" I say. Donald nods but says nothing. He looks away quickly but I'm sure I spotted tears in his eyes.

Wait. Someone's missing. "Donald, did you forget to pick up Montrose at the kennel?"

"Not exactly. I decided we could keep him there till your Mom gets back."

"Yesss! What a good idea. It's a first-rate kennel with a vet and everything."

I'm overjoyed with Donald's arrangements. Dennis is gone with George Bush: that means no dogs in the house!

Oh my! I'm suddenly in danger of falling back in love with my clever husband.

"For what they charge, he'd better be fine. Uh, we don't have to say anything to your Mom?"

"Cross my heart."

***

Argggh. I wasted my entire morning struggling with my word processing program which has decided to play the computer jungle game: the processor monkeys around with my files while I go bananas trying to find them. Meanwhile, frequent interruptions from the kids have triggered a steady drumbeat in my temples.

Jack is pestering me for the latest game, called something like Ninepin. At first I thought it was nice little bowling game but research revealed that I should be thankful that the best virtual disembowelment games can only be run on the latest version of Windows, which we don't have yet. According to Jack, our "new" computer, only six months old, is "totally useless."

Windows phobia persists. The thought of trying to install the latest operating system on my computer makes my brain cringe. I've heard awful rumours about the penalties faced by morons who tried switching platforms on their own. After six grim months on a steep learning curve, I've only just come to grips with my new system and now everyone wants me to watch all my favourite programs crash because I have lots of things to learn about the latest platform. Just because they dinked up their computers, they want me to suffer too.

All I know is "upgrading" will cause sudden downbreaking, i.e., most of my programs won't work any more. Infuriating windows will pop up to warn me that the jock strap has fallen off my interruption request device module and I will have to spend days figuring out what *Terminal*

Error 9Bpartition103c means and downloading fixes and gludging them together only to discover new glitches with the gludges that I will duly fix only to discover that, by now, the gludges for the fixes screwed up programs that were working fine before.

***

Between being in computer hell all day and regular Brownie meeting hell tonight, there's no time left to read Ondaatje's *The English Patient* for CanLit class tomorrow. I've given it a good crease. I started reading it, four times now. No doubt it's a wonderful novel but I kept falling asleep. Oh well—I'll just rent the video and read the text later.

***

All the women in today's tutorial class kept talking about how gorgeous looking the longhaired bomb disposal guy was in *The English Patient* last night. We all liked him so much more than the burnt guy who abandoned his woman in the cave. But it was bound to happen. She was doomed the minute she began screwing around. You can only get away with brazen acts of adultery in real life, but never in movies or books.

After class, Michael, unsmiling, suggests we grab a coffee in the Student Concourse. I accept quickly but with a gloomy feeling that he is about to abandon me in a cave.

I place an order for a tall latte while Michael orders a short espresso. I wonder if this is a sign that he means to dump and run? The lout. If so, I ought to preempt him and ditch him first.

On the way over to the table, our coats accidentally brush, thereby paralyzing my tongue. We sit facing one another and silently stare at our coffees. I hope I won't burst into tears when he says goodbye. The first silly tears are already forming in my eyes.

"Sorry about your coat," I venture. "But the insurance is going to ..."

"Forget the coat. Uh, Pauline—I can't stop thinking about you."

***

Sigh! Twenty-four hours later and I can't stop thinking about the fact that Michael can't stop thinking about me! Isn't life delightful?

***

Forty-eight hours later and I can finally stop thinking about the fact that Michael can't stop thinking about me. Now I am thinking about the fact that, although he admits that I'm a huge distraction, he can't allow our teacher-student relationship to be compromised by unprofessional behaviour on his part. Damn. Life is a poxy joke.

***

Donald, in an unprovoked attempt at Valentine's Day romance, offered dinner out at a classy restaurant, no kids. Graciously, I accepted his invitation as I can't recall the last time we visited a dining establishment which doesn't boast a drive-thru window.

Come to think of it, I would glom on to any offer involving food, the greasier the better, as my weight-loss diet is getting to me big time. To hell with living on love: I would trade away a whole week in bed with Michael for a double-bacon cheeseburger, large fries, chocolate shake and a side of onion rings.

I'm starving. The basket of warm rolls on the table is

delicious. And apparently, Donald knows a thing or two about fine wines and cozy bistros. The aromas coming from the kitchen are tantalizing. My husband is speaking hot and delicioso tonight. There's no need for him to whisper herbed garlic nothings in my ear—all he needs is a pat of pesto butter and he'll have me licking his hand. Looking around, I realize that he is the tastiest-looking man in the room. Maybe a romantic night on the town is just what we needed.

Alas, between scarfing down all the rolls and digging into my Chef's Special Antipasto Platter (Mesquite Smoked Salmon and Soy Rapini with Organic Red Peppers Grilled in Virgin Olive Oil and Baked Garlic and Four Black Olives Garnished With Fresh Coriander), I realize I can't think of anything to say in the way of intelligent conversation.

The romantic date with Donald is already veering towards disaster. I can't remember the last time we made dinner table conversation without extensive interference from the kids. I wish Donald would spill my drink or at least yell, "Yuck, I'm not eating this crap."

We can't continue staring at each other over an expanse of linen, crystal and candlelight forever. I'm painfully aware that this fancy romantic meal is financed by the fire insurance payout (proving I'm too ironic for my best black minidress and heels).

Here goes: "So. How was your day?"

Donald: "Terrible."

Me, with real concern: "What happened?"

Donald: "Nothing. The usual pricks."

The usual pricks? No, Donald must be mistaken; the usual pricks all work in the Office of Student Programs at Sir Oliver Dingwall. I launch into a tirade about the incompetent Dingwall dinks who exist solely to make my existence miserable. Somehow this cheers Donald up.

By dessert Donald has warmed up past monosyllabic

communication and, changing the topic, utters a complete sentence: "I bought us a satellite dish today."

Me, swallowing hard: "What?"

"It's better, we can pick up way more channels and stick it to the cable company."

"But we don't need more channels. We don't need more rusting crud stuck to the side of the house."

So this is why he's being so smooth, taking me out to dinner and all: to butter me up. We already have working cable plus two rusting satellite dishes, thirteen assorted converter boxes and five TVs. I'm sure Donald is trying to drive me apenuts. I'll end up mute and gibbering while he beams around the globe looking for sports broadcasts.

"Take it back," I hiss across the table. "I thought we agreed to buy a new couch with the insurance money ..."

"*You* agreed we were buying a new couch."

"Don't raise your voice at me, you jerk, people are looking at us."

"THEN DON'T CALL ME A JERK."

Donald grabs for his coat. So do I. The argument continues out to the car and all the way home.

***

I'm still not speaking to Donald but it looks like Serenity and Dennis, at least, patched things up last night. Serenity's bedroom door is firmly closed with a leather tie draped over the doorknob. There's been no actual visual of Dennis yet but the sight of her pickup truck parked back in the driveway and George Bush parked back on my bed with wet muddy paws, confirms.

***

It's not always possible to keep up a campaign of not-speaking. When Donald walked in from work tonight I had to know: "The vet just called to ask when we were planning to pick up the cremains."

"The cremains?"

"Yes, from Montrose."

"Montrose is dead?"

"Yes—the vet said you told them to have him put to sleep."

"I TOLD THEM I'D *LIKE* TO HAVE THE DOG PUT DOWN, NOT FOR THEM TO ACTUALLY DO IT."

"My mother is going to flip."

"Shhhhhiiiittt."

"When you go to pick up the ashes, maybe you could take the satellite dish back so we can pay off the vet bill."

***

Donald and I have decided to put off telling Mom about Montrose for now. Why ruin her vacation?

After Donald threatened to sue the kennel people, they decided to waive the cremation fee plus the entire kennel bill. With all the extra cash in the coffers (thanks to Montrose), our family dispute has been happily resolved: instead of a couch or satellite system, we signed up for high-speed Internet and bought another computer! This new-new one is six months newer than the old-new one which makes the old-new one practically obsolete. The whole family is in ecstasy: Donald can write everything off against his taxes, Jack and Olympia got their disembowelment game after all and I don't have to install the latest Windows myself. Yahoo!

***

Oh Tuesday, wonderful Tuesday. I've just floated home from a dynamite study date with Michael at the back of Dingwall's library. While being extremely sexy and attractive, Michael has managed to bring CanLit alive for me—truly a challenge since much of CanLit has to do with gruesome blood-spattered deaths on snowy deserted roads.

Why are Canadian writers so inclined to the dismal, the depressing, the dark side? The whole literary world must be creeped out by Canadians, especially by our bizarre sexual practices as depicted by our most popular narrators. I'm sure the average reader in, say, England or Australia or even a reader from a free, sexually progressive country like Sweden, must think that if we're not ghouls hungering for corpses, we're yahoos whooping it up on someone's face after a car crash.

In England, the popular authors are fun broads like Jilly Cooper who regularly leads her readers to imagine having sex with minor royalty who still have pulses if not warm blood, and in more interesting settings too, say in the temporary stalls at polo games with the ponies looking on.

* * *

Mom's on the phone. She wants to speak to Montrose: "Put the phone up to his widdle ear so I can tell him how much I miss my sweet widdle poopy-pup."

Covering the receiver with my hand, I call Donald. "Hey poopy-pup, come over here and pant for my mother." I hold the phone up to Donald's ear while Donald pretends to slobber on the receiver. Best part of my day.

* * *

Besides being loaded with leisure-time entertainments, our powerful new computer is proving to be an awesome timesaving research tool for school. The new system can download information from the Internet way faster than the old system. For example, downloading the Harvey Keitel screen saver takes at least twenty-four minutes on the old slow system where the time needed by the new speedy system is barely half that.

I love having instant access to vast realms of useful information at the click of the mouse: this morning while researching grammar for my CanLit course, I was drawn to explore the university-based "Save the Adverb Site" by a Mr. D. Alexander Garrett, who is seriously working hard to stamp out adverbial abuse—I couldn't agree with him more so have firmly resolved to henceforwardly respond properly to all inquiries as to the progress of my health, etc. with the correct "well" or, even better, "goodly" rather than the improper, adjectival "good." I didn't have time to read everything, so I printed all the related pages on the site while moving on with my research.

The Adverb Site led me to an informative page on pig Latin which I had to download and print for later, and then from there it was on to The Women's Drumming Circle, where I found a neat link on "The Broad's Bagpipes" (curious, so I printed that too), which in turn led to a fascinating source of info on Celtic Goddess music and how to build uilleann pipes which I printed for future reference. I wrapped up my session with a quick recreational stopover at the "Toaster Oracle" to request a reading from the all-seeing Toaster about Michael. In response to my query whether things are getting too hot to handle, The Toaster told me my "muffin is burnt."

In the dreary pre-Internet days, an English student would've been stuck poring over a single dull, static grammar text all day and probably not get anywhere at all.

***

Lewis Morris Boriston is back on my doorstep, hopping with rage. He's insisting that George Bush broke through his fence and "raped" his "purebred" poodle yesterday. Poor Fontine had to take a morning-after shot, a smart precaution as the prospective parents, 'Tine and George, together couldn't even produce the genetic intelligence of dog kibble.

I inform Mr. Boriston that although I agree that George Bush needs to be fixed, I refuse to pay for his trampy poodle's contraceptive measures seeings as 'Tine and George have been seen whooping it up in every yard around the entire neighbourhood. No means no is Boriston's department: he'd better keep a chastity leash on his prize pooch when she goes into heat from now on.

***

Panic stations time. The deadline for my completed writing portfolio is less than seven weeks, or forty-eight days, away. My calculations show that, due to the relentless daytime presence of the kids (on average, three out of seven days each week), and two days spent attending classes, my available working days per week equal two. Multiplied by 6.8 available weeks, I have 13.6 available days.

Given that, on a good day, no serious writer can honestly be expected to produce more than one decent page of prose, and that half that decent prose will eventually prove to be worthless trash, only 6.8 pages of prose can be produced within the remaining allotment of time.

Since Coach Stool is demanding a minimum of twenty-five pages, and thus far I have only completed seven, I'm going to be short by at least 11.2 pages. Instead of working on creative writing, I'd better craft a creative excuse.

***

One of the hockey women is throwing a party: the theme is Can't Afford To Go To Florida. We have to supply appropriate tropical foods and beverages and dress up in our best cruise wear. The prize for Most Excellent Costume is bound to go to the goalie who is wearing a life size cardboard cutout of Tom Cruise's head strategically bobbing under her grass skirt. Aloha!

I'm terribly fond of rum-laced drinks but I have to refuse the fruit salad made with kiwi fruit. Kiwi fruit causes numbness and swelling around my lips. One of the forwards suggests it could be a sign of an allergy to latex, as kiwi fruit is loaded with it. Another forward inquires if I've been exposed to a lot of latex in the past citing that doctors and nurses are lately reporting increased sensitivity due to over exposure to latex gloves. I can only think of over exposure to latex condoms during my wild oats days but I hold my tongue on this point.

The thought of experiencing anaphylactic shock during my next condom-related enterprise causes deep concern, however. Not that there's much latex exposure happening these days but why take chances?

As soon as I arrive home, I express my fears to Donald: "I could die in your arms."

"I might not notice right away," he says.

Then he throws his head back and laughs like the nasty old hyena he is.

"Very funny," I say. "But we can't use latex any more."

Donald shrugs.

***

The first hint that spring may be on the way: Donald arrived home tonight wearing a sly grin and bearing a small gift—a box of natural non-latex condoms. His sap must be rising.

I inspect the box. The box says that natural sheaths are made of sheep's membrane. "What is this, Donald?" I yell, "Sheep's membrane?!? Ugh, from what part???"

I feel slightly sick. Anaphylactic shock is beginning to be preferable to a love glove made from some unmentionable sheep body part. This is probably Donald's idea of a cruel joke. Now I'm certain the Ship of Romance has drifted from its marital moorings and I'm beset by a sailor on land leave from the Ship of Fools.

I glance at the price sticker and feel even sicker. "Holy shit, Donald, we can't afford sex, these cost a fortune."

"Hey, it's not that bad—*for a whole year's supply,*" says Donald, his voice dripping with sarcasm.

"We could be talking *two* or even *three* year's supply."

"More if we reuse them."

"Never mind, it says right on the box: *Condoms not to be reused.*"

So much for a green glove revolution in the Daley-Parril bedroom, thank goodness. I'm free to slip back to mooning around over Michael.

Come to think of it, the last busy spell around here was the time I read that hookers can sneakily install condoms with their mouths, onto customers who might otherwise object. I couldn't believe it. I asked Donald, "How in the world do they do that?" Donald bravely volunteered to be a guinea pig for an experiment. I'm always game for learning new skills. The next day Donald rushed home with a plentiful supply of condoms in a wide range of flavours such as raspberry, strawberry and even Swiss chocolate. I've always had a terrible weakness for Swiss chocolate.

Trouble began when Donald noticed his giant supply had dwindled far more rapidly than could possibly be accounted for even given the Swiss chocolate. One night, after wading into my stash of medicinal Lagavulin, he said, "So, where'd they all go? *Someone's* obviously used them all up."

"Me? Nope. I thought maybe it was you."

"Maybe it was the kids," he said, backing down quickly.

"It's really awful that we're so suspicious of each other that we just interpret each other negatively all the time," I said.

***

Every night I go to bed, hoping for a passionate dream about Michael. Instead, last night I had a perverted dream about Harry Frick, the pimply young poet from Creative Writing class.

Now I won't be able to look Harry Frick in the eye for fear of blushing uncontrollably. The dream involved me as Titania being seduced by a manic woolly Puck-like creature with Harry's face and sporting an alternative brand of condom for sheep. Ugh. I wish Shakespeare would butt out of my dreamscapes—it could be worse, so far there's been no sign of nightmarish CanLit influences. Please, may I at least be spared from erotic dreams about "The Dog Who Wouldn't Be."

***

Jack is "working" on his science fair project about cats and complaining bitterly about school: unfair homework assignments, cruel teachers and all the other outrageous aspects of academic inquiry. I'm deeply sympathetic as I have unfair homework assignments and cruel teachers of my own. The trouble is, I can't do my own homework until I help Jack catch up with his. (Childcare responsibilities are a convenient excuse that works way better on politically correct profs than "the dog ate my homework"—even though George Bush actually did eat my homework last week.)

While attempting to kick the legs off the desk and simultaneously balance on the two rear legs of his chair, Jack asks: "What's the use of school anyway?"

No use explaining to him that one must obtain a sufficient education in order to find a job in order to obtain financing for a car in order to get to the job in order to repay the educational loan. Jack declares, "In school, you don't get nowhere."

I correct him: "In school, you don't get *anywhere*."

Secretly, I'm convinced that he is right. Kids aren't learning anything in school. I recently calculated, based on 365 days of the year, and subtracting weekends (104 days), two months summer holidays (62), three weeks for Christmas and Spring Break (21), plus parental aggravation days (14), statutory holidays (6), assessment and examination days (10), school trips (5), track and field days (3), "play" days (3), elective days (5), Christmas choir and other intramural performances (10), snow days (3), and sick days (5), that 109 instruction days remain.

According to further calculations, based on a school day of 6.5 hours, and subtracting lunch (one hour), two half-hour recess periods (one hour), opening exercises and announcements (half hour), attendance taking (fifteen minutes), collecting of lunch money, book sale money, fundraising etc. (half hour), dealing with inappropriate student behaviours and violent altercations (half hour), student assemblies and school spirit rallies (one hour prorated daily), 0.5 actual instruction hours remain.

Multiplying 0.5 instruction hours by 111 instruction days equals 55.5 hours of actual instruction in one year. Which are, no doubt, delivered by substitute teachers who don't know what they're doing.

I figure I have personally delivered at least a hundred hours in the past year assisting Jack, Olympia and Serenity with homework. Therefore, assuming a base starting teaching assistant's salary of approximately $24,000, I conclude that the school board owes me at least $48,000 for ancillary teaching support. Before expenses.

Time to rein in the bitter complaints and personal

resentments against the school board and get back to Jack's cat project, due tomorrow. Somehow I've been suckered into gluing the cat kibble lettering to the backboard. Jack is supposed to be doing the writing and research parts while I'm crouched down on the floor working on the display. Two hours of backbreaking work and so far Jack has done nothing but dither and complain. All we have to show for it is a hunk of cardboard covered with cat food.

I look around. Jack has disappeared out of the room again. That's it. My patience is gone. I storm the living room where I find Jack sitting in front of the TV. After negotiations, Jack agrees to (1) keep the television volume down to a dull roar while I work and (2) not fight with Olympia over the TV remote. Without Jack underfoot to distract me, the project will be done in no time. I'll make a pot of coffee.

***

Back in the den I discover George Bush has gobbled all the cat kibble right off the backboard leaving it glistening with dog saliva. Now I have to start over from scratch.

nine

All Appropriate Action

The phone rings and I snatch it up, hoping against hope that maybe Michael is calling me at home with news of a sudden volte-face on his frat policy. No luck. The caller is Mom. She's just arrived home and wants to talk to Montrose. But first she wants to tell me about her world tour. Fidel Whosit turned out to be a two-timing slime bucket and she dumped him, but that's okay since she's not selling the house after all and is seeing Jesse next door now.

"He looks just like Phil Mickelson, you know."

It's time to confront Mom. Since Dad died, she's gone completely off her tee.

"Mom, don't you think Dad would be upset that you're running around with all these different men?"

"Not at all. Your father says he doesn't mind me dating."

"What, you've asked him?"

"Sure." She lowers her voice to a stage whisper. "I think he likes to watch actually."

"You've *talked* with him? Mom, this is going too far. Dad's dead. How can you know what he thinks? I mean, he doesn't think anything. He's dead."

"I know he's dead, dear. But we chat regularly. He isn't taken with Jesse. He thinks Jesse's a bit young for me."

"Mom, Jesse *is* too young for you. He's too young for *me*."

"Not to worry, it's all very innocent. I gave up sex for lent this year. Now can I talk to Montrose?"

"Montrose," I yell. "Come! Your Mommy wants to talk to you again." I hand the phone to Donald.

I never want this to end.

***

Mom's on the phone again wondering why Donald sent her a giant arrangement of flowers. That coward. Guess it's up to me to break the news to her gently. "Mom, when you're talking to Dad, do you sense anyone else there with him?"

***

As tutorial class wanes, I'm studying Michael's rear end as he writes notes on the board. So cute. Maybe after class, I should suggest another cozy library study meeting, another innocent but deliciously flirtatious boning-up session with Michael. I wish he would leave off the silly "professional ethics" shtick. It's terribly frustrating, all this firm self-control. I'm dying to taste his succulent lips upon mine again, while—oh God—if Michael were tempted to steal a forbidden snog today, my lips will taste of that heap of fried onions topping my pita at lunch.

I rummage frantically through my bag looking for a package of breath mints or the like. Amidst crumbs, loose change and empty wrappers, I find several stray pieces of Olympia's pink bubble gum and a handful of chewy, fruit-flavoured candy. I can't decide which to try first so I palm the whole lot into my mouth at once.

Never eat chewy, fruit-flavoured candy and bubble gum at same time. Due to a special anti-gum chemical additive, the candy turns the gum into a sticky, billowing glueball. Now the glueball is stuck on my cosmetic caps.

I attempt to swallow the glueball but no luck—the ball

seems to be increasing in volume and stickiness with each passing moment. Hiding my face behind my binder, I surreptitiously try to scrape the gum off my dental work with my fingernails, but I only manage to transfer a portion of the glueball onto my binder. Now I have sticky pink ropes of gum stretching from my teeth to my fingertips to my binder and back again. From my binder, the gum easily makes the leap to my desktop.

At this point, the gum seems to come alive with horrible long pink tentacles reaching blindly towards my hair and the floor and everything beyond. The students nearby me are pretending not to notice as I try to stuff all the untamed gum back into my mouth, without much luck. Michael turns from the board and glances in my direction.

Ducking my head, I bolt from class to the privacy of the women's washroom. The glueball, as if by evil magic, continues to cling fast. I attempt to use toilet paper to scrape the gum bits away with the result that I now have strips of toilet paper adhering to my mouth and fingers. I can't possibly return to class, let alone meet Michael, with toilet paper hanging from my teeth.

It's better to go home now, before a boning-up session with Michael turns into a sticky situation.

***

Mom phoned again. To celebrate International Women's Day, she's decided to sleep with Jesse after all. He's the best feminist male she knows. And Dad says it's okay with him after all.

"I thought you said you were giving up sex for lent?"

"Oh I did, dear, but you're allowed on Sundays. Remember when you were little and gave up candy? You saved it up in a shoebox and I let you eat what you wanted on Sunday. You usually ate all of it at once and threw up."

"But today's only Saturday."

"I know. I told Jesse we'll have to wait till midnight for penetration."

***

I just received a phone call from my old army detachment pal Regina: I'm invited to be a bridesmaid in her wedding, come April.

Due to being deployed to remote army posts during my coming of age years, I've never been a bridesmaid before. Wicked! I've been granted an opportunity to appease my appalling girlish longings to participate in this feminine rite of passage. The best part is Regina has assured me that the costumes will be simple and won't look at all like bridesmaids' dresses.

I assured Regina, in turn, that as long as the dresses don't have giant puffed sleeves, I couldn't care less what frippery she wants us bridesmaids to wear. Since Regina wore the same worn-out combat uniform every day for five years during our service time, I'm sure her wedding will prove to be a low-key, unfripperous affair and bridesmaiding will be a hoot like the good times we had back in the day. The only trouble is that Regina wants Jack to be her ringbearer.

***

En route to the first bridal dress fitting, I secretly feel that Regina is making a colossal mistake giving up her single status. I will be a proper, mannerly bridesmaid, however, and bite my tongue rather than advise Regina to skip directly down to the nearest feminist family law practitioner to seek premeditated counsel on the division of property.

I have to bite my tongue hard though. All I got out of

my first marriage was Serenity and a heap of turquoise jewellery we bought in Mexico on our honeymoon.

Now my second union is lapping at the doors of the nearest couples counsellor. I would suggest going for a session or two except, as far as I can tell, couples counselling is the leading cause of messy and expensive divorces. I'm sure a life sentence with Donald is a way better deal than sole custody of three kids. We're better off just trying to get along, rocks and all. After all, no doubt Lindsay-baby is a minor stone in the path, a sharp bit of crushed gravel in my shoe. While Michael is a featherbed in my step.

And who knows? Perhaps observing Regina and Brad embarking on their blissful journey of love will inspire me to rekindle some romance with Donald: I remember the thrill of trembling kisses and shyly proffered bouquets of bluebells. Okay, forget the bluebells. Trembling kisses maybe. Like the time we did it in the backseat of the Cutlass one winter. Perhaps Regina and Brad's tender vows of commitment shall fan our dying embers of passion and romance and bring forth a newfound bouquet of spring violets. Perhaps my purple thought passages could be transformed into a short story for creative writing class.

My thoughts are diverted from spring violets when I realize that I'm late for the fitting. The downtown core is grid locked. I fume at the red light until I notice the attractive man beside me in an awesome blue Boxster. He is checking me out. The nerve of these guys, thinking they can go around in their expensive-ass sports cars all day ogling women.

I don't mind at all actually.

My imagination settles me in the seat of his convertible and into the arms of the Boxster man, as a carefree life of jet travel and chi-chi ski resorts flashes before my eyes—third time's a charm right? Of course, as soon as we're hitched, I'll have to insist on a proper grown-up car, say a mint '59 Cadillac Coupe de Ville. I raise my chin and give him the saucy hair toss. As the light turns green, I flash him a sidewise vampy look, at which he squeals away, but not before it dawns on me that he has been picking his nose all the while.

At the bridal shop, Regina is busy trying on gowns and numerous sour expressions. Unbelievable: Regina has seven attendants, including me, but not counting the twin flower girls, Jack the ring bearer and the groom's seven ushers.

All B.M.s are either engaged or already married. They've convened in a huddle to compare their wedding rings: each size and setting is studied—the winner of the rock contest, Jocelynn, glances at my naked ring finger with disdain. I won't reveal that I lost the diamond chip years ago and the wedding band is buried somewhere in the kids' sandbox—I think. I tell her my priceless jewels must be stored in the family safety deposit box. All the B.M.s look peeved and insist I display the hardware on Regina's big day.

Regina summons all the B.M.s to consider the options for our gowns. Camilla and Judith declare themselves to be "Springs," so they can't wear red and deep green tones. Lynne is "Winter," Natalie and Janet are "Autumns," while Jocelynn is a "Summer." The choice is narrowed down to nothing but Saran Wrap. I've never had my colours done, but I'm sure I would turn out to be "April Mudslide."

Jocelynn, who could twirl her wedding band all the way up to her skinny shoulders if she wanted to, declares her refusal to wear short sleeves as they will make her arms "look fat." Judith refuses long sleeves because the weather in April might be too warm. The rest raise a solid chorus against elbow-lengths. Prolonged discussions on style, skirt length, fabric and trims reveal a firm seven-way division on preferences.

Regina announces that she has the problem licked and

motions the staffer to show us a gown she preselected for our consideration: our eyeballs bleed at the sight of ankle-length fire engine red satin with fringed sweetheart neckline, twenty layers of crinoline and *gigantic puffed sleeves*. The rig is generously bombarded with beads and bows. The only consolation is those sleeves appear roomy enough to conceal Regina's body after I murder her.

Regina appears to have made up her mind, but I'm spurred to venture comment given the horrified looks on the faces of the dumbstruck B.M.s. I point out that seven women standing in a row wearing enormous puffed sleeves might require the photographer to pack an extreme wide-angle lens out onto the football field. Regina's eyes brim with tears. All the B.M.s shoot me drop-dead looks. All proceed to wax enthusiastic about balloon sleeves—although the neckline might be altered. Jocelynn resumes campaigning for lace inserts and slits up to here, both up to the minute she insists.

The choice narrows down to Streetwalking Firefighter or a $1200 polyester slip with balloon sleeves. I wonder how many years I will get for gunning down the whole bridal party?

***

I'm losing my marbles. Jack, Olympia and Serenity are all home for March Break. Both the cats and George Bush are circling me to be fed, Serenity is hogging the kitchen phone and Jack is inches away, bugging Olympia into a screaming frenzy: sweeping the kitchen floor never fails to attract all available household members underfoot. I have 2,000 square feet of squalid housekeeping and everyone insists on standing around the same dust ball.

My only consolation is Donald is away on a week-long Training Convention, an annual event which always just happens to coincide with March Break, thereby gaining him a respite from the worst parenting week of the year. This situation normally makes me so mad I could bite him. Especially since I'm still *almost* sure he takes full advantage of those hopscotch hotel room opportunities. This year I was happy to wave him off to convention playground with good old Lindsay. I have ample opportunities to square off here at home with Michael with the additional advantage that now he can call me on the landline without risk.

A pang of anxiety strikes: who's zooming who now? What if my suspicions concerning Another Woman are unfounded? What if Donald is *not* fooling around with Lindsay-baby or anybody else for that matter, now or never? Heaven forbid that Donald is actually faithful to me—especially now that I desperately need go-ahead revenge points, a clear green light to fun and games with Michael.

Long wailing meows drive away my introspections. Time to feed the cats and George Bush (I'm tempted to feed the cats *to* George) and pack them all outside. Jack and Olympia start whining, "We're bored."

"Find something to do quick or I'll think of a job for you."

Olympia quickly settles down to plan funerals for family pets in case one dies. She declares that she hopes one might conveniently die after March Break so she can miss more school to grieve.

Jack's agenda, besides bullying Olympia, suddenly shifts to pestering me nonstop for an iguana. I can barely hear his pleas as Serenity is screaming at Dennis on the phone.

Serenity has been in a complete snit all morning as Dennis stormed out last night yelling "Hasta La Bye Bye Forever This Time." Sure. Those two are constantly fighting and reconciling. No doubt Dennis will be back in time for supper.

Serenity yells, "I'm keeping George Bush, he's at least half mine you know." I wish she would take custody of the back yard also. In between iguanal pestering, Jack begins yelling at Serenity to give up the phone today already.

I yell at Jack: "Quiet down and go help your sister arrange a funeral for George Bush," the pet I'm betting Most Likely To Be Murdered This Week, upon which Olympia takes a break from funeral planning. She slides off her chair and comes to stand beside me: "Did people have four hands once?"

Me: "You mean, like, did they have hands where we have feet?"

Olympia: "No, four hands. Wait, no, I meant four fingers."

Me: "People *do* have four fingers ..."

Olympia: "No, we have five, stupid." She holds up one hand and waggles her thumb and four fingers.

Me: "That's four fingers and a *thumb*." (I think. I'm not sure. Is a thumb a finger too?)

Olympia: "That's what I meant."

Me: "Does that answer your question, then?"

Olympia (wailing): "You don't get it."

She's right. I don't get it.

Olympia, bored with fingers, wants to know what would I say if I didn't know the answer to something? Ah—a question I can answer.

Me: "I would try to find out for you."

Olympia persists: "And if you still don't know the answer?"

Me (getting cross): "Then I'd make something up."

Olympia, not liking the answer, scowls and storms off to design cemetery layouts. Serenity is still shouting into the telephone. I tap her on the shoulder. "Here, take the cordless and stop yelling in the kitchen." She stomps upstairs to her bedroom. Jack remains behind to discuss iguanas.

I'm growing tired of Jack's continual pestering for an iguana. An iguana is just the fun family pet I need. I'm sure it would dislike me and grow into a 100-kilogram lizard with a long spiky tail, sharp claws and a grudge. I tell Jack to think of a new weird pet I can prohibit. "Rather than hassling me for an iguana, how about inviting a friend over to play? *One* friend, mind you. Maybe that one who *looks* like an iguana?"

Jack promptly calls three buddies and Olympia, two, from the privacy of Serenity's bedroom before I cotton on. I confiscate the phone and put an end to the free for all, but it's too late to cancel the impending invasion by neighbourhood kids: their ecstatic parents are, no doubt, in blistering fast transit by now.

It isn't long before Jack and three friends are hunkered down in front of the television with video games, cans of pop and a large bag of mini chocolate bars. I step into the room just in time to see Jack flip a candy wrapper aside and say to his friends, "Just throw them on the floor, my Mom will pick them up."

I tell them to pick up the mess and go play in the basement, a bad move as they soon commence a practise session for the school talent competition using Donald's ancient amp, an electric guitar, keyboard and my new bongos. The band, newly christened My Sister Sucks, is busy proving that their main talent is being loud and obnoxious. I can hear Jack continually repeating the refrain (and only line) of his first original rock and roll composition: "My ugly sister sucks." Olympia, no doubt, is becoming ticked, but the band is drowning out her and her two friends, a remarkable accomplishment that results in Serenity's sudden defection to parts unknown.

I'm grateful for Serenity's disappearance and for the loud and obnoxious music as now I can sneak into my bedroom to phone Michael in peace. Michael, my darling Michael of the honeyed thighs and angel eyes, has proved to be the best T.A. a schoolgirl could ever wish for. I can't wait for those wonderful Tuesdays, a day full of romantic anticipation, a day when we might steal an hour after class for scholarly pursuits, for private meetings of probing minds, etc., study carrel to frisky study carrel, thigh to teasing thigh, in the dim recesses of the library stacks where no one else ever goes. Thanks to Michael's remarkable effectiveness as a teacher, I have fallen in love with school.

Alas, being a noble, honourable and guilt-ridden T.A., Michael has remained true to his vow that our friendship shall remain firmly platonic until our teacher-student relationship has fully dissolved—that is upon the final delivery of marks in late April. Furthermore he will ensure that Professor Greshen grades all my tests and essays. I think Michael is over-PC'ing with the honour bit, but I admire him—and his thighs—all the same.

CanLit has become a front for passing friendly notes and secret emails back and forth, a pet topic of discussion being where and how soon can our friendship be properly and honourably consummated? I never thought academic pursuits could be so stimulating.

During Greshen's last lecture—and before this nasty March Break—Michael boldly sat beside me and slipped me a note describing, with pointed detail and a diagram, how desperately happy he was to see me, daring me to consider the evidence close at hand, and could we possibly let things get out of hand the minute this course has ended come April?

When, where and how is becoming an exceedingly difficult conundrum given that April's winds are too cruel to slip away into the nearest forest. And I don't like the idea of a motel—too ticky-tacky. I want romance and spontaneity even if I have to plan it down to the last tickle and lick.

Our last (privately exchanged) online "class discussion" email debated the merits of lovers' lanes and the back seat of Michael's car, but I overrode his suggestion on the grounds of space considerations. I need more room to comfortably spread out the middle-aged spread. These are the ugly consequences of being too cool to buy a family-size van. And as for when, well, April remains long weeks away. Arggh. I may die with waiting for this dopey course to end. I hate school.

I dial Michael's office: the English department's ditzy secretary, for once, answers the phone: "Sorry, Mr. Doorite is away from the office until tomorrow—would you like to hold?"

* * *

Damn March Break. If the aim of childhood is to stockpile sufficient toys, then Jack and Olympia have met their objective with distinction, turning the whole house into a nuisance minefield. It has become impossible to navigate from one room to another without puncturing a heel with a Lego piece or tripping over a soccer ball left on the stairs.

In sheer disregard for the futility of my own objective, I have decided to tackle the chaos in the kids' bedrooms. I'm normally afraid to venture into Jack's room, as one never knows what disagreeable woodland creature might be cornered within. I have a package of green garbage bags, a pair of rubber gloves and I will keep the cordless phone at my fingertips in case of an emergency or if anything asks to "phone home."

Upon sight of the garbage bags, Jack switches into collector's Code Red Alert. He forbids me to throw anything out without a full consultation. Now I'm entirely sure Jack is Donald's child. Jack is a meta-collector: he collects collections.

Jack counteroffers: he'll sort out his room himself. No way. The last time I insisted Jack shovel out his room himself he emerged after two hours with nothing but a length of baseboard trim and three pop cans. The cans were unwanted low value "denteds" from his pop can collection and the trim just "fell off" somehow.

Olympia, not one to be outdone, has a room that Stephen King could've invented. It's a whole new terrifying spin on *Toy Story*. Bored to ever spiralling heights of fractiousness by March Break, she commences useless arguing with Jack about who has "more stuff." How convenient—now I can slip away, unnoticed, to commence the reduction of their stuff.

I enter Jack's room tentatively. Flipping on the light, I experience the sudden cold chill you get when things that creep about in the dark come to a sudden halt. I think I can hear eerie jungle noises, roars and screechings in the distance, but it's probably just my hearing receptors buzzing with a morning caffeine dose massive enough to poison the Amazon River. Rapidly, I fill two laundry baskets with gym clothes that are stuffed under the bed when the phone rings.

I stare at the phone with trepidation. I don't want to answer in case it's Regina. She phones me every blinking day with updates for the wedding. She puts me to work at every opportunity. This week I have to research table toppers and ways to keep guests from tinkling their glasses during the meal.

But what if the caller is Michael?

Answering quickly, I hear Michael's voice. "Look Pauline, I just have to see you today. Forget everything I said about ethical teacher-student relationships."

I swoon with delight. Sweeping everything off Jack's bed, I lie down feeling faint. I'm pressing the phone to my ear so hard it's making a dent in my skull.

"I don't know ... I have the kids here and I haven't a clue where Serenity is and ... I suppose I could make up some excuse and get a sitter ..."

Michael says, "I have a key to a friend's place, we could meet there."

"What? You told a friend about me?"

Michael told somebody??? This is the crocodile moat around our relationship—i.e., nobody knows about it but us. It's our only rule so far excepting that I don't do motels and we can't sleep with anybody else but our spouses. And I make the rules. Michael is already breaking the rules and we haven't even signed the constitution yet.

All of a sudden Olympia breaks into our conversation from the playroom extension: "I don' wanna sitter. I wanna go with you and Michael."

How on earth did Olympia know I was talking to Michael? His name wasn't mentioned so far in *this* conversation. "Olympia, hang up the phone," I yell and I wait to hear the confirming click.

Michael's voice gets all edgy. "You told your kid about me? What for?"

I don't like his tone but he's right to be worried. What has Olympia overheard? None of our conversations tend to bear a family rating. If we were a movie it would be entitled, Pauline Wants to Ride 'Em Cowboy or What Naughty Things Michael Can Do With His Tongue. My head spins as a panic attack looms: I feel like I should lie down except I already am.

"Never mind, call me tomorrow, I have to go."

There's no time to properly consummate our first lover's quarrel because I better go deliver damage control to Olympia and possibly to her buddies, Jack and his buddies, and who knows who else.

***

Oh joy! Michael presented a raincheck right after breakfast. After I thoroughly disabled all the extension phones in the house, we confirmed our plans using code language: Michael will await me to commence the primary research session in his friend's condo. I'm feeling much better this morning, since last night I told Olympia a new kind of bedtime story. The tale was laced with numerous bald lies regarding the identity of my phone friend. I discovered she could repeat some choice phrases gleaned from three separate instances of eavesdropping. With any hope, by the time she grows up, she will have forgotten that Michael the "vacuum cleaner salesman" wanted to lick her mother all over.

Thank goodness vacuum cleaners can do things like turn on, vibrate and suck things up.

***

The condo turns out to be a chi-chi townhouse in a classy part of town. I hesitate in the Jeep for a moment and breathe deeply. I'm wearing my sexy new Georgette blouse, unbuttoned all the way down to wantonly reveal my sexy new pink and green half-cup bra (a very creamy "C" cup). I reach into my coat and button my blouse all the way back up to the neck, check my lipstick and unbutton my blouse again.

I can barely climb the stairs to the front door what with my knees—and resolve—gone all weak and crumbly but some unseen force propels me forward—or maybe it's just a premenopausal last-chance-for-fun flash. I fluff my hair into a seductive tumble with trembling pre-adulterous fingers, take a deep breath and knock.

Michael answers the door almost immediately, seizes my hand and pulls me inside. He hangs my coat on an elegant antique hallstand equipped with a marvellous mirror that reveals the recent disappearance of ten years from my face and ten pounds from my butt. Uh oh. My cover is no doubt blown. It's dead easy to tell when a friend or neighbour has either left her husband or is having an affair: excess pounds are effortlessly shed and out trots the flirty new up-do. The reappearance of untended curls and stretch denims signals a return to the regularly scheduled marriage. Bibienne narrowed her eyes at me the other day. I better cancel a tanning bed or two.

I tear myself away from the mirror and pause to wander through the spotless living room, tastefully decorated with original artworks on immaculate walls. Antique tables overflow with marble slabs and expensive looking collectables. I'm tremendously impressed with Michael's bachelor friend. I wonder what *he* looks like?

Then I experience a sudden panic at the thought that *he* could be a *she*. Another "other" woman? Now the condo seems suspiciously fussy and effeminate. Michael's friend could be gay. Maybe Michael is bi. Hope not. That's twice the competition.

Michael pulls me quickly into his arms. I can feel his heart beating against my chest and his breath on my skin as he commences kissing my neck leaving behind several brand new pulse points at each nuzzled location. Our progress up the stairs is halted at frequent intervals to remove items of clothing. On the landing Michael pauses to remove his jeans.

***

Michael believes that falling down the stairs was his just punishment for engaging in an unethical fraternization with a student. He also believes I'm a big klutz. I was only trying to help. And he wouldn't have fallen down the stairs if he hadn't been hopping around with his foot all tangled up in his pant leg when I accidentally tripped him.

I wish I knew how bad the break is, but I couldn't find it out as I had to quickly skulk away from emergency when Michael's wife arrived.

***

The gods are punishing me by breaking my men. I just found out that Donald has met with disaster on the slopes beside the Convention Centre. He is in a foul humour as the broken ankle "hurts like hell" not to mention he had to cut short his "convention agenda." Oh yes, and Lindsay is driving him home.

***

Good times, good times. I spent the day tending to Donald, in addition to Jack and Olympia who have reached the zenith of March Break ennui. The kids wiled away an hour or so trying to teach George Bush how to balance treats on his nose. Now I know that the dog is horribly allergic to beer nuts.

I'm in a vicious mood. Why do dogs always have their violent allergic reactions on new living room carpets? I send the kids outside to play, warning them to stay away from the creek and all muddy areas. The warning is probably a complete waste of breath—no one in this house ever listens to me. Yesterday Olympia lost her new "indoor" shoes—the school pair I told her weren't to be worn outside—in the mud beside the creek. I wasted an hour digging for them with the result that the shoes are still missing, but now I have a body sized trench in the most secluded section of the park.

Donald is the worst listener of all. This morning, in an attempt to be solicitous in light of his broken ankle, I offered to make him a hot breakfast. Three times, to no avail, I asked him which he preferred, "Tea or coffee?" I gave him both, all mixed together in a large mug with a twist of lemon, cream and sugar.

***

At last. It's Sunday night and March Break is over. I sit up in bed with Donald and watch the late night news. Recent studies indicate that famine, poverty and pestilence are surging worldwide. And Canada is predicted to go to the polls again. Worst news of all, the right wing is gaining major footholds Canada wide: nothing like the promise of a homegrown surge of famine, poverty and pestilence.

The weather report displeases as usual. Since Donald broke his ankle, he can't negotiate icy sidewalks on crutches. Every single damn day it snows, providing him with a continuing excuse to stay home from work. There's more snow on the way, but I'm comforted by the thought that the kids return to school tomorrow signalling the end of March Breakdown.

***

A special 7 a.m. bulletin just came in from Serenity: it's a snow day and the school buses are cancelled. Peachy. I can look forward to yet another day of Jack and Olympia leaping around the house like gazelles on uppers. At least I can stay in my warm comfy bed later than usual even though it probably means listening to Donald moan on about his ankle again. I tell him I hope he can handle making his own breakfast this morning since I'm desperately in need of resting up from the rigours of March Break.

The peace and quiet of my warm comfy bed is interrupted by the sound of a thud in the hallway just outside our bedroom door, which is quickly followed by the sound of Jack and Olympia howling accusations at each other. They storm the bedroom yelling:

"Jack ran into me."

"No, Olympia ran into *me* first."

It's too early in the morning to determine who ran into who first. I explain to Jack and Olympia that the laws of physics apply—they obviously ran into each other at the same time. Both wander away scratching their heads indicating I've reached an advanced level of child handling skills or else they've contracted head lice.

Looking outside, I can see the driveway is socked in again with snow. I need a vacation. I'd like to run away from home—it would be neat to test the laws of getting physical as in my body colliding with Michael's on a beach in Mexico. If only the roads were passable. If I can but hold on till tomorrow, I will at least get to see Michael in class and learn the extent of physical damage that occurred during our last collision.

***

The buses are running this morning, but Olympia woke up complaining of a sore stomach. I wonder how far advanced her complaint might be—these types of situations always result in an eruption of one kind or another so the question is whether to administer Gravol for one end or Imodium for the other.

Whatever the outcome, I'm forced to keep her home from school. All my hopes to see Michael today are toast. I don't have the nerve to phone him at home either so I can only continue to guess as to his condition.

I would take Olympia to the doctor, but I think she might recover faster if I keep her in bed and skip the medical attention.

***

Yesterday, after two long days of intensive nursing, I broke down and transported Olympia, at death's door, to the Urgent Care Clinic. Two hours in the crowded waiting room, where everybody coughed their germs at me, was just the ticket: the moment the doctor walked into our cubicle, Olympia perked up and all her symptoms vanished. Doctors are miracle workers.

Olympia has gone back to school today, thank goodness, as the deadline for my Creative Writing portfolio is looming.

Five incomplete short stories are rotting in the depths of my new computer. I call up the most promising narrative onscreen for a redrafting session. Ratfarts. I can't think of anything more compelling to occupy my two main characters other than making them fall in love with each other. I would give them a hot rod sex scene except I can't quite get them into bed together.

Writer's block is no longer my only problem—while at the medical clinic with Olympia, I showed the doctor my sore arm and received a diagnosis: Repetitive Strain Injury. I offered the doctor a convincing RSI explanation: the demands of Rigorous Scholarly Inquiry have forced me to withstand long hours at the keyboard power-pointing the mouse. I got a prescription for anti-inflammatory drugs and a stern warning to give up mousing until my arm is healed.

I'm too embarrassed to admit the truth: too many sessions of Tetris, FreeCell and Spider Solitaire are to blame. Donald is, as usual, all warm sympathy: upon my return from the doctor, he hopes out loud (from the comfort of the couch with his ankle propped up on the ottoman) that my "delicate little elbow" won't prevent me from doing my share of the housework not to mention keeping up with my studies and watching the kids.

Somehow I will have to unplug from my FreeCell addiction. My writer's block is to blame. Every time I can't think of a thing to write, that game seduces me. I'll play one last round before my final swearing off.

***

I'm beginning to wish it were me with the broken bones. Ever since March break, I've been on deck for all the driving, laundry, shopping, cleaning, cooking and childcare. All without any contact with Michael.

Donald spent the whole week lying on the couch tapping away on his laptop, watching game shows, tying up the Internet line all day and napping, his cell phone clutched in one hand and the TV remote gripped fast in the other. Every few minutes he calls for some needful thing: his newspaper, coffee, a banana, a pillow, another pillow, another banana, water, pain tablets.

I've been checking my email hourly for days. Finally, just now, Michael emailed me an update on his prognosis.

Until today, I've had no contact with Michael since leaving him in agony at emergency when his wife arrived to transport him home. Poor Michael. The doctor said that thigh bone fractures tend to be slow to heal, but depending on the extent of the damage, he's hopeful Michael can graduate from a primary cast to a walking cast quickly, and return to work, maybe even by next week.

I also learned that Michael's wife is launching her gunboats because, as it turns out, the admitting nurse remarked to her that everyone thought that *that other woman* who brought Michael into emergency was the wife. Then everyone looked at Michael who couldn't respond because his bruised testicles were still affecting his voice.

Today, the world will simply have to struggle on without me as I'm drowning in late assignments. I've just warned everyone to keep back. I intend to stay locked in the den with all pertinent reference books and special resources (chocolate chips) until I have completed a dynamite portfolio for creative writing class.

There's nothing like pigging out on chocolate chips for sparking tired old brain synapses: the secret is to eat the entire bag in one go.

Voila! I've invented an ingenious trick to circumvent

writer's block: the idea is to take a deadly novel and turn it inside out and backwards by switching all the words around and substituting selected words with their antonyms. The result will be an original piece of writing (or at least such a well-disguised fake that no one could suspect plagiarism) expressing groundbreaking ideas entirely opposite to the tired old ideas expressed in the original.

From the bookshelves I snatch down D.H. Lawrence's *Women in Love*—an immensely tedious novel by a most tiresome, misogynistic male. The process of bastardizing Lawrence's work should be satisfying indeed. Now I'm bursting with creative juices.

I begin with the title, *Women In Love*. How about *Lust in Women*? Very grabby. I'll turn all the male characters into women for starters. Birkin and Gerald could be Bernice and Geraldine. Ursula and Gudrun could be middle-aged lesbians.

Or were they already? Perhaps Lawrence was toying with us all along. It goes with my theory that all male giants of English literature are, at core, pretentious two-bit scammers.

***

Things are looking up—Donald hobbled back to work today and I saw Michael in class, his leg solidly encased in plaster. Michael is bummed because his wife has been driving him back and forth to work everyday—because of his leg he can't drive yet. She isn't speaking to him because she thinks he's having an affair.

If only she were right.

***

The pregnancy test was positive.

Looks like George Bush is going to be a father. Now

Boriston's on the warpath: he's demanding compensation and damages. Donald remains adamant: Boriston's dog is a roving, trespassing slut, and her pups were conceived (twice), not in Boriston's yard, but in the middle of our front lawn.

***

I'm home alone when, unexpectedly, the doorbell rings. I'm overjoyed to open the door to find ... "Michael ... How did you ...?"

Muttering something about, "I can't wait a minute longer," he steps inside and, shutting the door behind him, grasps me tightly and begins to kiss my face and neck while slipping his hands up under my sweater. We sink to the floor where my sweater disappears and Michael starts a slow sweet tongue slide all the way down to ...

I'm awakened from a deep sleep—and the best dream of my life—by Olympia bursting into my bedroom yelling, "The bus just went by."

Olympia isn't dreaming but, dammit, I was up until this very moment. I recall Donald saying 'bye at 7:10 at which I appealed to him to set the alarm, please, so I could grab twenty minutes more sleep. I grabbed an *hour* and twenty even though the alarm went off according to plan—only it was set to "radio" and the volume was set to "low" so the moth-eaten old brain burlap filtered it all out as quiet meaningless muzak to sleep by.

I don't blame any of this on my brain or the alarm though. I blame it all on the Internet. I stayed up late last night downloading and installing a "net patrol" program all because Olympia decided to surf the net in search of boy band sites and some of the options that popped up had too much to do with free pics of boy bands dropping their pants online.

Although Olympia insists she didn't have enough

time to actually visit the Nude Male Celebrity Sex Tape Place, I don't like that she's still burning with curiosity to see what's behind those smutty links.

Actually, I installed a net filter thingy weeks ago. It failed for some reason, possibly something to do with having to disable it so I could surf for smutty links of my own. And when I attempted to restore the original net filter, I couldn't remember the secret password nor even where I stowed the software on the computer, so I thought, with my big brains, I'll just download another program. It'll be simple, as there are dozens of these porny filters out there, right? As of 3:30 a.m., I had accomplished my mission.

I hustle the kids into the Jeep and off to school, but we arrive too late and I'm forced to explain to the principal that our lateness is all because of the Nude Male Celebrity Sex Tape Place.

The principal is unamused since he had to get out of bed on time, long hours ago. His all-powerful principal eyes burn through me, and I have no choice but to admit the truth: I slept in. Sir.

I feel like a little kid again. I wonder if I might have to write 100 lines of *I promise to wake up on time from now on.*

As fast as possible, I drive home to rouse my wrinkly old brain with an extra-strong cup of coffee. Funny—my email and the Internet are down. Soon I discover why: the new net patrol software has gone to war with the old net patrol software preventing all access to the net whatsoever. Nettlesome error message windows are popping up everywhere, like dandelions going to seed. I swear the new program worked fine last night. Enraged, I erase both net patrol programs in a matter of seconds and find myself back, cybertorially speaking, where I began, in raw surfing mode. Except my computer is still sore at me and is still firing off error messages, except now they're big, dire error messages instead of pesky, little error messages so it will be a miracle if Michael ever gets another slutty email from me again, net patrol software or not.

I think I should go back to bed. Perchance to dream.

***

I spent most of yesterday restoring email capability on my computer so now I'm even further behind with my homework. I have to stop pissing around. But it's tough working on a dull CanLit essay when thoughts of Michael keep popping up. I'll just take a few minutes' break to fire off, to Michael, an email containing the Open Book Question of the day: *Are you an anteater or a mud turtle?*

Ten minutes later, I check my email to find a reply from Michael: *Which would you prefer?*

What, do I have a choice here? Hmmmm. Just how far would he be willing to go in the name of love? Maybe it's a good thing (for Michael's sake) that I'm hoping for an anteater. I've never had an anteater.

But what if he *isn't* an anteater? I better take care with my reply: *No special preferences. Just curious. Do you have a scanner?*

Moments later, I open another email from Michael to find a scanned-in pencil sketch of a huge, erect, smiley-faced penis with a long tongue waving from its distinctly anteater mouth-tip. Snatching up my sketchpad, I scan back a quickie rendering of a well-hung Michael and me, leaping nude, hand in hand, through a patch of flower-power type daisies.

I love doing homework with a computer.

***

Dammit all to hell. Another snowstorm. The wind is trying to rip the roof off the house and the driveway looks like a scene from *Dr. Zhivago* again. I feel like Lara waiting to be Yuried.

Despite the snow, I'm elated to have just managed to complete my final CanLit essay. Knowing that Michael will be applying his angel eyes to my naked prose made my fingers tingle as they typed a finely crafted (I hope) analysis of Susanna Moodie's literary works. I could go for some roughing it in the old bush right about now. Essay writing is becoming tinged with the erotic: I'm tempted to insert some lascivious reader response passages including instructions for marking, such as *this essay should be read in bed*. I could even go all the way and include graphics and a scratch n' sniff strip.

I have to stop myself from adding salacious annotations, as Michael will merely be proofreading my essay before passing it along to Prof. Greshen for marking. But how can I resist scanning in that sexy photo Bernie snapped of Bibienne and me, when we were sunbathing tops down in her back yard last summer? Lucky I have a photo fixer-upper program to touch up the cellulite patches and crop out Bibienne (who arguably has better boobs, etc.). I will toss in the photo with a caption as a "For Your Eyes Only" alternative "cover girl" page for my essay. Two hours of touch ups later, I'm ready to add the caption: A *good teacher always keeps on top of the student body.*

I print out my alternative cover page. I wouldn't want Donald to see this so I meticulously erase all traces of the Michael's Eyes Only file by rewriting its contents with zeros, deleting it and then deleting the directory to boot. Uh oh. My carefully erased directory was also the one and only last resting place of the final draft of my CanLit essay.

I spend a panic-stricken hour attempting to recover the lost directory. Turns out the computer retained the entire essay in the form of "deleted files" in a backup to the backup trash bin. I guess I will have to let the computer live. After setting the program to print the reactivated essay, I find a perfect copy of the final draft lying in the printer tray, printed hours ago just before I printed my two-timing note.

Then I notice that my incriminating cover page is also retained in the state of the art computer memory in the form of a "deleted file." Now what? Every time I try to overwrite the note, my smart-ass computer makes *another* backup copy of it. A flash flood of computer rage is engulfing me. Why the blazes don't computers come equipped with needful components like a benzo wizard, ready to dispense at the click of a mouse?

Several more hours get burned while I research an idiot-proof method to permanently remove all "deleted" files from the computer's elephantine memory. Exhausted, I drop into bed only to remember that, come dawn, Jack and Olympia will be expecting their annual Easter egg hunt and Mr. and Mrs. E. Bunny forgot to buy the necessary sweets again this year.

I heave myself back out of bed. The glow of the bedside clock illuminates Donald's immaculate ankle cast, which is poking out from the blankets and propped up on a pillow. It's 2:35 a.m. Thank goodness for all-night drugstores.

***

Despite the lack of sleep, I woke up in an unusually inspired, creative mood. I devoted my artistic energy to setting out coloured markers, stickers, glitter, glue, bowls of dye and three dozen boiled eggs for decorating while Jack and Olympia gobbled down their Easter bunny bounty.

Olympia occupied all of five minutes in decorating her egg, accidentally cracked it, flipped out and refused to do any more. I just finished decorating the thirty-five remaining eggs. I think I did a very nice job. I can relate to Easter: deep down it's all about ovaries and fertility and the rule of female hormones. Estrogen dominance is forcing me to eat a whole flock of chocolate chicks. I feel terrific as a result despite the persistence of Easter egg dye stains on the kitchen floor and countertops.

ten

Action Deferred

April Fool's day. It was no joke when Boriston's legal beagle served us with notice that we're being sued for $10,000 for loss of breeding opportunity, veterinary services including examinations, tests, inoculations, whelping fees, etc. I'll have to make Donald sit down in the living room when I show him this so when he grabs for his chest, he can expire in the comfort of his favourite armchair.

***

I'm flat out *furious*. Donald has invited Lindsay Bambraugh and her partner over here for dinner Sunday night. He said, "It's okay, Pauline, you don't have to do anything, I'll cook the dinner, and clean up and everything, don't worry."

He gave me his best Bambi eyes and temporary insanity took over, causing me to pledge a helping hand. I have no desire to cook for Donald's secret squeeze but, I must admit, I wouldn't mind another good look at her. Could be, she's put on a few pounds recently.

How infuriating: entertaining means planning a meal, shopping, tidying up the place. Where to begin? I sit on my newspaper-strewn couch in the living room to stew. All my furniture suddenly looks outdated. I hate my living room. Not to mention the ugly pesto-coloured flocky wallpaper, leftover from the previous owners: it's so godawful, I would rather die than expose myself on the anvil of Lindsay's decorating judgment. That's it. Time to undecorate the living room. Leaping off the couch and seizing a loose corner of paper, I tear off the first length.

After ten minutes of satisfying ripping, boredom sets in. In some places, the paper is refusing to come off. My fingernails are no longer adequate to the task. I need buckets of water, drop sheets, scraping tools. Since Donald's been engaged all evening on the phone with Boriston, both yelling about lawyers and suits and carrying on crazy, now I have to finish stripping all the flipping wallpaper without any assistance.

Donald runs into the room, holding his hand over the receiver of the cordless: "What does 'Baise mon cue' mean?"

Merde.

***

Bibienne has volunteered to help me shop for new wallpaper. On the way to the mall, I'm sorely tempted to come clean with her about Michael. Just as I prepare to open my mouth Bibienne says, "There's Chapters."

Michael and the wallpaper can wait. Bibienne shrugs into her favourite chair, and turning the pages to find where she left off last time, settles down, tall Cinnamon Latte in hand, to read *Mars and Venus Together: Going Down On Uranus.*

I'm thinking of plunking my money down on a funky book about the mystic art of Feng Shui. No wonder a cloud of misfortune hovers over my head: according to the book, the placement of every object in my house is all wrong. For one thing, my marriage bed is a Zen-free zone because it's situated in the wrong corner. According to this book, large mirrors on the ceiling to redirect the universal flow of chi are supposed to help.

In fact, our entire house is dissed by the universal flow of chi. For instance, our back door is smack dab in the middle of our relationships / marriage area and our wealth and abundance area is entirely missing. I better buy this book. It's a steal at $49.95.

***

The only decent wallpaper I could find turned out to be the most expensive, a zillion dollars a roll, but I don't care because the new paper will do wonders in the living room. Donald's eyes bugged right out of his head when he saw the receipt. He doesn't appreciate my excellent taste.

Last night I voluntold Donald to help me put it up. While papering the alcove I explained to Donald that, according to the principles of Feng Shui, our toilet is inauspiciously located. We should relocate it elsewhere. Or at least keep the lid down from now on. Otherwise, our wealth is going down the drain according to the book.

"Wealth? What wealth?" howls Donald as he yanks a dripping roll of paper from the soaking tray. "You just maxed out a credit card on a ton of wallpaper." Without warning, he launches all his chi into a tirade on all the reasons we will never have any wealth, forget the f'ing art of placement, how about the f'ing art of budgeting and principles of planned purchasing?"

"Be more careful Donald. You just crushed the edge of that roll. Now it's ruined."

"Fine, I'll just throw the fucking thing away." Donald yanks up the window and flings the roll onto the front lawn. For the rest of the evening I refrain from mentioning that our career corner needs redecorating, with metal and fire elements, for fear of further huffy outbursts and boring lectures on the topic of Why The Ambitious Financial Planner Shouldn't Be Making Public Applications For Protection From Creditors.

***

Lindsay and friend, and Bibi and Bernie, are all expected at 5 p.m. for predinner cocktails. I'm amazed that my dinner party agenda is running smoothly. The house looks decent, the kids are dressed and under control, and food prep is well underway. Even the insanely fiddly puff pastry canapés turned out perfectly: golden brown and stuffed with smoked salmon and St. Andres cheese. Entertaining usually leaves me feeling rushed, stressed and uptight. I think I've mastered this nasty business after all. All that's left to do is nip over to the grocery store and pick up toilet paper, strawberries, French bread sticks and fresh dill for the canapés.

In the checkout line, I check my watch: goody, it's still early, only 4 p.m. There's plenty of time left to make a side trip to Dairy Queen for my super efficiency reward. While debating whether to go with butter pecan or chocolate fudge, I overhear a snatch of conversation between two cashiers: one is pleased to be getting off work in ten minutes while the other replies that she gets off at 6 p.m. "But hey, that's only an hour away, right?"

In the parking lot, I'm still diverted by the idle thought that those dodo-brained cashiers can't tell time: 6 p.m. is two hours away, not *one*. Right? RIGHT? OMIGOD, it's ME who can't tell time, it's ten minutes after 5 p.m., not 4, I'm a twenty-minute drive from home and with any luck my guests are going to be fashionably late because I'm going to be too. And DAMN daylight savings time.

I speed home, feeling rushed, stressed and uptight. En route, I stop at the quickie convenience store for a giant blueberry Freezie—I need to chill out a bit. Sure enough, my guests await me, the Freezie has leaked all over my best white blouse and Donald, his daylights still an hour behind in another time zone, looks dazed and perplexed. In front of everyone he asks, "Did you remember to get the toilet paper?"

My sole consolation is that, in her next life, Martha

Stewart is probably going to come back as me, and that will be her just punishment.

***

At dinner last night, Lindsay refused to try my Smoked Salmon and Cheese Puffins. She's on a special bodybuilding diet. Pulling out her so-called "hip carafe" of high-protein meal replacement shake, she took a swig saying, "This is all I can have for six more weeks." She twirled about in her sleeveless mini dress to show off her calves and then thrust out her bare arms. "My trainer says my muscle definition is like iron draped in silk."

I refrain from hoping out loud that her arms won't rust off in the next rainstorm.

Bibienne glanced at Lindsay's upper arm and shrugged. "I hear those protein drinks are full of lympho-melanomial steisotopes." I'm sure she made that up.

Lindsay's dinner "partner," a tubby computer analyst, polished off all the Puffins, then quaffed a whole bottle of Barolo's finest while ploughing through half a leg of roast lamb and two kilos of asparagus because he only likes the tips. After dinner was demolished, he swilled down half a bottle of Scotland's peatiest while Lindsay tossed aside her plastic carafe and sucked up the Drambuie and Donald.

Bernie, after a short time in the presence of Lindsay's carved silky legs, became delirious and Bibienne sent him home with a headache. I must admit, Ms. Bambraugh has style. She looks sleekly steamy like a woman who has just had sex in a sauna. One peep at the porcine programmer, a legless drunk if I ever saw one, was 100 proof enough that she's not having saunas with him. If not him, then who?

For his part, Donald soon gulled back enough grape juice to forget his table manners: before long he was salivating over Lindsay and addressing her rather familiarly, as "Zee," an interesting nickname for one's boss that wasn't lost on Bibienne who led me out to the kitchen and offered to teach me how to administer an instant headache via her famous "rapid cranial rotation" massage technique.

My head already hurts and, besides, I'm supposed to be the ever-gracious host-person. Donald will most certainly pay for his caddish behaviour later. For now, I'm happy to let Bibi take her on.

After a trip to the washroom, Tubby the analyst returned, and remarked mid-belch, that asparagus "sure makes your piss smell funny." Then, all done with offering conversational gems, he heaved his body onto the couch, threw his head back and fell asleep in seconds. Lindsay slithered across the carpet, slipped off her shoes and curled up in front of Donald's recliner with her head practically resting in Donald's lap. She kept saying things like "I shouldn't wear shorty outfits when I'm not wearing any panties," and "Pauline, you have such a cozy little house, it has that comfortable, lived-in look."

Bibienne raised her eyebrow ever so slightly and asked, "So Zed, where do you live?"

"In a condo near Greenpark."

Bibienne stared at her as if she were under glass. "I never knew anyone who lived way out there. Now I've met one."

Lindsay replied tartly, "I'm hardly ever there. I need something close to the airport." She stretched and rearranged herself so her stocking foot nestled against Donald's. "The stay-at-home married life isn't for me. I mean, variety is the spice of life, don't you think Pauline?"

I had no idea how to respond. She's right: it's true that Michael would certainly spice up my life, but I hate to agree with Lindsay on anything.

In the silence, Bibienne abruptly stood up and crossed the room, saying, "I could use a top-up." As she passed

Donald's chair, she somehow managed to stamp her high heel directly into Lindsay's instep, leaving her shrieking, "Oh my God, my foot, it's bleeding."

Bibienne leaned over to inspect the damage. "I'm so sorry. Wow, I think that's going to leave a scar."

***

I'm in despair: today is last day of classes with Michael. School is fascinating. I've learned so much.

After class, I slip away with Michael to the library for a final Dingwallian embrace. While swooning lip-locked in the back of the stacks, I decide that Michael's mouth tastes wonderful—like a really good book, one you can't put down. Or is it the musty smell of the august tomes around us? Whatever. Today's stolen kisses are better than any D'Arcy, Rhett, or any other great kisser in this whole library could possibly deliver. If we're star-crossed lovers in a book then I can't wait for the denouement—that is, as long as our tale proceeds to its joyful climax.

Five minutes in Michael's arms and I'm cured. All symptoms of heartsick longing for this very moment disappear along with anxiety, fear, cancer-prone cells and the need, of late, for an eye test for reading glasses. I can clearly read every adorable thought radiating from Michael's eyes. If I mash my face any closer my eyeballs might intrude into his eyeball sockets.

Too soon Michael stops kissing me, and pressing his lips to my ear, he whispers, "What are we going to do?"

I don't know.

The misery of reality returns along with stress, an exploratory party of free radicals and the first pangs of longing to be back in Michael's arms before I've even left them.

***

Oh joy! It's the last day of Creative Writing Class. I deliver my writing portfolio to Coach Stool. In the end, I succumbed to Stool's base dictates regarding style and rewrote my entire portfolio with help from Jack and Olympia who speak the Stool lexicon with ease.

The poem most likely to win Stool's highest praises is entitled "What's Sperm?" and begins, "Sperm is …," followed by an all-inclusive shopping list of short adjectival stanzas which should make Stool drool.

I have to admit, my tasteless sperm poem was inspired by Olympia's quest for knowledge—while we were eating dinner the other night Jack insisted that my gelatinous vichyssoise was "totally gross" because it looked "just like sperm." After a stunned silence, Serenity and Dennis, gagging, excused themselves from the table as Donald turned green and Olympia uttered the inspirational phrase.

Jack was right of course, carelessly prepared leek and potato soup is unsuited for family consumption.

***

Blah. Regina's wedding machine is gearing up to full throttle. She's booked us for no less than three wedding rehearsals. A collective boredom at today's rehearsal appears to have produced man-eating urges. All seven bridesmaids and one of the ushers are badly smitten by the groom's masculine charms. All of us are jostling for advantageous rearview positions up and down the aisle.

I'm muscled to the back, the perfect location to overhear Jack, huddled with the flower girls in the last pew, teaching them how to swear: "If you want to be cool you have to say 'fuckin' in every sentence. If an adult's around, just say 'frikken.'"

Wedding rehearsals are turning into a full body-contact sport. The maid of honour, Jocelynn, is constantly hip-checking Regina out of the way to wriggle up to

Brad. Last week Camilla elbowed Jocelynn resulting in a bruised rib. My only consolation for missing Michael and for entrapment in endless rehearsals is the secret pleasure of fantasizing about the groom and observing Jocelynn closing in for the kill.

***

Bother. Now I'm stuck at a wine shower. Another dullsville wedding-related all-call. Perhaps the wine will perk things up. Lord knows I've tried my level best to be friendly to the other bridesmaids at past events, but none of them are cooperating with the possible exception of Camilla who just now smiled at me and offered to fill my glass when she rose, somewhat unsteadily, to pour her fourth glass of sherry. I kinda like this other bridesmaid. I wonder if she plays hockey?

Jocelynn is eyeing Camilla too. She walks over and in a loud voice, coos, "Ooh, Camilla, I adore your dress. It looks fabulous on you, I mean, the goth look is soooo slimming."

Camilla turns up the sides of her mouth and looks at Jocelynn sweetly. "Thanks, you look trendy yourself. My daughter is right into emo too."

Camilla's Betty White veneer is wearing thin. I drain my glass and go for more, with a sidewise glance at Camilla. She nods.

At the buffet table, I notice Camilla heaping the vegetarian bean soufflé onto her plate and skipping the barbecued chicken wings. Here's my chance to start a friendly conversational thread: I'm hopeless at initiating clever social chit chat, but I could ask her if she's into vegetarian-style eating, and maybe draw her out to talk about herself as a skilled conversationalist might well do.

But maybe she'd be offended if I ask a personal question? What if she thinks I'm prying or am about to judge her eating style? I better speak up though, as Camilla's plate is almost full. Plunging in, I say: "Are you vegetarian?"

Camilla pauses, and smiles agreeably at me: "No, not really. But I adore vegetarian-style foods. What about you?"

Whoa. This is going well. I quickly respond with a safe, "Me too."

Camilla picks up the thread, another good conversational sign: "I mean, who has the time for grinding groats and all that jazz?"

"I agree!"

Uh oh. I can't leave it at that. I sound so simple. I have to extend the thread, promote the next round. Camilla is looking at me, quizzically. I opt for the jokey filler line:

"Some people take it a bit far, you know, like those diehards who even make their own dog food." (Chuckle, chuckle.)

Camilla's smile disappears. "I make my own dog food. It's much healthier for the animal. Do you have *any* idea what they put in commercial pet foods?" she asks, shooting me with a frosty glance that clearly says she believes I'm slowly murdering my pets kibble by kibble, which, yes indeed, as a matter of fact, I would actually like to do.

"Ahahahaha, uh, no kidding, well of course, ahahahaha, making your own would be *much* better. So, uh, what do you put in it? Horse meat?"

Camilla glances down at her plate. Without even bothering to reply, she turns on her heel and stalks away leaving me to wonder if I should just be a drunken monk for the rest of the day and if a vegetarian pet food chef sneaks in ground up horse guts or beefs up the menu with tofu burgers or tabouleh salad or what.

***

My final exam for CanLit is this morning. I'm in a complete panic. Hungover too. I should've studied last night instead of downing a thousand quarts of sherry at the shower. I couldn't help myself. The bridesmaids began telling war stories about men and, with a common enemy, everyone started to get along. Even Camilla and Jocelynn drank until they almost liked one another. We're all flying to the Bahamas right after the honeymoon to get us and Regina properly laid.

I'll just wing the exam.

***

Snork. It's a drizzly day both outside and in, due to spring rains and a terrible head cold causing my sinuses to weep and my nose to run. I feel all weepy and runny inside too. I'm sure I flunked the final. Most likely I didn't use enough high-impact intellectual terms like *antiphallogocentric ecriture* and *foregrounded discursivity*. And, worse, now that my courses are all over, I will have no further regular contact with Michael.

Perhaps I should stop thinking about Michael anyway and start thinking about looking for work. I have to do something about my money troubles especially since the old Jeep is acting up again: the brakes are squeaking and the transmission has a slow leak; every day I must top it up with another spoonful or two of transmission fluid.

Spoon feeding the miserable heap is raising my bile: I want a new car, no, make that two new cars because Donald's old clunker is falling apart too. That'll be at least $100,000 for two roadworthy vehicles plus a double garage to put them in. Say $50,000 for a bigger garage.

Plus there are all the bills and credit cards. That's another $35,000. And the basement is still a half-finished mess, $25,000 would get me an aesthetically satisfactory basement.

So there—adding it all up, I only need $210,000 to put me in a civil frame of mind today.

***

The rain has stopped, but I still feel like murder, an ideal state for tackling my garden. I go outside and stab at the weeds with my trowel for a while: that's it, if the garden refuses to shape up I'll plant boulders in it. Maybe I can handle a rock garden.

The frikken weeds are everywhere. At this rate, I'm looking at days of hand weeding. Or a quick blast with some nasty environmentally unfriendly weed killer, but I'd die of the guilt.

If it weren't for my overactive guilt-producing glands, maybe I'd be further ahead with Michael too. I'd love to cultivate a lush patch of romance. There's just this little problem of kids and a husband.

This morning some big mouth on the radio claimed that spring has arrived, but I don't believe it. Peter Gzowski would never have lied about this.

I'm protected against the elements with my winter jacket and thick gloves. One would think Canada had never heard of global warming. I'm sure Americans are already enjoying the effects, but Canada is always ten years behind in things.

***

Another umbrella day. Last fall I pitched all the decaying umbrellas in a fit of de-cluttering, then forgot to buy new ones. Worse yet, I caught a flea on my pillow this morning: the spring flea season is starting up in spite of the cold damp weather. Not surprising, fleas like to get a jump on things. I better hop to it myself and declare open season on pests especially as the house is still overrun with the annual winter invasion of spiders and mice and innumerable stragglers from the annual fall invasion of ladybugs. Plus, the ants of summer are mustering. It's getting so I hate every lousy buggy season of the year now.

Too muddy in spring, too cold in winter, too hot in the summer. Fall would be tolerable if it weren't so depressingly close to winter. A fountain of negativity is welling up within: is it my cold? Premenstrual bloating? Crappy weather? Single Malt Deficiency? Michael deprivation? All of the above?

It's probably the bloating. It's no fair that I have a cold *and* bloating at the same time. It was the same damn thing last month, like having menstrual déjà vu.

The calendar confirms: my sap is about to fall rather than rise. Women should come equipped with an on-off spigot instead of an inconvenient great gaping hole. With this thought I run to the bathroom cabinet: yup, I'm flush out of plugs again. Dennis must be back in residence. She and Serenity break it up and make it up so often nowadays that I never can guess who's coming to dinner any more.

At any rate, I wish those two would time their breakup-and-reconciliation routine on a more convenient and predictable twenty-eight-day cycle so I will know how many tampons will need to be dished out.

It's time to stock up in earnest. I wonder where the nearest Tampax factory outlet might be? Probably Mexico. Mexico sounds more wonderful for the menstruating woman all the time: daily siestas, double margaritas, loads of chocolate and cheap tampons. But I would hate to face an annual household invasion of Gila monsters, scorpions and fat hairy tarantulas. Is there no bleeding compromise in the whole western hemisphere?

***

That's it. A person can take only so much premenstrual bloating. I've just come away from the car dealers where I've cooked up a sweet deal for a shiny new Jeep. I've already handed over the down payment which comes from a little stash I've been hoarding that Donald doesn't know about.

I'm set on a blue one with silver trim and the sliding moon roof so it's going to be a couple of weeks till I can pick it up. Wait'll Michael sees me cruise by in this sexy little thing. I'll need to get a new spring outfit to go with it. My mood is transformed.

I won't tell Donald about this yet. He might wig out. I'll wait till I have the keys in my hot little hands. I'll just have to soften him up a bit first.

I'll tell him I'm willing to share it. I got a good trade-in on the old Jeep so now we can put a little money into fixing up Donald's car—he's bound to agree that we should swing the payments together somehow. I began my campaign this morning when Donald started up again, complaining about a dinked wiper blade motor: "Three weeks the parts are on backorder, it rains every damn day, do you think the damn garage gives a shit? No, they ..."

I broke into his rant and said, "Why not look into something new? There's plenty of great deals out there for spring."

To my vast surprise, he nodded and said, "I think it might be time, actually."

I better not mention the cost of Regina's wedding, which is soaring lately. So far I've shelled out for a B.M. gown, matching shoes and clutch, a permanent wave for my hair, makeup, plus five shower gifts and a wedding gift chosen from the most wallet-slenderizing bridal registry I've ever seen.

To date, I've attended five monster showers in which Regina received all the major appliances, furniture, his 'n' hers leather recliners, seven complete sets of china and *cash.* (I'm crying. *Crying.*) My lone wedding shower garnered me three potato peelers and a bathmat.

I can't decide which shower has aged me the most; however, I'm certain Jocelynn's lingerie shower alone shaved several healthy years off my sex life. The B.M.s were invited to show off our best peignoir sets and entertain the guests. I haven't the stomach for parading around in baby dolls so I opted for playing my usual "Not Tonight, Bub" self while modelling long purple underwear and my zebra stripe slippers. Jocelynn invited Bradley to attend and then she strutted around all night in her Victoria's Secret leather teddy. I hadn't known that Victoria had an evil twin.

During last week's pre-rehearsal, I was moved to offer to furnish the cake for tonight's stag party. A surge of creative juices has resulted in a humongous tit cake, lavishly decorated with protruding red nipples and a titillating push-up bra.

***

I'm gratified by a good report from Donald on last night's stag: the groom was so pleased by my tit cake efforts he licked the nipples off first and then buried himself up to his toothsome neck in the centre of the bodacious double fudge mounds. Lucky tit cake. I wish someone would ice me and leave me quivering on Michael's pillow—I would love to feel Michael's tongue licking off all my icing and poking into my cake parts.

Due to being trapped in endless wedding preparations, I have had no opportunity to attempt a rendezvous with Michael. I have just returned from the ninth and, thank God, final dress fitting where I took possession of my B.M. dress from the shop. The post-honeymoon trip to the Bahamas is off. The infighting has become so complicated, I can no longer figure out which bridesmaid is still speaking to which. The configuration of alliances and hostile takeovers changes daily. All attempts at conflict resolution have been dismal failures, but communication has been somewhat facilitated since the decision that B.M.s are entitled to bring support persons to any meetings involving any combination of members of the bridal party.

But, hey, I've conducted myself with outstanding self-control, under the circumstances. The only exceptions of undue behaviour involved a regrettable teddy-strap snipping incident with Jocelynn at the lingerie shower. And, of course, the blowout at this morning's final, final dress fitting. Legal counsel representing the seamstress insisted, "Absolutely no further alterations would be done." Jocelynn must've thought she said, "Further altercations would be fun."

The constant conflict is all a tad unsettling considering Regina, Jocelynn and two of the maids served together on a peacekeeping tour.

* * *

The bridesmaids aren't the only ones at pains to get along lately. Dennis and Serenity's forty-third reconciliation ended with a bang late last night as Dennis gunned it out of the driveway in her truck, backfiring as always. Serenity wasn't willing to discuss the matter except to say that Dennis took her toolbox, her collection of zines and will come back for George Bush "later." It's final.

Huguette Boriston just phoned: Last night George Bush became the father to eight healthy pups. The mother is doing fine. When did I wish to take my half of the litter off her hands?

* * *

Jack and Olympia are jumping for joy over the thought of four puppies. I'm ready to simply jump myself.

"No way," I say. "We are *not* taking any of the puppies. We already have George Bush and he's too much dog as it is."

I don't add that if Dennis's promise of "later" ever comes, we will be completely and wonderfully dogless.

Olympia isn't speaking to me ever again as I'm a twisted dog poo.

***

Disaster. Huguette invited Jack and Olympia in to see le petit chiens today. I'm a *double* twisted dog poo now.

***

Donald just pulled into the driveway in a brand new Jeep. "A sweet lease deal," he says.

His new ride is black. With the sliding moon roof. And the leather interior. Mine has cloth. The slick bastard.

How dare he just go out and buy a new vehicle without consulting me first? Where did he get the down payment? And how did he manage to get his deal done so fast? My Jeep won't be ready until Monday. I can't tell him yet. I better think this through first: on the one hand, we could keep his new wheels and I could quietly cancel my deal: it'll be like having a secret hatbox full of cash as I could then justify making a future big expenditure without prior consultation. But if I let him keep his Jeep he'll gain the psychological advantage regarding ownership. He'll have to let me drive it, but it won't be *mine*. He's already signed off and everything. This isn't fair. I want a new toy too. We can't afford two new vehicles? Can we?

Donald pats the hood and says, "I didn't tell you anything because I wanted to surprise you."

I don't believe it. Donald's taking over Lindsay's job, a position which comes with a big raise plus a signing bonus. He can expense the Jeep to the firm, all thanks to Lindsay who is moving up to become a regional director. He's still going to be working directly under her though. Damn that Lindsay.

The sun slides out from behind a bank of clouds and Donald's Jeep gleams like a bandit's gold tooth. He opens the door for me and I slide behind the wheel and check out the console. The buggy is fully loaded. God, I love that woman.

***

Michael just emailed me to say he can get away to meet me tomorrow at the Dingy Coffee Cup if I'm game. Tomorrow is the goddamn wedding. I hate Regina.

***

Regina's Big Stupid Wedding Day: it's damp, cold and drizzly out, after days of a steady downpour. A late exit from the house means Donald is in shortcut mode. I asked him to take the main route, but he won't listen to me. He's in love with his new SUV and wants to take it for a little back road spin.

Last night I paid Jack and Olympia extravagant retainers for good behaviour with a written promise of the balance of their fee afterwards. To earn full fees, they must dress up, sit still during the service and use actual cutlery at the reception.

Our shortcut is deteriorating: sections of the dirt road are covered in water, but Donald hammers through the washed out areas determinedly. Ahead, I can see that the road is missing. I implore Donald to turn back: "Look, up ahead, that's a lake."

Donald stomps on the gas. "It's only a puddle."

In the middle of the washed-out section, the Jeep stalls as any self-respecting SUV does when asked to double as a submarine. The front end is almost submerged, the water is seeping in and the interior will soon be flooded to the level of the steering wheel. Another bad entry gate decision, Donald.

"Everyone out, quick," Donald yells as he climbs through the driver's side window to wade around to open the rear door.

Olympia is crying and won't go. Donald climbs back in. He grabs her and hauls her out. Yanking off my strappy high heels and nylons, I shove everything down the front of my bodice and, lifting my dress, proceed to wade through the waist-high washout to dry land.

Now the edges of my crinoline are dripping wet and smeared with mud. "Gimme the cell," I growl.

I'm in luck—the dealer says they'll come fish us out of the road and, guess what, my Jeep is ready! At the dealership, I sign everything with barely a glance, especially in Donald's direction. His mouth is working up and down like a trout, but nothing is coming out. Grabbing the keys, I can only hope my beautiful new blue baby can get us to the church on time. Donald refuses to come with us—he wants to wait for the garage to deliver the prognosis on his mud-brown SUB—so I race down the highway while combing my hair and reapplying my lipstick.

I arrive at the church doors, dripping mud blobs, and stagger to the women's room to discover Regina, surrounded by the B.M.s, collapsed in tears. Goody, a bride in crisis out-trumps a psycho bridesmaid any day. Now maybe I'll have a chance to rinse my feet and legs in the washroom sink and perform an emergency resuscitation on my mud-spattered dress without anyone noticing.

As I attempt to sneak past the huddle, Camilla announces in a syrupy voice, "Look, Regina, Pauline's here."

"She needn't have come. Brad is a two-timing prick. The wedding's *off*."

Camilla pulls me aside and whispers: "Regina caught Brad with Jocelynn last night, in his car. Giving him a hoodwash.

Regina stops sobbing to gape at me: "Christ, what the hell happened to you?"

My recently permed hair is, apparently, having a near-death experience: the dampness has caused frizzy cork-screw-curls to project weirdly into space around my head as if going towards the light on some invisible plane. I wish the rest of me could escape on a timely astral junket too. I hope that the unwelcome effects of my out-of-hair experience will subside before the photo-sessions, if there are any.

I say to Regina, "Never mind Bradley, think of this as a gift, my dear, now you can freely take a lover."

Regina perks up enough to decide that I will be perfect to sub in as the Maid of Honour—the wedding will go ahead only on account of the gifts and the promise of a Girls' Night Out right after the reception.

* * *

The best hangovers can be expected after wedding celebrations. But this morning's pounding headache cannot override the happy feeling that comes with consigning Regina's wedding day to that portion of my brain reserved for wedding reminiscences and similar disasters: that dark lobe is also crawling with difficult and painful memories such as my high school years, family vacations and the time I underwent a pap smear and my (ex) family doctor introduced me to the "big toothbrush."

The best part is Donald's Jeep was so full of mud that the dealer wrote it off under his insurance and Donald can expense my new Jeep under his account at the firm. Meanwhile we will put some money into fixing up the old sedan for Donald to drive. I get to keep my new blue baby!

***

Election Day: I better get down to the polling station and cast my vote. I wonder if exercising my franchise is a good idea though? Voting is, after all, the leading cause of politicians.

Plus, I'm still undecided about which direction to cast my vote. Because of losing the smoking bet with Donald, if I vote, I'm honour bound to vote Conservative. However, there were no stipulations that the loser can't check off *all* the names on the ballot and vote for everyone. Or I could lie to Donald and vote my conscience—which insists one must never vote Tory if one wishes to vote responsibly. Or I could draw happy faces on my ballot. I'm leaning towards the happy faces. The country could always use more happy faces on Election Day.

I'm always uncertain which way Donald is voting. Donald waxes secretive when it comes to politics—it's as if he suspects I'm keeping a secret notebook on him to hand in during the next bloody revolution so he will be executed for his subversive voting habits. (Not a bad idea actually.)

By 10 p.m., as the election results pour in, I can see that the country is still an unruly but viable patchwork of solitudes and that's well worth the raising of stemware. Bibienne charges our glasses in a tribute to her beloved Bloc and then joins me in a toast to all the old and new officials of the nation: "Here's to nasty old political hacks: may they never wallow in family values!" We then pause to shed a few womanly tears of nostalgia for Trudeau. Momentarily overcome, I allow Jack and Olympia to light their giant

Mexican sparklers in the living room, a stupidly impulsive move as now my lovely new Heritage Green carpet is dusted liberally with burn holes.

eleven

At My Command

The first decent spring day has arrived. The weather is gorgeous: warm, dry and picture perfect for—a tasty picnic in the woods with Michael! Now that his cast is off, I could kiss all his bruises better. I wave Donald off to work and lunge at the phone. With fingers all a-tremble, I dial Michael's office. Drat—no Michael, only his voice mail. I leave a brief message—call me!—and hang up, dejected. The phone rings immediately. Could it be …? I snatch up the receiver.

The school secretary is calling to say Olympia has bonked her head on the climbers: could I come immediately? I speed to the school in panic mode to find Olympia looking and feeling perfectly well. Nonetheless, the teacher, in her most dangerous say-it-with-me voice, suggests Olympia should be kept home a day for observation. Driving home, Olympia bouncing happily in her booster seat behind me, I have the sinking feeling that now that I have an energy-ridden child underfoot, my day will turn out to be no picnic.

Olympia, surprisingly, agrees to watch television. While she is occupied, I suppose I could slip outside and do something about the yard. The tulips are drowning in the flotsam of last year's delphiniums and asters: I better rescue the flowerbeds first.

An hour's digging later, Scratches appears and sniffs around at the freshly dug bed, her legs crossed in anticipation. I remember last year's experience of communing with nature, barehanded in the spring-warmed earth, discovering suspiciously well-textured chunks and the soil drenched with cat pee. A search of the garden shed yields nothing but an empty container of pet repellent granules. Damn. I return to find Bitesalot hellbent on scraping up peony roots. That's it. With Olympia in tow, I'm off to buy cat outsmartant.

In town, Olympia demands ice cream. I say yes in hopes that once indulged, Olympia will behave like a model child in Canadian Tire. But I can't find the repellent. I wander about the aisles, Olympia trailing behind me, glad-handing her drippy cone. A young store clerk points out a shelf that offers unfamiliar liquids and gels—but none of the granules that I prefer. "How does the liquid stuff work?" I wonder aloud.

The clerk, shrugging, uncaps a container of chalky-looking substance and sniffs. "Ugh, it stinks," she says.

"I don't know," I say as the clerk holds up the bottle to my nose and points out that anything that smells this bad has to work. She recaps the bottle and I agree, resentfully, as now my beak is full of the disgusting odour. Olympia tugs on my shirt and complains that the liquid has dripped on her.

"No, it hasn't," I say. "Your ice cream cone is just drippy," and grabbing her cone, I attempt to reduce the ice cream fallout by licking, in one giant lick, the broad melty top and sides of the cone. Olympia begins to scream that I'm "eating it all up" when I discover that Olympia is right. The cone is contaminated with pet repellent.

The taste of pet repellent is brutal. The clerk backs away as I clap my hand over my foaming mouth and spin about in circles, squeaking piteously. I'm attracting the notice of other customers in the store. Spying the service counter, I dash over, toss the cone in the garbage and demand tissues, water, poison control, etc., as ice cream drools from the corners of my mouth.

What to do? Maybe I'm going to die. Is this my punishment for Michael? For some reason, all I can think of is Madame Bovary: the poison and all this drooling isn't unlike Emma Bovary's terrible exit scene. It's not fair. I didn't get to do all the horny Bovarian stuff yet.

Olympia wails at the sudden loss of her ice cream. She squirms past me in an attempt to steal her cone back out of the garbage can, while I try to block her. More people are staring, pointing and gathering around in curiosity.

The counter staff, all useless teenagers, first have difficulty interpreting my distress, then have difficulty suppressing their laughter as they grasp what has happened. They stand back to watch me coughing, spitting and sputtering. One kid informs me that the customers aren't encouraged to sample the pet repellent product line and another reluctantly offers me a chair beside the counter.

How toxic is this stuff I wonder? I try to make it up with Olympia, who is in the throes of a full-bore temper tantrum, but she remains uninterested in making deathbed reconciliations with me. I promise to buy her another cone, another *bigger* cone.

I wonder if it's safe to drive under the influence of pet repellent? Out of corner of one eye, I spy Michael approaching the checkout counter with his cart. What the hell is he doing here?

I try to hide my head, but too late: I've been spotted. I'm barely able to speak what with the awful taste in my mouth and Olympia wailing, but nevertheless I attempt to explain, as gracefully as possible while spitting flecks of foam-covered phlegm, what's happened to me. Michael listens and pats my shoulder, which is now an unbelievably active erogenous zone, perking me up with the offer of coffee, elsewhere, to wash away the taste.

Sounds good to me. I gather up Olympia and my purse, plus two free bottles of repellent from the staff. Soon we're resting under a shady tree in the park with two tall iced cappuccinos. What extraordinary good luck—I waxed my legs last night and I'm wearing my sexy gardening shorts. As Olympia is occupied with a Sugar Tail ice cream cone, Michael is free to tease me by twirling grass across my silky smooth shins. After a while, he whispers in my ear that the healing of all his broken and bruised parts has advanced to the stage where he doesn't need a painkiller to think about me again. "When can I see you alone?" he asks.

It's too late to venture out on a picnic today, but that's okay—Michael has an even better suggestion—perhaps we might wish to pay a visit to his cottage? Now that the back roads are passable in the north, his rustic family retreat might well serve as our playful love nest.

***

I hate modern communications. In the good old days, I'm sure it was much easier to arrange the sneaking around. Nowadays, what with call return, call tracing and call display, the "sorry, wrong number" game is bollixed. Not to mention cell phone spies are everywhere. I'm sure if Alexander Graham Bell were alive today, he wouldn't stand for it.

Just so I can get a secure landline connection, I have to drive to the nearest pay phone and remember to bring my prepaid phone card. Then I have to hope and pray Michael answers instead of his maddening voice mail service. It's difficult to have satisfying phone sex with a pre-recorded message, especially in a public booth.

However, I've confirmed our cottage tryst with only five phone booth treks and one call display near-miss the day Michael called when Donald was supposed to be at work. Donald thinks I'm taking a hockey skills weekend up north. Puck handling and power skating. Funny, yesterday our goalie caught me exiting from my steamy booth—she jokingly charged me with making an illicit call to a lover which I deftly turned aside by confirming her accusation complete with horny details. People never believe you when you tell the truth.

At last! Tonight's the night! I only have to get through the grocery shopping—unfortunately I have the kids in tow—and then it's time to blast off to bliss. I can't wait. Stupid red light. C'mon lights, c'mon.

I've cooked up a foolproof sneakyboots plan for the rendezvous: Michael will be waiting in the parking lot of the doughnut shop at 6 p.m. When he sees me drive past, he will follow me to a prearranged quiet spot where we can hide my wheels for the weekend and carry on to his cottage. The thought of carrying on sends an exciting shivery feeling up and down the base of my spine. No wait, that's Jack in the back seat sticking his Freezie into the nape of my neck.

I wish I didn't have Jack and Olympia with me. Years ago I vowed to never again go shopping with kids. I've stuck to my resolution, except for last year's trip to the hardware store where Olympia used the demo toilet for a gigantic number two. I'm forced to take them with me as there's not enough time to drop them off at home before a quick trip to the store to stock up on fast dinner essentials. Love makes us do crazy things. I need to learn to plan ahead. I had the whole week to prepare yet there's nothing in the cupboard at home except two cans of beets and an ancient bag of dried chickpeas.

I never did get the hang of the Guiding motto, "Be Prepared." If found out, I could lose all my Brownie Leader pins, but so what? I'm aiming to earn a more interesting distinction, a secret, special-interest badge all my own.

The clock on the dash reads 7:29 p.m. There's no need to panic since the clock is running fast by forty-three minutes and daylight savings time was set twice by accident. I have no clue how to adjust the time on my clock. Too complicated. And it will sort itself out—if I don't get round to readjusting for one too many "Spring Forwards" then the next "Fall Back" will catch me up. Since "Double Spring Forward" I must mentally subtract sixty minutes (to 6:22) and then subtract forty-three more minutes to arrive at actual local time (5:46 p.m.) Customized time management allows the illusion of extra time to race against.

Since Serenity's birth, I've deliberately set all car and household clocks fast to provide for comfy psychological time zones. No woman I know goes by standard time. Becoming a mother means adopting ALST (Acceptably Late Standard Time).

I have precisely twenty-nine minutes left to dash through the grocery store, grab frozen pizza, pop and milk, zip home, toss the meal on the table, ensure Serenity is on hand to babysit Jack and Olympia, and fly out the door to Michael's sweet waiting arms. I'm wildly excited.

Jack and Olympia are wildly excited too, as they haven't been into a store for a dog's age. Both stop dead at the vending machines by the entrance. I promise them a rich reward of vending machine toys/candy in exchange for good behaviour in the store. If anyone threatens legal action as a direct result of their behaviour, then *no treats*. Jack grabs a cart, Olympia hops in, and they zigzag off to plough down as many seniors as they can find. I couldn't care less. I'm in love, love, love. I plough down a few seniors myself in front of the frozen food section and check my advanced timetized watch: twenty-four minutes till the happy takeoff to the love nest. I should pack an overnight bag but clothes, I hope, will be totally unnecessary.

Grabbing the milk, pizza, etc., I charge over to the checkout. Twenty-two minutes to go. My heart is all a-flutter while the cashier makes a maddeningly slow price-check. Where did Jack and Olympia go? There they are: attempting to jam their carts out through the automatic entrance. I'm glad they're, at least, running amok in the right direction. I pay the cashier and run the kids to ground in the foyer in front of the vending machines. Miraculously, I have exactly the right amount of change for the good behaviour rewards. I've no idea if they're deserved, but there's no time to quibble. Fifteen minutes to go.

After excruciatingly long deliberations, both kids opt for giant jawbreakers. I feed the machine two loonies. The machine releases one jawbreaker for Jack, chokes on the second loonie, refuses to cooperate further and withholds the candy and the coin. My last loonie. Tarnation. I jiggle the coin return. I thump the coin return. I swear and hoof the vending machine. Olympia is waiting impatiently, about to burst into tears. I crouch down and peer into the opening. Ah—I can see the giant jawbreaker stuck partway down the chute. I thrust my hand hard into the opening in an attempt to knock the candy loose from the jammed mechanism. My wedding ring gets caught on something. And now my hand is stuck in the vending machine.

I twist and pull on my hand but no way. Panicky tugging and wrenching almost causes the machine to topple over. I'm close to tears. Olympia, upset that my hand is blocking the passage of her giant jawbreaker, begins to wail.

A crowd gathers offering advice. The head cashier consults with the produce manager. The produce manager consults the box boy. My hand, especially the ring finger, is beginning to throb. The produce manager hurries away to call the vending machine operator while the head cashier calls for the store manager. The produce manager returns to say the vending machine operator is out of town, but he should get here within a few hours, maximum. "I can't sit here for hours," I yell.

The store manager puts in a call to 911. A bunch of paramedics arrive on the scene with an ambulance, all lights flashing, followed by a police cruiser, volunteer firefighters and more flashing lights. The flashing lights draw additional onlookers from the mall followed by several local reporters toting cameras. Many onlookers seem to think that a candy heist was, no doubt, in progress before my timely arrest.

Umpteen professionals are on the scene, but none can agree on the correct procedure. Words like "tamper-proof" and "specialized tools" are bandied about freely. The onlookers suggest that the firefighters could employ the Jaws of Life. The store manager is full of care and concern. The machine could be damaged. He prefers to wait for the vending machine man's authorization to pry open the machine.

The store manager suggests coffee, doughnuts and perhaps a low stool. The police officers look all hopeful upon the mention of doughnuts. Scowling, I fish my cell phone out of my purse. "I'm calling my lawyer."

I call Bibi. "Put him on the phone," she growls.

After a series of Yes, Ma'ams and No, Ma'ams, the store manager hangs up and gives the nod. The firefighters produce hammers, wrenches and crowbars. The police officers stand back, looking terribly disappointed about the doughnuts. I wish they would demonstrate some techniques of crowd control.

I'm released in a hail of glass and giant jawbreakers. A joyous free-for-all breaks out just as the disgruntled vending machine man arrives. Grabbing Jack and Olympia, I flee the scene. The rendezvous time for the love nest meeting has long since passed. I discharge the evening hours nursing my tender swollen hand with several tall compresses on the rocks while Jack and Olympia mount a sugar and tooth challenge against their giant windfall of free jawbreakers.

* * *

The minute Donald leaves for work on Monday morning, I phone Michael. Hooray! Michael refuses to forgive me for Friday's no-show unless I meet him in half an hour! There's no reason we can't slip up to the cottage for the afternoon and be home by suppertime, right?

Right! I hang up quickly—I have ten minutes to shower, shave my legs, select a sexy outfit, fix my hair and apply some make-up. A message from the Stodgy Old Responsibility Bureau in my head bursts through my serious thoughts of wearing a kicky little skirt to go with my freshly shaved legs: *Whoa down there, Ms. Kicky Legs, what if during your absence the school calls to say Olympia has bonked her head once more or Jack has been suspended again? Perhaps you ought to notify the school that you won't be in your "usual place?"*

I hate having a conscience.

I should notify the school but what do I say? *Hi there, I'll be tied up (I hope) all day today with my new lover and won't be taking any calls,* won't do. Scratch notifying the school. Donald can handle all barf- and headbonk-related disasters today. He'd better be taking calls in his "usual" place for once.

The damp drizzly weather can't touch my extraordinary good mood. My extraordinary good mood upgrades from tropical storm to hurricane status upon receiving a long passionate kiss of greeting from Michael. Michael nips into the deli for sandwiches and coffee to go, but I have no appetite for anything but M.'s mouth-watering charms.

We race through the storm to the cottage. I wait in the car while Michael runs through the downpour to unlock the door. After a long interval, he re-enters the car, drenched and perplexed. "I brought the wrong key and I can't get in."

***

Men can't find things. They just can't. It's a genetic thing, resulting from countless years of the female of our species getting stuck looking after the kids. Back then, if we had to go out and leave the kids behind in the cave, we'd better remember which cave. And if we hid the baby under some leaves while hunting and gathering we had better know enough to look *under* the leaves to find the baby again.

Michael is certain his wife has stashed the key in some key location, but he can't ask her where without arousing suspicions. I suggest to him all the places I would put keys—on my key ring or in my purse for example. I don't tell him I have fourteen purses and thirty-odd keys on my main key ring, twenty-six of which I don't remember what they're for.

***

Jack and Olympia flew off the bus today waving a note from school and yelling, "If the strike goes on more than three weeks we might have to go to summer school." Strike? More than *three weeks*?

I snatch up the note and read with mounting horror: teachers will commence a strike action Friday morning if their contract talks remain deadlocked. What stinky timing—I have a beauty salon appointment Friday morning, my first chance in ages.

The hairstyling is critical too as I also have a job interview downtown. The job sounds dicey, but it still constitutes a fine justification for a haircut at the most expensive salon in the universe.

The worst thought of all: what if Michael finds the key? How will we escape to our country love lodge or at least to a picnic blanket in the woods with the dang kids hanging around the house all day?

Paranoid. No doubt, this is just the teachers' way of

controlling us parents using fear. I'm sure management can come up with a stall tactic: they'll still be on the job Friday, I'll get my haircut and the job interview'll be a breeze.

***

The radio news guy says the school board talks have broken down and the teachers have hit the bricks. Jack and Olympia are ecstatic. Serenity remains unaffected—she's been skipping school since mid-April.

I direct the kids to clear away the breakfast dishes while I get dressed. I will go straight from the beauty salon to my interview and leave Serenity in charge at home. I wonder if I can get away with a "casual Friday" outfit for a Friday interview? Well, why not? I couldn't care less about this job anyway. It's bound to be a pathetic joke like all the rest; why do I even bother?

Checking my watch I see that I'm running right out of racetrack to get to my critical beauty appointment on time. Arggh. I can't find my new lipstick. I rummage through the bathroom cabinets and vanity drawers while ignoring the sounds of a loud argument in the kitchen: Jack and Olympia are fighting over who should clear the last glass from the table. I hear a glass shatter, then a brief silence, and then a fresh battle emerges over whose fault it was.

"Jack, I hate you, you shittybumhead."

"Don't say 'shittybumhead.' Mooooommmm, Lumpy's saying swear words again."

I run downstairs to break up the fight and clear away the broken glass. Jamming the shards into the overflowing garbage, I attempt to tie off the garbage bag at which one of the shards rips through the bag and jabs straight into my wrist.

Jack and Olympia stop fighting to watch their mother trying not to faint at the sight of blood spurting all over the cuff of her favourite casual day blouse. *Shit, shit, shit.* Now I'll have to find something else to wear. Oh God, the blood is going everywhere. Except to my legs. I better lean over the sink. I wonder how long it takes to bleed to death? Need doctor. Possibly very soon.

I feel woozy: maybe it's too late for the doctor? How many klutzes like me slash their wrists by accident and in so doing deprive their heirs of the pots of insurance money? No sane adult would doubt my motivation given my slovenly house, joblessness, teachers' strike, etc. "Shit, shit, shit."

"Mommy, don't say 'shit'," says Olympia.

"Never mind. Jack, where's Serenity?"

"I dunno. I think she went out."

Wrapping my wrist in towels, I lurch off to Emergency with Jack and Olympia in the backseat of the Jeep complaining about missing all the cool weekday morning game shows on TV.

***

I'm in *agony.* Four stitches were required to close my wrist wound. I'm now incapable of lifting heavy objects like dishcloths and cupfuls of laundry soap and the like.

The job interview was a complete disaster. My hair was a rat's nest because of missing the salon appointment and I was forty-five minutes late because of long lineups at Emergency where, when my turn came around, bunches of nurses started clucking over me with gobs of understanding and then they called in a social worker, "Just for a quick wee chat."

I flew home to change out of my blood-soaked outfit. I could find nothing else decent to wear but my winterweight wool suit the bottom half of which I located under the cat in a heap on the floor at the back of my closet.

Serenity was still nowhere to be found so I was forced

to bring Jack and Olympia along to the interview. In desperation, I stopped into Becker's on the way and blew $40 on comic books which they read lying on the reception room carpet with their feet up on the chairs while I sat on the far side of the room frantically picking cat hair off my skirt with my good hand.

Then I had to face down a forbidding panel of seven interviewers. Seven. For me. Hahahahaha: I'll be wanting a cushy job in management in my next life, yes indeed, please, and thank you very much. Everyone looked knowingly at the bulky cotton bandage on my wrist while I, slowly boiling to mush in my winter-weight suit, mopped my red, dripping face with the bandage since there was nothing else at hand. When they asked me about my salary expectations I lost my head, and snortily told them of course I expected a salary, and a damn good one too since I wasn't planning to work for peanuts.

After the interview debacle, Donald received the news with a concerned shrug and then smirked. "Most people slash their wrists *after* having a bad day."

***

I wake up all perky with the knowledge that Mother's Day has arrived on the hateful Hallmark Parade of Holiday Tortures calendar. Once again I must endure the annual rituals celebrating timing errors gone awry due to biological urges. I should've checked the calendar *then*.

Someone should convince Hallmark that the world wants a new special day to observe. They could devise an annual Marrieds Freedom Day or better still, a Virtue Open Weekend. VOW could be an annual time of renewal when all marriage contracts are declared temporarily null and void: a carefree, guilt free, no-questions-asked time of exploring one's inner adulteress. It would be a time to celebrate the diversity of the split personality. We all disassociate at some time or other. Trapped inside every married woman is a horny alter broad who bellows "Hey Sailor" to every male on two lips between 16 and 106.

Time to get this hush-hush thing out of the closet. Indeed, I know many marrieds who have been secretly celebrating VOWS holidays for years. More men than women may admit to a VOWS orientation, but women'll come out from all walks of life, I'd bet my strappy new CFM'ers* on it.

I lie back in bed and think how wonderful it would be to consummate a VOW Power Weekend with Michael. I'm getting so desperate, I would even settle for a VOW POW! Hour. All of a sudden the kids burst in to deposit Breakfast On Bed despite last year's assurances from Donald that this kind of thing would never happen again.

I would much prefer sleeping in and having Lunch In Bed. Or, better yet, having Michael delivered for a change of menu. I haven't had a decent hot breakfast in years. The thought of a full-bodied breakfast causes my hormones to surge and wipe out my appetite. I slip the rounds of cold toast and rubbery eggs to George Bush; for once his unyielding presence on the end of my bed is welcome.

I am resigned to the truth: Dennis's dog is permanently installed in the house, no doubt for many years to come as the vet said he is barely beyond puppyhood, and is vibrantly healthy, and then he added, ominously, "He'll be really big when he fills out."

Unfortunately, George Bush is still prone to chewing and chain barking. Fortunately, Lewis Morris Boriston dropped his lawsuit over the puppies when he grasped that he was barking up the wrong bank account. Last week he changed tactics with an offer—likely bogus—to pay our moving and real estate expenses if we agree to sell the house and move elsewhere. Donald took offence,

*Come Fuck Me shoes

exchanged a few snarly words and universal gestures with him and, as a result, he allows George Bush to roam at will again.

At least George Bush has caught the clue regarding housebreaking. Actually, he trained up better than the kids and Donald, none of whom have yet learned to close the bathroom door, flush or replace an empty roll.

Also on the plus side, I've discovered the best way to deal with a yardful of dog droppings: like Mary Poppins says, you make a game of it. Usually I play golf. I can drive a turd almost fifty yards into the ravine behind our house using a lowly five iron. No need for a tee up as George Bush makes high chunky turd balls. All one needs is a hot, dry spell so the balls harden off properly. Since that damn dog moved in, I've shaved several strokes off my fairway game.

Donald likes turd golf too. He prefers to lay up with a seven iron and aims for Boriston's eaves troughs. Donald has a wicked slice but he'll never admit it. He *claims* he's shooting for the pool. Like most low-handicap golfers, he's a shameless liar.

I better get up, get dressed. It's time to pack up the crew for the Mother's Day Visit with His Mother. Serenity is flat out refusing to go; she says she has to study but I know better: I overheard her on the phone arranging a down low date with Dennis's new lover.

Jack and Olympia are demanding to know why they have to go to Grandma's house when Serenity does not. I promise them a cash reward for compliance and good behaviour. "How much?" says Jack.

"Two dollars?"

"Twenty."

"Okay, five."

"Fifteen and a Power Pez."

"Ten and the return of TV privileges."

"Done."

I congratulate myself on crafty deal making: I have every intention of reinstating TV privileges as soon as we arrive at H.M.'s.

I think H.M. hates Mother's Day too. If only she'd admit it: a shared hatred could become the foundation for improved relations. The list of Safe Topics to Discuss has dwindled down to two items: How Bad the World is Getting (who can argue with that?) and what bothersome pest is eating up her garden this year. I can but hope that a decent invasion of earwigs has hit recently so we can make sympathetic conversation last a bit.

***

H.M. turns out to be in top holiday form with a special Mother's Day List of Unsafe Topics to tempt me into a disagreement. I commit a serious tactical blunder by mentioning the Internet.

"What good is the Internet?" she asks, producing a handful of clippings from her vertical files to back up her contention that the Internet will raid your bank account, have a high time on your credit card and reveal all your private business to untold millions.

"There's all kinds of educational information on the net."

"There's all kinds of pornography too. I hope you don't let the children look at Internet pornography."

"Of course not," I say, "they have filters for that."

"But do they have filters for the pedophiles who lure children away?"

We argue fruitlessly all day.

In the car, I try to ignore Donald's wrath over my bickering with his mother so much, then I give in and bicker with Donald fruitlessly the rest of the way home.

At midnight, I discover a message from Mom on the answering machine: she's hurt and disappointed with me.

I forgot to execute the critical Mother's Day telephone call to her as I was too engaged in arguing with His Mother all day. Caving in to my preferred unhealthy stress response, I steal into the backyard for a decent smoke, spitting my anti-smoking gum into the bushes on the way.

Most of the time, anti-smoking gum works too well, and I'm now addicted to the gum. I'm still chewing dozens of pieces a day. The constant chewing has caused my jaw muscles to balloon. Now I can ripple my cheeks like a bodybuilder.

The doctor advises cutting back on the gum. Lately, I've taken to smoking the odd cigarette in order to wean off. I may wind up on the nicotine patch to fight the gum/cigarette habit and then what? I could end up covered with patches while chewing a large box of gum per day and chain smoking. A hardcore nicotine junkie. I might have to turn to crime to support my habit. I can see the headlines: Local Mother of Three Raids Pharmacy for Nicotine Gum.

***

Mom calls first thing in the morning, full of forgiveness. She says she dreamed I died last night. Great.

"You fell into a pit of poisonous snakes."

"I have to go now," I say quickly, hanging up.

Turning on the radio I hear the news report: the teachers have rejected the latest offer and have left the bargaining table.

***

Woe is me. Another Tuesday without Michael. And a check of the scales this morning has only served to increase my wretchedness.

Strange. Despite a strong desire to be ravishingly slim

and sylphlike (in anticipation of slinking into Michael's arms), my commitment to diet and exercise is beginning to wane lately. I'm as fat-positive as ever though increasingly less cheer-positive: the judging season of shorts and swimsuits is looming and so am I.

I've heard that yard work is slimming, so I've informed Donald that from now on, all lawn and garden care will be under my firm jurisdiction. That's it. I'm going on a survivor diet starting now: it'll be nothing but white rice and water until I'm thin. I'll work my chubby butt off, starting with the task of trimming the outposts of grass interspersed among the burdock and dandelions.

Lewis Morris Boriston's chemically hopped-up lawn is a perfect green rectangle: obviously all his dandelions applied for refugee status and emigrated to our yard. Despite Boriston, or maybe *because* of Boriston, I've grown rather fond of the sight of those glad yellow heads bobbing and ducking down in the path of the mower.

The decomposing lawn mower is a long-standing source of conflict between Donald and me. All the safety features on the mower fell off long ago. All that's left of the thing is bockety wheels and the tendency to backfire oily blue smoke at regular intervals. Last week's claims that we either buy a new machine or call a realtor were greeted with a venomous stare. "It's just my opinion, Donald," I said, "but if we can't cut the grass with a reasonable margin of safety and reliability, then we aren't coping with home ownership and it's time to move into an apartment, preferably a seniors' residence where they do stuff for you."

After ten minutes mowing, upon meeting up with a mature burdock tree, the mower quits with a loud kerpow. The sight of a mushroom cloud of blue smoke and a large gaping hole in the side of the motor makes me feel all warm and happy inside. Perhaps this means it's time to call a realtor?

***

The assembly of the new mower was accomplished last night in the middle of the kitchen since the garage is too full of junk to get inside.

I drag the new mower from the kitchen to the yard in anticipation of a rare afternoon of mechanical cooperation: the machine roars to life with a single pull and the lawn submits to a good whacking. Trimming the grass is a welcome chore: the loud rackety drone of the mower motor is soothing, meditative, especially as it drowns out loud grating household sounds like yelling, whining and barking. (Racking, fracking teachers' strike.)

Today's lawn-cutting meditation is focused on my usual delicious problem of How To Make It With Michael. My fervent daily prayers to St. Anthony about the missing cottage keys have gone unanswered so far. Obviously, he and St. Dorothy, the patron saint of gardening, are in cahoots against me. Either I'm not praying hard enough or it's time to appeal to the administrators of another belief system, preferably one without a capricious power elite.

I could try out some occidental religion that promotes the self as the godhead, but if Western theology is incomprehensible—and male dominated to boot—whatever sense could I make of Eastern canons not to mention that guy with way too many arms to be good for him?

Unquestionably, letting my soulmate Michael get a good grip on my godhead would be an all-encompassing experience. I'm sure he'd fill me up with satisfaction, like perfect soul food, like heaven and nirvana all rolled up in a big existential nonfattening chapatti of bliss, or to switch metaphorical gears, like going from zero to Zen if you're from the East, or if you're a Christian capitalist, like landing on free parking in paradise.

Michael would laugh at my musings considering he rejects all forms of organized religion, preferring to call himself a philosopher, a fan of Mr. Negativity himself, Nietzsche. Despite Michael's off-putting Nietzscheian bent, I tolerate his unenlightened attitude ever since he recently revised his stance by saying he's, "Still into nihilism but in a positive way."

My meditative state, the illusion of mechanical cooperation and horny thoughts of heaven's parking lot are shattered with the appearance of Donald, home for lunch and complaining that his car has decided it doesn't want to back up any more. We just spent a fortune on the engine and major bodywork. But what else can we do? I suggest contacting a mechanic at which Donald nods in a reluctant manner as if questioning whether a full-featured transmission is absolutely necessary. Perhaps reverse drive is a bit of a frill after all.

I think I have reached the edge of my loaf, that all-crust state in a woman's domestic life where it's time to buy a chainsaw and practise crazed grins.

Everything I own is either:

1. Whooped in some way: cracked, torn, stained, or missing an important bolt.

2. Deadlined but we're keeping it just in case it can be cannibalized.

3. NS but Donald wants to keep it in case it could have collector's value some day.

4. Cobbled together by duct tape or glue (which disintegrates frequently, especially with kitchen appliances like food processors, usually with catastrophic results).

5. Making an unbearable clanking, screeching, or ratchety noise that indicates a breakdown is imminent (car, washing machine, self).

6. Scruffy, tacky or otherwise aesthetically provoking (living room couch, back yard, self).

To gain a sense of control over the situation, I should go out this minute and break an important part off the new mower.

***

As I prepare my measly bowl of white rice for lunch (three days of survival dieting and I'm in ketosis now, baby!) I glance out the window and see Boriston outside in his shirtsleeves digging a sizable trench in his back yard. What's he up to? Also, I can see it's a beautiful warm sunny day, perfect for another weed-related workout. Groan. All my puny muscles are complaining after two days of hard-core attempts to beautify the backyard landscaping, but I must be firm with them or they won't be firm enough to beautify my backside landscaping. Reluctantly, I pull on my grass stained jeans.

While digging in the garden, I wonder why Boriston doesn't let the puppies out for some health-giving fresh air once in a while? Why? Come to think of it, Boriston refused to allow Jack and Olympia in to see the puppies yesterday. How suspicious.

***

I'm sick to death of white rice. I feel a bit strange and light-headed, but reality TV shows don't lie. This diet will work. I'm sure of it, so I'm sticking to it. I devoted yet another entire day to the garden, but saw no sign of the yapping brats.

I'm worried. What has Boriston done with them? The situation has become deeply suspicious. Boriston's trench, just the right size for eight dear little pups, is neatly filled in. When did he do that without my noticing? No doubt, late last night, under cover of darkness.

***

I'm tempted to go over to Boriston's this minute and outright demand to see the puppies. But, if I did that, Boriston might take that as accepting responsibility for the blasted little mutts.

A better idea would be to sneak over and check out Boriston's trench.

***

I can't stand it any more. No doubt a quick trench inspection will reveal the horrible truth: Boriston is a puppy murderer. Wait'll the Humane Society finds out. I'll be a hero. I'll be lauded as a great animal rights activist. Maybe I'll even earn a special prize or commendation. Together, we activists will see a cruel killer put behind bars.

I fidget beside the window: as soon as the Boristons head off to the farmer's market, as they always do on Saturdays, I will slip over the fence with my trusty spade. I can't wait to expose Cruello De Boriston. Poor Huguette probably has no knowledge of this. She'll just have to get over him in time. It's possible I could be averting senseless tragedy: by this brave act, I may be preventing a terrible escalation in Boriston's criminal career; for all I know, Huguette could wind up buried in Boriston's next trench.

It's just a short wait: soon both Boristons emerge from their house and scoot away in their hatchback. Time to swing into action.

I'm in the clear as Donald has taken the kids to their swimming lessons and Serenity is still in bed. With a pounding heart, I climb the fence and begin digging.

Funny. Boriston's trench is empty, end to end. No gladiolus bulbs, no plumbing pipes and no furry bodies. Boriston is obviously up to something but what? I begin filling in the trench when, out of the corner of one eye, I spy Boriston, coming around the corner of his house. Oh God. He stops short upon sighting me. I'm caught, muddy handed.

Boriston's face curdles with rage at the sight of his trespassed trench. "Qu'est ce que fuck?" he growls at me.

The only thing to do is blame everything on the usual suspects—Jack, Olympia and George Bush. I offer up the lame explanation that I'm attempting to repair the damage done when "Le chien et les p'tit enfants" were attracted by the new muddy patch in Boriston's yard even though we have enough attractive muddy patches in our own yard to keep a hundred kids and dogs forever occupied.

My apologies go unheard as Boriston sputters and fumes over how the damn kids and mutt have destroyed the special new flowerbed he'd so painstakingly dug and seeded with chrysanthemums and lavatera just this past week. I promise to reseed and restore the bed—the whole yard if need be—but Boriston refuses my offer saying, "Merde. Aller, aller, vous êtes comprendez? Merde, le p'tit Chris."

***

Despite the absence of bodies, I'm still feeling wildly suspicious. At bedtime, I casually ask Donald if he has noticed that Boriston next door is acting strangely lately. Donald commences the emission of bizarre strangled sounds through his nose, so I quickly qualify, "You know what I mean, more whacked than usual."

"No."

"I haven't seen the puppies lately. Boriston won't let Jack and Olympia over to play with them any more. And just a few minutes ago he put out five big bags of garbage. Do you think ...?"

"No."

"I think we'd better check his garbage."

"NO."

"Gee, I wonder what the media would do with it?"

At this Donald looks up, rubs his thumbs together and, with cunning spreading across his face, says, "We're going in."

Under cover of darkness, Donald scurries out to the curb with a bag of our garbage and, sidling fast across to Boriston's pile of bags, snatches a couple and hustles back to the safety of the house. Breath baited, we open the bags. Both contain grass clippings.

"Better go get more."

The next two bags reveal the usual coffee grounds, carrot scrapings, *adult* dog food tins (but NO puppy food or puppy bodies), etc., plus a real grab bag of powerful odours from real, but entirely innocent, garbage.

"C'mon, there's just one more …"

We tear open the last bag. I can't believe my eyes. I'm left shocked and gasping at the sight. Way down at the bottom lies another smaller bag containing a brand spanking new designer bathing suit with the tags still attached.

How disgusting. Our throwaway society has obviously sunk to its worse depths of wastefulness yet. Time to take a bold stand. I will liberate this suit and deliver it to the nearest women's shelter. Some ragged and wanting feminine soul will be delighted to own such a fashionable new garment and all because of my kind generosity.

I examine the price tag. I had no idea designer bathing suits could be so expensive. What with all the starvation and yard work, I might just squeeze into it.

Spiffy bananas! The suit fits like sun to shine. And it has fabulous butt and bustline support. Donald even bestows a grudging compliment. I might as well keep it to prop up my own sagging feminine soul—and everything else besides.

***

Donald shakes me awake with the news that Boriston is, at this very moment, out at the curb tearing through his garbage bags. Donald is actually wringing his hands. "I think he saw me watching him from the window, too."

I peek out from the side of the bedroom window. Donald, too nervous to risk being detected lurking at the window again, hangs back.

"What's he doing now?" whispers Donald.

"Huguette just came out of the house and—whoa, does she look mad. I'll bet Boriston shot her bathing suit into the garbage by accident and she just found out and now she wants it back."

I'm in possession of stolen goods. Now what? I can't very well go over there saying, "By the way, look what I found when I was snooping through your garbage last night …"

I'm frozen with horror as Boriston straightens, turns and stares at our house with a suspicious look upon his contorted features. I hold my breath as he turns his gaze back upon our pile of refuse. Our bag count mysteriously increased by one bag since last night because numbnuts Donald was too lazy to return the last bag all the way back to Boriston's heap.

Worse, under the cruel morning sunlight, the new impostor bag is a different shade of green compared to our own budget bags, a detail I'm desperately hoping Boriston won't be observant enough to notice.

"Now what's he doing?"

"I don't know. Omigod, I think he's coming over here."

I suck in my breath as Boriston makes a brief furtive step toward our pile and stops with another peep our way. I watch him with horrified fascination: would Boriston have the nads to inspect our garbage in broad daylight while we cowardly scoped out his trash under cover of darkness?

Then, a miracle. Here's the unmistakeable sound of the garbage truck clanking around the turn at the end of our road and, a glance confirms, in a few short moments, all the evidence will be whisked away. Boriston hesitates, then turns and boils back up his driveway. Phew. Close call.

***

Huguette Boriston called this morning wondering why the children haven't come over to see the pups lately and to complain: "Maudit merde! veux tu ben me dire pourquoi this stupid Lewis a jette mon maillot, euh, what do you call it?—bathing suit?—last week by accident, c'est un idiot, mon mari, maudit merde!"

***

Damn. Damn. Damn. Last week's flummoxed job interview has produced a serious offer. It's a sweet deal with a plump pay scale, decent benefits plan and possible occasional travel. I can picture myself touching up my nail polish and relaxing on a comfy hotel room bed while coolly parenting long distance over a cell phone and then charging it all to an expense account like those neatly tucked in business women on television ads. I'd work for free if they'd guarantee the travel. Jack hopes I'll go for it since he wants a wave pool for his birthday. Donald snorted, but then he urged me to accept since we're drowning in bills.

But working means never having a minute to myself again. Back to cranky bosses and office politics. Back to fluorescent lighting that gives me headaches and makes my skin look terrible.

What to do? Back to school next fall could mean the resumption of yummy library study dates with Michael.

And shouldn't I finish what I've started? I will think about it tomorrow.

***

I'm so depressed. I haven't heard anything from Michael about the missing key yet and there's no sign of my Grade Report.

That stupid university. I can't decide whether to take the job offer or go back to school next fall or what. On the one hand I'll puke in my backpack if I have to listen to any more pseudo-intellectual babblefests invariably referred to as "discoursing." On the other, I could go back to the workaday woman's Work-24-7 Marathon. The horror, the horror.

***

A police officer appeared on our doorstep around dinnertime to warn us about a recent rash of break-ins in the neighbourhood—just last night Lewis Morris Boriston's house was hit. Did we hear any noises?

"No," I tell the officer, "but our dog might have."

I explain to the officer how, late last night, George Bush jumped up and bolted, whimpering and shivering, down to the basement, exhibiting his usual craven response to thunderstorms and, no doubt, demented axe murderers attacking next door. His crazed barking routine is reserved for warning us of peril lurking nearby in the form of evil neighbourhood cats on the prowl or fiendish blowing leaves. Otherwise, George Bush is a cringing coward. He swings into terrified retreat at the sight of new and potentially hairy objects such as incoming bags of groceries. Most any odd household object can strike terror in his quivering breast. If a thief busted in here brandishing, say, a feather duster, all would be lost.

The officer receives all this intelligence with a look of suspicion, then he makes a brief note in his book. He wonders aloud what's with Boriston that he thinks we might know *much more*. I'm paralysed with the alarming thought that Boriston has turned us in for stealing his garbage and that the police are poised to produce a search warrant for Huguette's bathing suit, hanging in *my* closet at this very moment.

"Mr. Boriston said ..."

"That fucktard Boriston can bite his balls if he has any," yells Donald, pushing past me and the officer and out the door to glare at Boriston's house.

"Never mind," the officer says as he snaps his notebook shut, pats his gun holster and nods at me sympathetically. "Just let me know if you hear anything, okay? "

***

Donald and Bernie are gone on their annual fishing weekend. I invited Bibi and the hockey women to come over for a barbecue and a few drinks. Big mistake.

As soon as they crack open the first seals, they begin gearing up for the annual survey. *How many men have you done it with? Who likes women? Are you back of the bus? Who LIKES sucking a guy off? Do you spit or swallow? Where's the most unusual place you've done it?* And—the biggie—*Who is having an affair?* If I told the truth, it might get out, but I've never before lied like this in the company of women. No can do. They'll know. They'll see the old green in my eye. I better drink till I turn green and pass out first.

***

Amazing—I managed to keep my mouth shut all night about Michael. On the other hand, Bibienne opened up wide and told us all why she loves watching basketball on TV so much, using words like "orgasmic" and "climax" and terms like "exploding into play" and "tight buttocks." I wish I had a warped sex thing about TV basketball too.

***

I'm in heaven. Donald came home from fishing empty-handed and is now gone off to Calgary on some course and—just in time to prevent my having to play at being a single mother with no support from the Ministry of Education—the teachers' strike has ended, as the negotiators struck an agreement over the long weekend. Teachers are clever ones indeed: they're schmoozing back just in time to avert the possibility of summer school.

***

Tonight, for once, I've managed to get the kids off to bed on time. I love being a single parent. Donald and Serenity arrived safely in Calgary and all's quiet, serene. I've just spent a wonderful, sex-charged half hour on the phone with Michael doing da phone dip and wishing he could come over here this minute and pick me up off the floor where I've sunk, all hot and sloppy with desire. Michael, too, wishes he could slip over here and mop me up. No luck, he can't get away. Oh well. I'm all primed now to climb back up onto the couch with a snort of Donald's VSOP cognac and try to get my groove back with the basketball thing.

Moments later, a suspicious muffled thump on the back deck stops me cold. The noise could be a skunk or a raccoon. Or a cat. Trouble is, none of the above can jiggle door handles. The door-jiggling noise is more likely to be the work of a bad-ass, woman-raping and throat-slashing robber. Or could it be Boriston's burglar, come back to continue his neighbourhood spree? Did I remember to lock the doors?

I'm frozen in terror. So is George Bush who is quivering beside me. One of us manages to snatch up the cordless and dial 911.

While waiting for the police to arrive, I lock myself in the upstairs bathroom and cringe in the dark, listening to the sounds of stealthy footsteps circling the house and trying the windows and doors. I remember now: the whole trouble with single motherhood is having to cope with the eerie bump in the night thing rather than that other bumping in the night thing single mothers freely enjoy.

* * *

Damn, damn, damn. I have truly blown it this time. While I cowered indoors, the police arrived, ran down the "prowler" and as they shoved him, handcuffed, into the cruiser I caught a glimpse of his white, terrified face: it was Michael.

I ran out to the cruiser. It pulled away before I could stop them, while the tow truck passed me, pulled up at the end of the street, and began to winch up Michael's car (which was parked well down the street away from prying eyes so he could slip around to my back door to jump me).

I hurried down to the station where, hours later, the officer in charge yawned and dismissed Michael as a case of unfounded arrest.

Michael is somewhat disconcerted at the thought that a police report with his name and "suspected prowler" written in block letters on the intake sheet is on file downtown. He looked unconvinced when the officer on duty assured him that he is no longer a person of interest, never mind the incident report, it's routine paperwork and will always be kept fully confidential. Michael claims he's not bent any more, but he still wouldn't look me in the eye as we left the police station. Course it was 3 a.m. and he was worrying about going back home to the big dog house again.

twelve

GO NO-GO

Michael isn't returning my calls to his cell. Serenity lost my cell phone in Calgary last week, but he could still email me or something.

***

Olympia has been trying to make friends with a skunk family. Last evening, I caught her kneeling at the back door, tossing out cat treats to a Mom and two youngsters, who were all within two feet of coming right into the house. "They are going to be my new pets," she said with bright, happy eyes.

What to do? Call animal control? Buy a shotgun? Lure them over to Boriston's yard?

Perhaps making friends with the skunks is the answer. Skunks are supposed to be cute and friendly if they're handled properly. I could join Olympia in the treat giving and they will grow to love me too.

Animal control is busy.

Guess I'll try Michael's office again.

Sorry, there's no one here to take your call, if you wish to leave a voice mail message, please dial the extension of the person you wish to speak to ...

For some reason, when I dial his extension, I keep getting redirected back to the opening message. All my emails to him are bouncing back.

Wait a minute. Why has his email been down for so

long? Is he blocking me? Has his patience run out? Maybe he's found someone else already? The stinker.

Maybe making friends with skunks is NOT the answer after all.

* * *

Days of waiting. Why hasn't Michael contacted me? Why? Why? Why?

* * *

I've wasted every morning this week waiting for the mail carrier in the wasted hope of a communiqué from Michael. This morning I rushed out only to find what looks like my long awaited Grade Report nestled among the bills and other junk. I tear open the report immediately: top marks in Thigh Chi and Feminist Drumming, good old Stool passed me smoothly enough with a solid B and, best of all, Greshen has awarded me an A for my extra-special efforts. He must've appreciated the alternative cover page after all. No thanks go out to Michael, the rat bastard.

With such glowing grades, I must continue on the scholarly path. Perhaps I'm not destined to graduate Magna Cum Laude (more like Mondo Cum Latte), but I'm still a heck of a fine student.

I walk back to the house in triumph over my marks, but in despair over Michael.

* * *

I waken in the middle of the night, struck down with grief. I can no longer deny the truth: Michael has ditched me for good. I'm crushed. My useless life is over. I have no assets, no career, a dull loveless marriage, delinquent kids. And a fat bum. It's hopeless: how can I return to Dingwall while creep Michael is still roving the campus, preying on innocent women's hearts? How can I diet when everyone knows diets don't work?

My hip new relationships therapist is suggesting I could try smudging Michael out of my life. Last week, in a native handicraft store, I purchased the works: pouches of sage, sweet grass and cedar plus a cunning little pottery smudge pot and special long wooden matches for the have-it-all sacred ritual, but I haven't got around to trying it yet. Now would be the perfect time: while everyone is asleep, I could slip out onto the deck underneath the stars and cleanse myself with the purifying breath of the Great Spirit and Mother Earth. Afterwards I could top off the ceremony—I will think of it as a celebration to release Michael's bad energy—with the appropriate refreshment, say, a bowl of chocolate ice cream with hot fudge syrup and a sprinkling of pecans.

I step onto the deck to find a perfect warm June night, a clear starry sky above and a gentle breeze lifting the edges of my cotton kimono. What does a person have to do to conduct a proper native cleansing ritual? Perhaps I will feel freer without my kimono so I take it off. The gentle breeze feels deliciously cool and playful on my bare nipples. Michael would enjoy this ritual: he'd probably start off by caressing my erect ... Wait, wait, wait, I better get focused on the purpose of the ritual, the banishment of Michael-thoughts forever.

It would probably be best to begin by bowing to the four directions like I saw those native kids do once on North of 60. I don't know which direction is correct to bow to first, but I will take a stab at it and start by facing north. North is associated, no doubt, with wise old age and frozen things—the tundra, ice and snow and skidoos and suchlike. Intoning (under my breath, good grief, I wouldn't want Donald catching me at this): Oh Great Spirit of the North, um, oh wise Great Spirit, I bow to you and your, um, great old age, Oh You Who Knows What Is Going On Here, May You punish Michael, the One who has wounded me so grievously: please smite him down, yeah, trample him with your great northern caribou herds … Feeling better now, I continue round to the East, then South, before I grasp I'm all turned wrong: I'm bowing to the East while mouthing South-appropriate things.

Oh well. I finish off rapidly, with cursory nods to the South and West, as I want to get on with it. I hope the directions won't mind too much. Striking a wooden match, I apply the flame to the smudge mix with proper solemnity. The match immediately goes out, so I try to light another one. The match head pops off. I withdraw a third match from the box.

A whole box of damned expensive matches later, I've only managed to burn my fingers. The stupid smudge mix is refusing to catch, as the gentle breezes on the deck keep blowing it out. This is the least combustible smudge mix ever made, probably low-grade crap the natives set aside just to flog to silly white women. Those hucksters can forget me coming back next week to buy those sweet but overpriced fringy moccasins.

Uh oh—I have probably offended the Great Spirit, and all his demanding directions. Banish those uncharitable thoughts. My apologies to the Great Spirit. I will go to the native store first thing tomorrow and cheerfully pay full retail for those darling moccasins. I won't even go near the discount table. I'm sure I wouldn't wish to exploit any aboriginal person for quality handcrafted footwear. I will buy a handsome pair of slippers for Donald too. I add a hasty promise to visit Casino Rama and bestow heaps of cash onto G.S.'s charitable gaming tables one of these days soon. The smudge mix bursts into flames.

I bathe myself in the purifying smoke for a while. Far out: I'm getting a really not-bad little buzz off of this stuff. Very nice.

Nasty thoughts of Michael waft away on trails of smoke. I don't mind if he's my ex-would-be lover any more. I've discovered the Great Spirit and a promising new way to get high now.

I'm so glad I saved the ice cream celebration for last: now I have the munchies big time.

***

Stupid Donald found my smudge kit and laughed his fool head off. Well, fuck it. I'm sick of smudging anyway. And the late-night ice cream celebrations are already causing the pounds to pile back on. As if it mattered that I'm doomed to be morbidly obese. It'll all be Michael's fault. Stupid Michael.

***

I'm sliding into a pit of gloominess. I'd even call Mom to confide in her, but she's back with Brian and they've gone off to Vegas for a wedding-free honeymoon. She's got herself a digital camera and is uploading daily snaps to her webblog. I can see from today's pic that she's bought herself a snazzy new outfit. Camel Toes visits the Hoover Dam. Brian is beaming with pride. He's a pretty good guy. I'm happy that she's happy.

Of course, I'm unhappy that I'm unhappy. The best thing to do is find a quiet place to be alone, think, clear my head. After the kids get on the school bus, I drive to the Clearview Conservation Park and lurch off down a hiking trail.

That's it. I must accept that Michael is Just Not That Into Me. I hate his guts. If he thinks he can just ring up one of these days like nothing has happened, he's crazy. I will slam the phone down in his ear. Wait, no, first I'll tell him to crawl back under his slimy rock and *then* I'll hang up.

A blue butterfly flits by, and then lands on the tall grass beside the path. Breathing gently, I kneel beside it. I've never seen such a beautiful specimen. Its gossamer wings practically glow. I'm sure it's a rare creature. How fortunate I am to be granted this amazing glimpse of nature's most delicate citizen. Interesting. Without men balling up my whole life, I can open my mind to the majesties of the natural world, unencumbered. Clearly it's time I loosed myself from the sucking mud of relationshippery. Yes. From now on, I walk alone but free.

Invigorated with strength from my newly forged inner direction, I continue walking at a brisk pace along the path. That butterfly seems to be following me. Odd. This must mean something.

If the butterfly keeps coming on it's a definite metaphysical sign that ... Okay, yes, that Michael truly loves me. I walk along craning my head backwards. Come on, come on, butterfly. The butterfly lands on the path. Maybe I misread the portent being revealed by the butterfly flight path: okay, if the winged messenger comes closer, Michael loves me. If it flies away, I should forget all about him. I stare at the butterfly.

It flutters into the air and flies away. Damn. The ugly moth. I have a powerful urge to chase it down and stomp on it.

* * *

I finally have a new cell phone. It took me all day to get up the nerve to text the number to Michael. Within minutes, I receive an urgent text from Michael: "Call me on my cell ASAP. We have to talk."

I knew this was coming. No doubt Michael has found someone easier—and safer—to mess around with. I punch in his number. He answers immediately. Hot tears spring to my eyes, but before I can blow my nose and graciously bid him leave, he says: "Please, do something, anything, to get away this weekend, I found the keys to the cottage!"

***

Turns out Michael didn't call or email or text me before because I told him down at the police station that it might be too risky. He reminded me how I said he should wait until I called him.

Right. I remember now. I stammered out, "But I did try to call. To your office. I couldn't get into your voice mail and your emails kept bouncing back."

Michael responded that his access to email and voice mail stopped when his courses ended weeks ago. "Remember I told you that the office would be closed for the summer?"

Right again. Where're my brains? I forgot that part too.

Then he added, "Or did you forget ME? I never stopped thinking about you."

How sweet. I assured him that I, too, didn't forget about us and that I had nothing but loving thoughts of him as well.

***

I'm flat out determined to have my way with Michael this time. The entire day was devoted to making detailed plans, contingency plans and super-contingency plans. I've completed the Basic Mission Planning and METT (Mission, Enemy, Terrain, Troops—see DND handbook):

The Mission: Using KISS principles, to bivouac overnight with friendly troops (Michael) on secured ground (the cottage) and remain undiscovered and unsuspected by the enemy.

The Enemy: is determined to be members of The Block, i.e., our kids and spouses plus a multitude of spies, saboteurs, partypoopers and fools—practically all of the free world. The usual military objective is to engage and kill or at least capture the enemy; however, in this case, we feel it's advisable to simply disperse the enemy during the period of our operations.

Terrain: Our objective is to flee unfriendly enemy terrain (which is, ironically, home or in military terms, defence headquarters) and to avoid enemy fire and deadly physical obstacles (such as staircases).

Troops: Unfriendly troops must be subjected to extensive Diversion Plan so that primary objective—Horizontal Envelopment between friendly troops—can take place.

With the above Basic Mission Planning in place, it was simple to prepare a five-pronged Plan of Engagement:

The First Prong: The Tactical Plan

Careful tactical planning is critical to prevent failure of the adjunct plans (the remaining prongs). The top-secret bivouac location is Michael's old family cottage. The enemy brass (spouses) will be flanked by their own troops (offspring or "infant"ry), therefore they will be virtually paralysed behind their own enemy lines, continuously engaged in skirmishes with their own troops and possibly being mowed down by their own friendly fire.

Michael and I will deploy our forces in a surprise retreat manoeuvre and bunker down in the field of operations. Top-drawer tactical planners call this calculated approach *Hi Diddle Diddle, Up the Middle*. Therefore we have code named our Plan of Engagement *Over the Moon*. My operative code name is *Dish* and Michael is *Spoon*.

The Second Prong: The Mounting Plan

The Jeep needs an oil change. I will attempt to allocate the financing of the vehicle maintenance to the enemy.

The Third Prong: The Flight Plan

Troops are set to move out from a neutral ring location (doughnut shop) in convoy formation at 1300 hours. The enemy will be cordoned off with extensive high-tech

DVD bombardment. The estimated arrival time is 1530 hours. Due to possible resistance by unfriendly vehicles, the Flight Plan may have to be modified at the last minute and friendly troops may be forced to pool resources (in other words, go in one car).

The Fourth Prong: The Diversion Plan

The enemy troops are to be supplied with sufficient food and movie rentals to capture all their attention. The enemy thinks I'm going away on another hockey skills weekend. To practise my stick handling. Ha ha ha. The enemy received this bogus intelligence with barely concealed fury, but he (Donald) cannot deny that his weekends away—successfully executed Missions no doubt—have amounted to four so far this year alone while I've had a grand total of none.

The Fifth Prong: The Reconnaissance Plan

There will be a short reconnaissance necessary on arrival at the bivouac to determine if any spies are in the field (nosy cottage neighbours, essentially). Unexpected spies may cause a premature abort, thereby Tactical Plan B will be employed (divert the spies, penetrate the site under cover of darkness, etc.)

***

D-Day minus 1. The shopping was completed this morning without a hitch. I've supplied enough food and rented enough DVDs to immobilize everybody for weeks rather than just two days. I can't wait to meet my objective and commence the debriefing.

In the afternoon, I take the Jeep to the dealer for its oil change. Thoughts of going Over the Moon with Mr. Spoon are engaging me to the point that I'm indifferent to the charms of the cute mechanic.

***

D-Day: I rise at dawn and watch the sun offer up a brilliant greeting to its lovely mistress, a clear blue sky. Nothing can stop me now.

After waving the enemy off to work and school, I wait impatiently for 1300 hours, snatch up my rations (a bottle of bubbly) and flee enemy territory. I hope Mr. Spoon remembers to bring the extra battle jackets (condoms).

* * *

The Flight Plan is faultlessly executed, and we soon arrive at the cottage. I explore the waterfront while Michael waves the key with a grin and opens the cottage to air. Sitting on the sandy beach, I hug my knees and stare across the lake. The breeze coming across the water is chilly. I try to relax, but I'm overcome with a sudden attack of shyness. Now that I'm here, I want to run away.

My brain goes haywire and produces crazy visions: the image of Donald bravely toiling in his office, and then Jack and Olympia and Serenity dutifully bent over their lessons at school—well, perhaps that's going a bit far—especially as Serenity is at this moment speeding her way to the nearest womyn's festival—but still, what about all the good, hard-working teachers tending to the education and well-being of my younger children? What about the cadres of support workers, principal administrators, social workers, librarians, secretaries, indeed, all of society when one thinks about it: fire fighters, police officers, doctors, nurses, farmers and so on, all of them trusting that I, too, will be conscientiously engaged in an honest day's work, yes indeed, working in some way, great or small, for the betterment of society, for a finer future for all our children—while I sit sluglike at the water's edge lazily soaking my indolent sluggy toes, contemplating a sordid tumble in a dusty shack with a man, a man who isn't my lawfully wedded husband—a husband to whom